See How They Shine

See How They Shine

A Sadie Wagner Mystery

Joann Temple Dennett

iUniverse, Inc.
New York   Bloomington

See How They Shine
A Sadie Wagner Mystery

iUniverse books may be ordered through booksellers or by contacting:

iUniverse
1663 Liberty Drive
Bloomington, IN 47403
www.iuniverse.com
1-800-Authors (1-800-288-4677)

Because of the dynamic nature of the Internet, any Web addresses or links contained in this book may have changed since publication and may no longer be valid. The views expressed in this work are solely those of the author and do not necessarily reflect the views of the publisher, and the publisher hereby disclaims any responsibility for them.

iUniverse rev. date: 3/10/09

ISBN: 978-1-4401-1028-3 (pbk)
ISBN: 978-1-4401-1029-0 (ebk)

Printed in the United States of America

Acknowledgments

As usual, I owe thanks to many people who helped bring this story to fruition.

Eileen Edgren tirelessly researched everything from eyeshine to quantum computers. Mary Schramm Coberly, Patricia Weis-Taylor, and all the members of the "book club" are a constant source of encouragement. Faith Rogers, Patricia Lisensky, and Helen Brigham patiently read drafts, caught typos, and highlighted puzzlements. And without Sandra Rush's help, the final manuscript would never have been finished.

I am especially grateful to members of my critique groups: the Sisters in Crime group in Boulder, Thora Chinnery, Carol Dow, Sue Nash, and Vicki Rubin; and my on-line Guppies group, Shirley Jensen, Ottilia Scherschel, and Sarah Weismann. And to Bill Davis for his creative "engineering." Lastly, to Wally Clark, who actually made the production possible.

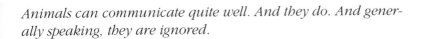

Animals can communicate quite well. And they do. And generally speaking, they are ignored.

—Alice Walker (1944–)
Am I Blue?

One

Eyes! Eyes shining briefly as the headlights caught them. Sadie Wagner braked, slowing the car to a crawl while she peered into the dark off the side of the road.

"What's the matter?" Mike Robb demanded from the passenger seat.

"Didn't you see them?"

"See who?"

"Those eyes. Someone is standing behind that fence over there."

"Don't be ridiculous. There's no one over there, it's just the old gravel pits. The ones someone gave the Institute a few years ago. Nobody's there. In fact, there's nothing at all there."

Sadie took her foot off the brake. The car inched forward and the gleaming eyes flickered again. She pulled the car off the road and parked.

"Okay, I saw them too," Mike Robb said. "But it's just a raccoon or something."

"Awfully tall for a raccoon."

"How about a raccoon in a tree?"

"Let's go see." She opened the car door.

"Wait, you shouldn't be walking around on dark country roads. Especially not by yourself."

1

"I'm not by myself. I have my own personal police lieutenant with me. You want to see a six-foot-tall raccoon up close and personal, don't you?"

He sighed. "Very funny. I'll go, but not until you put on your emergency flashers. This is supposed to be a driving lesson, if you'll recall...."

"Emergency flashers?" She'd forgotten about those. Were they really necessary out here? There was no one else around.

"You know, I'm not sure I'm the right person to teach you to drive," Mike said, punching the flasher button on the dashboard somewhat harder than necessary.

Sadie met him in front of the car. "I was just thinking that very same thing myself," she said. "Actually, I was thinking that I'm not at all sure I want to learn to drive."

"Maybe you shouldn't. It did enhance your suspect profile in those murders last spring ... Associate Professor at the Foothills Institute of Technology and Telecommunications, thirty-six years old, never married, homeowner, dog guardian, doesn't drive ... exonerated in hit and run ...," he reached over and tousled her short, red curls. "I could go on," he teased. "Five-foot-eight, well-nourished ..."

"Stop right there." Sadie didn't appreciate references to her almost appropriate weight. "Stop at 'exonerated in hit and run.' Or, if you must say more, you could add 'subsequently enamored of investigating officer.'"

Laughing, she grabbed Mike's hand. They walked toward the fence, the emergency lights providing a flashing backlight. Behind the fence, the eyes glowed again. It was an animal—but not, Sadie was glad to see, a raccoon. It was a donkey. A lone donkey huddled against a fence that barely enclosed a pond. A yellow and black sign on the gate ordered **No Trespassing. FITT Property.**

"Can this poor animal even lie down?" Sadie said, caressing the velvety nose that was now stuck through the fence in greeting. "Look, there isn't any room at all. The fence is practically in the water on this side and there are all those trees on the other side. What is this donkey doing here?"

"Probably the Institute put the donkey here to keep the weeds down."

"Weeds? What weeds? Those Russian olives come down to the water over there and there's no place for weeds to grow on this side."

"Call FITT public relations in the morning. They'll know why the donkey is here."

"On Saturday, I doubt anyone will be working. I hope it's not some sort of fraternity prank. What if no one knows the donkey is here? What is it going to eat?"

"Look, you can call in the morning. The donkey is safe for tonight. Nothing bad can happen to it inside that fence." Mike turned back toward the flashing car lights. "There's nothing we can do about it now. Let's go."

They returned to the car. Boulder glowed in the distance, nestled at the foot of the Rocky Mountains. Mike reached in the open car window and switched off the emergency flashers. Moonless darkness enveloped them.

"You drive," Sadie said. "This is way too dark for me." Too dark for that poor donkey too, she thought as she picked her way around the car toward the passenger side.

Mike attempted to get into the driver's side but the steering wheel was too close to the seat. Tackling the awkward task of pushing the seat back from the outside of the car, he succeeded enough to slide into the car and finish adjusting the seat to fit his lanky frame from the inside. "I wish you'd remember to push the seat back when you get out," he said. "I am considerably taller than you are, you know."

"Taller and bigger ... and a tad more crabby," Sadie added.

Two

The next morning, the telephone jolted Sadie awake. It was still dark. What time was it? Who could be calling so early? Early morning phone calls could only be bad news. Sadie's heart rate accelerated while she struggled to escape the duvet that so thoroughly enveloped her. She counted the rings—two, three. She knew she couldn't make it before the answering machine kicked in, but she hurried anyway. Surely, she thought, it must be Ling calling from the other side of the world.

But the voice that spoke from the answering machine wasn't Ling's soft, lilting Chinese accent. It was a loud, male voice. "I want it!" he said. "You say to make an offer. I'm offering a hundred dollars and I'm sure I'm the first caller. So call me back. I'll bring the cash right away. That's Tony DeMarques. I'm at four-eight-four-one-one-three-five."

Good grief, Sadie thought. I nearly broke a leg for a wrong number. Debating between staying up or going back to bed, she tuned into the worry that had been nagging her for several days. Ling Wang, her invaluable teaching assistant, had gone home to China for a summer visit. Ling's sister, also a TA at FITT, continued to assure Sadie that Ling was coming back, but fall semester was well under way and Sadie had not yet heard from Ling. Her absence was both a worry and a major inconvenience. Sadie relied on Ling for help in all of the language classes she taught for FITT's nonnative students.

This semester the English as a Second Language (ESL) Department had given Sadie a very odd schedule. Tuesday and Thursday were totally free—a situation that led to frequent requests from colleagues to cover one of their classes. The fact that she paid for the minor miracle of two free days with a horrendous schedule the other three days conveniently escaped everyone's attention.

Wednesdays were especially trying. In the morning, she taught three classes with only a ten-minute break between each one. The first two were in different buildings, a good five-minute walk apart—a significant problem in bad weather. And an inconvenience for any students wanting to ask one last question.

Pronunciation Lab at 10 was followed by ESL grammar at 11. At noon, she had drawn the short straw and the non-credit "extra help" seminar for TAs who needed to brush-up their teaching skills. Most needed to work on their English pronunciation as much as their syntax. Her hectic Wednesday ended with a required seminar: ESL Writing, a class difficult for both students and teacher. In short, Wednesdays were challenging, both physically and mentally. Without a teaching assistant, they were exhausting.

Mondays and Fridays, Sadie had three classes spread awkwardly throughout the day from 9 a.m. to 6:30 p.m. Her last class on Friday afternoon was ill-attended because Colorado's glorious mountains beckoned many students to start an early weekend. This necessitated so much review in the Monday session that Sadie was scrambling to figure out if she could somehow truncate the entire course. So, what looked like a luxurious class schedule was, in fact, a near-nightmare that threatened to be more than Sadie could handle if Ling didn't show up soon.

The phone rang again. Sadie glanced at the time on her caller ID. Five o'clock in the morning. She decided to let the machine answer this call. It kicked in after the fifth ring, and Tony DeMarques started speaking again.

Sadie picked up the receiver. "You've got the wrong number."

"No way, sister. Don't give me that. I'm sure I called first and I want it."

"I have no idea what you're talking about; please don't call again." Sadie hung up. In seconds, the phone rang again. No, Sadie thought. No more. Angry now, she turned the ringer off and headed back to bed grumbling, "What sort of nut calls at five on Saturday morning? Not once, but three times. And, for that matter, what was he calling about?" Sadie hadn't a clue what the phone calls were about.

Exhaustion erased her questions as she settled back into her still-warm duvet cocoon and returned to a sound sleep. Sound until a nightmare took over. A huge bear chased her around and around a pond. She couldn't get over the fence that surrounded the pond. The bear finally trapped her, and as its fish-laden hot breath washed over her, Sadie woke up.

The stinky breath was still there and, added to it, the heavy panting of a dog ready to go outside. Now!

Tiger bounced around the bedroom as Sadie struggled out of bed again. Bigger than his border collie mother, smaller than his hulking Lab father, Tiger was a good-sized dog. Consequently, his morning doggy dance took up much of the available floor space.

"Settle," Sadie said firmly. The dog obediently sat down. As Sadie found her slippers and put on her robe, she told the dog, "No more tuna fish for you. Today, we'll get you some real dog food."

Understanding only that she was talking to him, Tiger squirmed as Sadie headed into the living room to open the door. Once there, she called "Release!" and the dog exploded into action. He ran through the living room and straight out the now-open sliding glass door into the tiny fenced garden. After a quick patrol of the fence line along Arapahoe Avenue, he found his spot and balanced on three legs to begin his morning routine.

With Tiger thus occupied, Sadie shut the door and started her own morning routine. Water heating for coffee, paper retrieved from the mat outside her kitchen door, she headed back toward the bedroom. On the way, she noticed the answering machine. Two digits—2-6—blinked steadily. Twenty-six? Really? Twenty-six calls?

If Tony De-whatever called me twenty-six times, I'm going to call the police, Sadie thought. Well, maybe not the police exactly, but certainly Mike.

She hit the "play" button. Message number one was, indeed, Tony DeMarques again. Sadie pushed "next." It was an apologetic-sounding woman.

"Hi, I'm sorry to call so early but I wanted to get my bid in first. I guess I can offer you two hundred. Let me know."

The next call was from the same woman. "Oops, I forgot to tell you who I am. I'm Samantha Allcott. That's A-double L-cot with two t's."

The fourth call was Samantha again. Now she sounded really embarrassed. "Omigosh, I forgot the number. I guess it's too early for me," she giggled. "My number is …" Sadie shut her off.

Message five was—surprise!—DeMarques again.

What is going on? Sadie steadily pushed the "next" button on the recorder. Messages six through twenty-five were more of the same: people offering various sums of money. Some noted the time they called. Some demanded to be called back immediately. Some asked to be called whether theirs was the best offer or not. Call twenty-six was Tony DeMarques yet again.

I guess I'm going to have to call one of these people, Sadie thought. But not the insistent Tony DeMarques. No, that confused woman sounds more my speed. Sadie scrolled backward through the messages looking for Samantha Allcott's third message. She erased the others as she went, absentmindedly turning the ringer back on.

Just as Sadie found Samantha's number, the phone rang again. Snatching up the receiver, Sadie said, "What do I have that you want?"

"Well, I'll have to explain that in person," a chilly male voice said. "Will ten o'clock work for you?"

Something about the voice made Sadie shudder. "No! Of course not!" she protested.

"So, when is good?"

"No time is good. I've had twenty-six calls about this already this morning and I don't even know what *this* is...."

"Twenty-six calls? This is supposed to be a confidential investigation. How can you have had twenty-six calls about it?"

Fear morphing to confusion, Sadie replied, "Confidential investigation? What are you talking about?"

"As I said, I'll tell you when I see you. Now when is that going to be?"

Sadie was speechless. What was going on? Who was this guy? She shouldn't have answered the phone. She corrected that mistake by hanging up. As soon as she did, the phone rang again.

How could he call back so quickly? Must have auto redial, Sadie thought, as she again turned the phone off. Ringer, microphone, and recorder this time. For good measure, she yanked the phone cord from the jack.

Should have done that sooner, she thought. I'll plug it back in when I call Mike. He'll have some idea what to do about these weird phone calls.

It was still too early to call Mike, but as Tiger had been reminding her for some time, it was certainly not too early to go for a brisk walk. The crisp air and bright sunlight beckoned Sadie outside as she gathered her bright green running outfit from the back of the closet door.

Once dressed, curly red hair pulled back with a black headband, she had to cope with Tiger. Whoever coined the phrase "jumping for joy" must have been talking about a dog, Sadie thought as she tried repeatedly to snap the leash on Tiger's collar.

Quivering with anticipation, the prospect of a walk so joy inducing, Tiger ignored her repeated pleas to "settle." Obviously, the hyper-excited dog could not deal with any information other than the upcoming walk. Finally, when he executed a three-point landing from what had been an almost perfect axel, Sadie saw her chance and grabbed his collar.

"Anyone would think you haven't had a walk for a week," she scolded the enthusiastic dog. They set out through the lobby of Flatirons Vista and headed for the Boulder Creek Path, a paved, creekside trail that ran from Boulder Canyon through downtown and eastward some seven miles to beyond the city limits.

As they walked, she remembered the previous night and the donkey's woeful eyes. Her mind churned with questions. How many people drive by that poor animal every day? How many notice? How many fewer stop? What was it doing there? What could she do about it?

Sadie and Tiger passed the Dushanbe Teahouse, a unique gift from Boulder's sister city in Tajikistan and one of the best places in town for food, tea, and people-watching. The striking, colorful building was now in the midst of the hubbub preceding the opening of the Saturday Farmer's Market on the Civic Plaza that surrounded it.

They continued east to the edge of the FITT campus before turning around near the footpath up the hill toward the FITT Recreation Center. Dubbed the Ho-Chi Minh trail by activist students years ago, this dirt footpath was too steep for Sadie's dicey ankle. Too steep and, despite Boulder's arid environment, often too muddy. It was aptly named.

As she and Tiger neared the teahouse again, Sadie became aware of the growing background noise, foreshadowing the influx of traffic that would soon head toward the football stadium and the FITT Mustangs Homecoming Game at one o'clock. Traffic on the Creek Path had increased as well. In-line skaters, bicyclists, and joggers had joined the morning walkers.

Sadie returned vague smiles to those she hadn't seen before, nodded to those she had, and hurried on toward home and breakfast, thoroughly mellowed by the pleasant walk. She had managed to suppress her angst over the early-morning phone calls until she saw the two men waiting in the lobby of her condo.

One was Mike. Tall, sandy-haired, and dressed in an open-neck shirt, pressed blue Dockers and shiny black shoes, he looked every inch the tough guy. Reflecting, aviator-style sunglasses hid his piercing blue eyes and added to his stern image, an image belied by his broad grin greeting Sadie and Tiger as they approached.

The second man mirrored Mike's quasi-military stance. Stocky and balding, he too wore dark, well-pressed slacks and gleaming shoes. But unlike Mike, he sported a jacket and tie. The thick leather briefcase in his left hand and the scowl on his face made Sadie very glad that Mike was there.

"Your phone isn't working," Mike said. "Or it's off the hook. I just got here a second ago to see if something's wrong."

Sadie started to explain, but the other man interrupted. "Professor Wagner," he said as he took out his wallet and flashed an ID card at her. "I'm Sam Gross, Naval Intelligence. We need to talk."

Three

L ing! Dear God, don't let it be Ling, Sadie thought as Mike, Sam Gross, and Tiger crowded behind her into the kitchen. Tiger growled, issuing fair warning to Sam Gross, who was a bit too close to Sadie.

"Be careful," she said. "My dog doesn't understand ID cards."

"Very funny, but I'm more concerned about *this* guy. My business is with you … confidential with you."

"I'd prefer that Lieutenant Robb be here. In fact, I was going to call him as soon as I got home." Sadie turned to Mike and added, "I have a bit of a harassment problem."

"Harassment?" Mike echoed.

"Lieutenant? Lieutenant of what?" Gross raised a cynical eyebrow but Sadie ignored him while she explained to Mike the puzzling early morning phone calls.

"I was so angry, I erased most of the messages," she said. "Then I unplugged the phone and just left."

"What do you know about this?" Mike asked Sam Gross.

"Nothing, I called her once. She hung up on me," Gross answered. "I take it you're a cop? Not federal, I assume?"

"No, city. I think we should start over. I'm Mike Robb, Lieutenant, Boulder Police."

"And apparently a good friend of Professor Wagner?" Sam Gross narrowed his eyes.

"You could say that. Why, exactly, are you here?"

"I'll explain that to Professor Wagner when you leave."

Mike turned to Sadie. "Do you want me to leave?"

"No, no. I really don't."

"This is absurd!" Color rising in his cheeks, Sam Gross didn't stifle his curt response. "I need to talk to you privately, Professor Wagner. Not you and your boyfriend, even if your boyfriend is a cop."

"Maybe you could go see what you think about whatever's left on my answering machine," Sadie suggested to Mike. "And Mr. Gross can talk to me here in the kitchen while you're doing that. Will that be sufficient privacy for you, Mr. Gross?"

"It's Commander, Commander Gross. And I don't like it, but I guess it will have to do."

"Stay here, Tiger," Mike said as he left the kitchen. Tiger looked puzzled. He obediently settled down in the kitchen, but he was more interested in the high-pitched whirring that came from the living room when Mike rewound the answering machine tape.

"So, you want to talk, Commander Gross. Let's get it over with," Sadie said, sitting down at the kitchen table.

Gross sat down, opened his briefcase, took out a recorder, and spoke into it. "October eleventh, two-thousand-eight. Professor Sadie Wagner in the matter of Lee Hong."

"Lee Hong is a very common name. Are you talking about the brother-in-law of my teaching assistant?" Sadie asked.

"I don't know. He listed you as his employer." Gross shuffled through some papers. "Ming Fang Wang is his wife. Is she your TA?"

"No, she's my TA's sister. So you have the right Lee Hong except that he doesn't work for me."

"No, he said he did. Why would he say that?"

Sadie remembered the recorder. "Can you tell me what this is about, please?"

"We are conducting a routine background check on a national of another nation."

"Routine? Phone calls before seven on a Saturday morning? Showing up on my doorstep uninvited? Surely you can't say this is routine."

"It's unfortunately quite routine for a person who has to interview academics."

"What does that mean?"

"Look how much trouble you've put me to. You're not unusual. Getting an academic to sit still for a security interview usually isn't easy. You people act like you're too important to be bothered."

Put off by Gross's answer, Sadie spoke without thinking, "I don't think I'm too important to be bothered, but I do think I'm important enough to be told *why* I'm being bothered. Especially why I'm being bothered well before breakfast time on Saturday." She heard Mike's low chuckle from the next room and knew he was eavesdropping. She certainly didn't care, and Sam Gross either didn't hear Mike or chose to ignore him.

"Let's just get on with this," he said. "I am conducting a background check on a person who has applied for employment with a national security agency."

"Lee Hong? Really? I don't believe it." Commander Gross had progressed from scary to annoying to absurd.

"Believe it or not, it's true. Now tell me what you know about Lee Hong."

Sadie thought. What did she know about Lee Hong? He was Ling's brother-in-law. A talented photographer, Lee Hong worked for the women's basketball team at FITT. He also free-lanced and, last spring, one of his news photos was nationally syndicated. It was a memorable image of hoards of caged laboratory rats set free by student protestors at FITT's Animal Husbandry Laboratories. As hundreds of rats surged out of broken windows in the labs, Lee Hong had snapped his photo from Sadie's office across the street.

She told Sam Gross all this. She didn't tell him that Lee Hong had been in her office without her permission. She also didn't tell him that Lee Hong had been desperate for money because he had amassed a huge debt playing and losing in the stock market. She didn't tell him, but she didn't have to. Sam Gross already knew all about it.

"So, what about his debts?" he asked. "Did that one photograph make that much difference to him?"

"I think it did, actually. It helped him get a lot more assignments."

"Yes, that's what he said on his application. He claims he is now a free-lance photographer. He doesn't mention current employment with the Institute but he gives you as his former supervisor at the Institute."

"That's just not true. I'm sure there must be a misunderstanding." Remembering Lee Hong's less than skillful English, she jumped on the idea. "Probably he didn't understand the form. He thought you wanted a personal reference. And, of course, I do know him."

"Not just the form. He also told me that he worked for you."

"Well, then he didn't understand what you wanted. Did you ask for a reference? Probably he didn't know what a reference was."

"I asked him who he worked for at the Institute. That's a pretty clear question. And he gave me a clear answer: you. He also said that you had samples of his work. Do you?"

Sadie shrugged. "I don't know what to say. His sister-in-law is my teaching assistant, but Lee Hong himself doesn't work for me; he has never worked for me. And the only sample of his work I've ever seen is the picture of the rats."

"Hmmm, you're not helping him any, you know."

Not having a sensible response, Sadie changed the subject. "What sort of job is Lee Hong applying for? I'm surprised our government would hire a Chinese citizen. Especially, as you said, for a job in a national security agency."

Commander Gross was busy sorting through papers in his briefcase as he answered, "It's unusual, but sometimes foreign nationals have access to people that can be quite useful to us. Actually, he's already sold us a few photographs. On a free-lance basis, of course. Before we get more involved with him, we need to know more about his motivation."

"If all you're doing is buying photos from him, I really don't understand why talking to me before breakfast was so urgent."

Gross didn't answer, and Mike's voice from the living room broke the silence. Sadie couldn't make out what he was saying, but he was using what she called his "official cop voice."

Commander Gross had such a voice also, and that's what he used now: "It's important that we handle these things as quickly as possible. Before the parties involved talk to each other too much. I'm sure you understand."

Understand? Sadie was further from understanding than she had been when Gross first called. Parties involved? Who else was involved? And involved in what?

It was clear she wasn't going to find out. Commander Gross was packing up his recorder. He snapped his briefcase shut just as Mike appeared at the door.

"Have you got today's paper?" he asked.

The paper was right where she'd left it on the kitchen table. Sadie pulled it out from under Gross's briefcase. "I think Commander Gross was just leaving," she said, handing the paper to Mike.

"Oh?"

"Yes, he wanted to know about Lee Hong. He's apparently been selling pictures to the government. And now the government wants to know more about him. And it was important that this be found out right away before everyone involved can talk to everyone else."

"Oh?" Mike repeated skeptically as he looked at Sam Gross.

"Professor Wagner's summary is a bit uninformed," Gross said. "However, her information has been useful." As Gross stood, Tiger jumped to his feet also. "Thank you for your help, Professor Wagner, I can find my own way out."

Sadie held her breath until the door clicked shut behind the man. Tension left with Sam Gross. Mike opened the paper, spread it out on the table, and sat down to study the classified ads. Tiger, hoping for a tummy rub, rolled over and waved all four legs in the air. Sadie remembered that neither she nor Tiger had eaten yet.

"Have you had breakfast?" she asked Mike. He kept running his finger down column after column of the classified ads.

"Actually, only coffee. I was going to take you out for breakfast, but then I couldn't get you to answer your phone. Correction: I couldn't get your phone to answer at all." He turned the page and continued his line-by-line scrutiny of the classifieds.

"Breakfast out is a nice thought, but I'm really hungry. How about oatmeal? Or Four-Part Hominy?"

Mike looked up from the paper. "Four-Part Hominy? Is that what you said? That sounds good, if only for the name." He laughed.

"Okay, but first, coffee. Serious coffee," Sadie said as she poured water into the coffee maker she used solely to heat a carafe of water. If there was time, she'd then drip a cup through a coffee-filled filter. If not, there was always instant. While the water was heating, she collected a can of hominy, a can of chopped jalapeños, a carton of sour cream, and a bag of shredded cheese. All four were thoroughly mixed and in the oven before the heated water filled the carafe.

"I specialize in creative fast food, as you know. Never more than five ingredients, that's my over-riding principle," Sadie said. She gave Mike his cup of coffee and added, "In this house, humans eat first, then dogs, but I think we can count this as eating first. I'll go ahead and feed Tiger now."

The dog, who knew the drill, stood by his dish as Sadie filled it halfway with kibbles. Tiger waited until Sadie found some canned chicken in the cupboard, opened it, and spooned that on top of the kibbles. "No more tuna," she reminded him as the

Four-Part Hominy

1 16 oz. can hominy, drained
1 4 oz. can chopped jalapeno
peppers
1 C shredded cheese, any kind
1 C sour cream

Mix ingredients. Spoon into
greased casserole dish, pack
down. Bake at 350 for 20-25 minutes or until brown on top.

Sadie's notes:

If you don't have peppers, use
any green veggie—peas, aspar-
agus—whatever you have in the
cupboard.

Don't use nonfat sour cream or
cheese, but low fat is okay.

The oven temperature doesn't
matter. At 400°, it cooks faster. At
325°, it cooks slower.

dog gulped his breakfast down. "It gave you amazingly scary breath."

"The dog gets chicken? And tuna? And we're having *hominy*? What's wrong with this picture?" Mike asked.

"Hominy and jalapeños. Tiger doesn't do jalapeños very well." Sadie grimaced.

Mike went back to the newspaper. Sadie brought her cup of coffee to the table just as Mike found what he was looking for in the classifieds. "Here it is!" he said. "RV/camper, used by family of ten, make offer. And guess what the phone number is?"

"Let me see." Sadie leaned over his shoulder. "Where is it?"

Mike pointed to a small line ad in the classifieds. Sure enough it was her phone number. So, all those calls were a mistake. They were just people wanting to buy a used RV/camper. "Why would people call so early? And be so pushy?" she asked.

"I don't know. RV/campers must be really in demand. This one sounds well used. It doesn't even say how old it is. The lady I talked to said she'd been trying to find a used one for months."

"Which lady was that?" Sadie asked.

"Samantha. I called her and asked why she had called. I guess you'll have to let the newspaper know there's a mistake in the ad."

"Well, after breakfast."

The phone rang several times while they ate. Each time, the caller listened to only part of the new message Mike had recorded.

"Good morning," he'd said. "If you're trying to buy a used RV/camper, you have the wrong number. Actually, the wrong number was published. We suggest you check the ad again on Monday to get the correct number." It seemed to work. No one left a message. No one, that is, until Lila Simone.

"Eeeek," she squealed in her over-the-top French-accented tones. "Who *is* that? Sadie, who is this man answering your phone? What does he mean by saying '*We* suggest'? Sadieee, this is Lila. Call me if this is still you."

Four

"Who's Lila?" Mike asked between enthusiastic bites of Four-Part Hominy.

"Old friend, long story," Sadie answered.

"She sounded French. Like Dan whatsit, your Frenchie boyfriend. I mean ex-boyfriend. The French professor. What was his last name?"

Doubting that Mike had really forgotten Dan's last name, Sadie answered him anyway. "Simone."

"And Lila?"

"Lila what?"

"That's what I'm asking, Lila what? What's Lila's last name?"

"Simone."

"The professor got married already? Wow, fast work. Or is Lila an ex?"

"Neither, she's Dan's sister," Sadie answered just as the phone rang. Again, the caller hung up without leaving a message.

"This stuff really is good, by the way," Mike said, scraping the last of the crusty hominy out of the baking dish. "Watching you fix it made it look easy. Maybe I could even make it."

"Anybody who has a can opener can make Four-Part Hominy. I'll give you the recipe. Can I barter it for another driving lesson?"

"Hmm, the driving lesson will have to be tomorrow. I've got a wacko schedule today. Homecoming weekend always creates problems. So what are you and Tiger doing today?"

"Tiger doesn't have any plans," Sadie said. "But I do. First, I'm going to call the newspaper and get that ad corrected. Then I'm going to the grocery store after the game starts. And there are always class preps and housecleaning to be done. Guess which I always do first?" she said, looking around her cluttered kitchen.

"Okay," Mike said. "I guess I'd better go before the football traffic gets ridiculous." He stood, gathered up his dishes, and put them in the sink. The phone rang again.

"Maybe it's Lila calling back," Sadie said as she went to listen to the recorder. But it wasn't Lila. Or, if it was, she didn't leave another message. The caller hung up abruptly at the end of Mike's message.

"Probably someone else wanting a cheap camper," Mike said. "Good luck with getting that ad changed." Sadie and Tiger got similar pats on the head as Mike left, promising to call first thing in the morning.

"Hmmm," Sadie said to Tiger. "That was interesting. We both got patted on the head. Tell me, Tiger, does he kiss you too?"

The dog looked at her, his head cocked quizzically. "No, I doubt it," Sadie said. "And certainly not with your fusty tuna breathe. I wonder how long it's going to take for you to get rid of that."

In case all this talk had to do with more food for him, Tiger followed Sadie to the sink. "I suppose you might as well help," she said putting the casserole dish on the floor. Tiger attacked the browned-on crust with his agile tongue, and in less than five minutes, the dish was gleaming.

Sadie sat down with the paper, the phone, and another cup of coffee. Finding the number for classified ads at the top of the advertising section, she dialed it. A recorded voice answered.

"Our office hours are eight to five, Monday through Friday. Please call back at that time. Or, if you want to leave a message, touch five."

Sadie touched five and heard again that the classified ad department was closed. But this recording invited her to "Leave us a message and we'll call you back first thing in the morning."

At the beep, she began speaking. "There is an error in one of your ads. It lists a used RV/camper for sale but it gives my phone number. I am not selling an RV/camper, so please correct this ad. Thank you." Sadie started to hang up and then remembered she hadn't said who she was. "Oh, this is Sadie Wagner." She ended with a recitation of her phone number.

That task not completed but at least begun, she now faced a choice of other, unpleasant tasks. Returning Lila's call seemed the best option. Sadie hadn't talked to Lila in months but, since Lila hadn't said otherwise, she was probably still living in Dan's house as she had been since that day in May when Sadie sent Dan home with all the books and boxes he had moved into her condo. The final parting with her longtime colleague and much more recent lover had not been pleasant, and Sadie didn't want to talk to him any more than she had to. There were the inevitable meetings on campus. Dan was always so polite and proper and distant. Always the quintessential gentleman.

She punched in Dan's number, shoving aside the observation that she still knew it by heart. But she needn't have worried about talking to Dan. Lila's "Allo" came after the first ring.

"Hi, Lila. It's me, Sadie."

"Sadie! How are you? Who was that man? Is he living there?"

Who wants to know? Sadie wondered. You or Dan? Just in case it was Dan, she decided to be very explicit. "No, Lila, that man is absolutely not living here. I'm living alone with Tiger, just like always."

"But this man answers your phone?"

"He's my friend, Mike Robb. He's a policeman and I had a little problem with weird phone calls this morning. So Mike recorded that message. I'll change it soon but, until I quit getting these phone calls, I think having a man's voice on the recorder is good. Now, what did you call about, Lila?"

"What! I called because we are friends. And I do not see you since I moved here last spring. I thought maybe today is a good day to play with Sadie. I know Sadie will not go to the football game, maybe we can do something fun together."

"Dan is going to the football game, I suppose?"

"Oh yes, always. He and Rick. Always they go to the games. And to lectures. And concerts. And movies. And, just everywhere." Lila sounded decidedly lonely. "Daniel has his friend, Rick. So, I must find a friend also. Then I thought, I have a friend already. I will call Sadie."

Sadie laughed. Lila was as transparent as ever. "We had some good times together, didn't we?" she said, remembering Lila's annual forays to Boulder over the many years Sadie had known Dan and his late wife, Michelle. Sadie had been drafted into occasional relief service when Lila's effervescence became too much for Michelle. Lila would be packed off to the Denver Art Museum or a film or sometimes even the opera in Central City. And Sadie, Dan's ever-reliable colleague, was always the one who went along.

The last time Lila had come, she stayed far too long. Michelle was dying, and the cancer consumed her good humor even more rapidly than it ravished her body. Ostensibly there to help her brother and his wife, Lila had instead spent almost her entire visit with Sadie.

After Michelle died, the long-standing collegial friendship between Sadie and Dan had blossomed into something more, something that Lila clearly did not like. But all her subsequent hostility was forgotten now that Sadie and Dan were no longer a couple.

"Can we do it again?" Lila asked. "Have good times? Would you like to go to Denver today? Maybe to a play?"

"I've got work to do," Sadie said. "And I have to do it today because I have a driving lesson tomorrow."

"Driving lesson? That's perfect. I will come get you and you can practice driving today. Then you'll be ready for your lesson tomorrow."

Hmm, Sadie thought. What do I really have to do today? Class preps loomed, but Monday was two days away. The shopping could certainly wait. And the cleaning could always be put off.

"Sadie?" Lila trilled tentatively, "Are you there?"

"Yes, I'm here. I'm thinking. Maybe I could go somewhere around noon. Where do you want to go?"

"Anywhere you want is fine with me, Sadie. Is there some place you would like to go today?"

There was. Indeed there was. "How would you like to visit a donkey, Lila?" Sadie asked.

Five

"Sadie, I am so glad to see you. You and ... Tigger here," Lila was all smiles and hugs when Sadie buzzed her in from the lobby. Lila's looks were striking. Nearly Sadie's height, Lila was slender, but more wiry than willowy. As always, she was dressed with near couture élan. Her dark hair, barely flecked with gray, was close cropped. Tiny glasses with vivid green frames added to an overall elfin quality, albeit that of a somewhat aging, hyperactive elf.

Sadie and Tiger had been ready for half an hour. Lila had said noon, but she ran on continental time. Actually, Sadie thought, half an hour late isn't too bad. At least, not for Lila with all the stuff she has to do to her hair, and her face, and her eyebrows, and her outfits. Hmmmm, she thought, am I just a tiny bit envious? She glanced down at her Nike trainers, wrinkled blue capris, and yellow T-neck. Next to Lila, she probably looked like a plucked hen. And a clumsy plucked hen at that. She sighed.

"Is Tigger going with us?" The dog cringed as Lila patted him a bit too firmly on the head.

"I hope that's okay," Sadie answered.

"Sure, it is okay. I know Tigger rides in Daniel's car. So he cannot mind."

"Daniel's car?"

"Sure, he is not using it."

"I thought we were going in your car."

"I do not have a car. But Daniel is at the game. I told you."

"I'm not sure I should drive Daniel's car," Sadie said doubtfully.

"Why not?"

"Well, I guess because I don't have his permission."

Hands on hips, Lila said, "Look Sadie. Please can we forget my baby brother? I do not want him always standing between us. He gives me his car. I give it to you. This is permission, is it not?"

"Permission is what you get when you drive someone else's car," Sadie answered. "But you usually get it directly from the person who owns the car."

"*Mon Dieu!* You act as though you do not know the man. We both know you know him very well," Lila replied, waving her arms wildly. "Now come on. Let's go!"

Tiger heard the last two words. Let's go! More than ready to go, he started barking.

"There, you see, even Tigger gives permission," Lila said, jangling the car keys in front of Sadie.

"Okay, okay, but I'm not sure it's a good idea." Sadie pulled her door shut and they headed through the lobby toward the street.

The chili-red Mini Cooper was parked rather crookedly at the curb in the No Parking zone. Lila handed Sadie the keys and opened the passenger door. As she started to climb in, Sadie stopped her.

"Wait, Tiger has to get in first," Sadie said. When Lila looked confused, she explained, "I mean, he has to get in the back and he should do it from the curb side." Lila stepped back while Sadie pulled the seat forward. Tiger hopped into the tiny space behind the seats. Sadie snapped the seat back again. "I guess we really should have a seat belt for Tiger," she said to Lila as she went around to the driver's side.

"Seat belt? For a dog? Is that the law?" Lila asked as they settled into the little car.

"No, just a good idea," Sadie answered. She studied the dash-board. Nothing looked too unusual, although it was certainly different from Mike's Honda. More compact. Different icons. A huge, oversized speedometer. She adjusted various mirrors, strapped on the seat belt, and put the key in the ignition. "Everybody ready?" she asked.

"Indeed," Lila replied.

"What about you, Tiger?" Sadie asked, delaying the moment when she had to put the car in gear and attempt a smooth start.

"Tiger?" Lila said. "That's not what I said. What did I say?"

"You said Tigger, I think. Tigger is a tiger but he's a stuffed tiger. The one in *Winnie the Pooh*."

"Oh, I am so sorry," Lila said. She turned to pat Tiger on the head. "I'll have to practice. Tiger. Tiger. Tiger. There, is that right?"

Confused by the repetition of his name, Tiger whined.

"It's okay, Tiger," Sadie said, and the dog relaxed.

"You know, it is hard for me sometimes to get English right," Lila said. "And I am not so sure Daniel gets it right all the time either."

"He doesn't have to. He teaches French, not English," Sadie said.

"Ah, yes. I tell him that when he corrects my English. He tells me I should get someone like you to help me. Someone who specializes in teaching English just like he specializes in teaching French."

"Teaching English and teaching English as a Second Language are two very different things, you know," Sadie said. "My program at FITT is designed to help nonnative English speakers handle academic tasks, but there are a lot of noncredit ESL classes in Boulder. You might enjoy one."

"I think I'm too old for going to school, but maybe ... maybe I can talk to you about it. But, first, you are meant to be going to school—driving school. Let's go!"

Once again, the magic words. Tiger barked his endorsement, and Sadie eased out the clutch. They were on their way.

As Sadie drove east on Arapahoe Avenue, she marveled at the number of cars heading into Boulder. Westbound traffic was at a standstill from Folsom Avenue to the Foothills Parkway. The football fans didn't seem to mind. It was a good-natured traffic jam. Past Foothills Parkway, traffic was still moving westward, but slowly. Sadie was one of the very few drivers headed east. A stream of green traffic lights stretched into the distance in front of her and she tried to keep a steady foot on the accelerator. Mike claimed that the traffic lights on Arapahoe were timed for 45 mph. It seemed to be true. They made every light out to 63rd Street, where Sadie stopped and signaled for a left turn. She signaled … and signaled … and signaled. There was no break in the oncoming traffic. Finally, the light changed to yellow. Sadie inched the car forward, ready to make the left turn, but two cars continued through the light and blocked the intersection.

Exasperated, Sadie threw her hands up. "Now what? We'll never get to turn left."

"Oh yes we will," Lila answered. She unclipped her seat belt, opened her door, and got out.

"Come back here!" Sadie called, too late to stop Lila, who was determinedly stomping around the front of the Mini Cooper.

Lila rapped on the window of one of the offending cars, a blue Jeep sporting a FITT Mustangs banner on its doorframe. The startled driver ran his window down.

"Did you not see that we wish to turn here?" Lila demanded. "What kind of driving is this? Do you think it will make any difference if you wait one more light? This young woman is learning to drive. What do you think you are teaching her, driving so stupidly?"

The driver had no answer. Probably doesn't want to engage a mad Frenchwoman, Sadie thought. But Lila wasn't finished. "Now," she said, "I want you to pull over beside that car," as she waved at the car in front and continued, "and let Sadie turn left."

"There still wouldn't be room." The driver had finally found his voice.

"You just do what I say, there will be room," Lila retorted. "I will talk to him next." She waved at the second car in the intersection.

The people in the second car, an old white Buick, had been watching Lila. They were ready for her when she arrived at the driver's window.

"Lady, you shouldn't be walking around out here," the driver said. "You could get killed walking in traffic like this."

"I cannot be killed when cars are not moving," Lila countered. "And that's what I want you to do. Not move. Or, better still, you can back up," she said. "There are perhaps two feet back there. Go on, back up! Then we will turn left and be gone."

Just then the red light changed to green. "No, no," Lila shouted, jumping in front of the Buick. "You wait a minute!"

"Come on, Sadie. Turn, turn!" Lila waved at Sadie. "You can do it, there is room."

Horns began to blow. People behind the Buick didn't know what was going on, but they knew the light was green and they weren't moving.

As the blue Jeep pulled away, Sadie slid the Mini Cooper in front of the Buick and stopped on 63rd to wait for Lila. But Lila wasn't finished. She stood in front of the Buick shouting at the driver, who was now also blowing his horn.

Sadie couldn't hear what Lila was saying and, she thought, I probably don't want to know.

The driver of the Buick maneuvered around Lila, and one of his passengers made a rude gesture at Lila as they drove away.

Six

"MJD seven-four-two, MJD seven-four-two, MJD seven-four-two ... have you got a pencil?" Lila asked as she slid into the passenger seat. "MJD seven-four-two, help me remember this, MJD seven-four-two ..." Lila kept repeating her license-plate litany until she found a notepad and pencil in the glove compartment.

"There, now we will get your new boyfriend to arrest that man," she declared after writing down the license plate.

"Arrest him? For what? It's more likely he'd arrest you!"

"For what? For insulting me, of course. Did you not see that finger? I know what that means. In France, it is not the same. But here, here that is an insult."

"Lila, Lila. Don't you think maybe you deserved that insult, just a little bit?" Sadie admonished with a smile. She was trying not to laugh. "That was quite a performance."

"Performance, ha! If I had not 'performed,' as you say, we would still be back there hoping someday to turn. And, now that we have turned, where are we going?"

"It's just down here," Sadie answered, setting the car in motion again. They followed the road past the tailings of an old mine, through a steep left turn that approached Valmont Road. Coming from this direction, the gravel pits seemed to appear in the middle of the road. So, that's why we saw the donkey's eyes last night, Sadie thought. The road circles around this gravel pit pond.

When she pulled up next to the fence, the little car was nearly off the road, out of the way of the occasional passing car. Consequently, Sadie chose to ignore using the emergency flashers.

"This is the place? There are donkeys here?" Lila asked.

"I don't think there are donkeys plural, I think there's just one donkey," Sadie answered. "But I don't see it; maybe it's gone. Let's go see." They got out of the car with Tiger and started to walk along the fence. "It could be in those trees, I guess," Sadie said. She pointed at the thick stand of Russian olives. "But it didn't seem timid last night so I think it must be gone."

Tiger, however, did not agree. Hackles slightly raised, his growl a quiet rumble, he warned Sadie that all was not well.

"What is it, Tiger?"

The dog continued to voice his concern as the Russian olives parted and the donkey emerged.

"There it is," Sadie said excitedly. "It doesn't look happy to see us. Last night, it was very friendly. How do you call a donkey?" She whistled. The donkey looked at them. "Here, donkey, donkey," she called. The donkey continued to look at them.

"For heaven's sake, Americans don't know anything," Lila said. She began to make a clicking sound. The donkey's ears perked up. Lila repeated the clicking call. Definitely interested, the donkey began to edge toward them.

Tiger barked. "Hush, Tiger," Sadie said. He looked at her. Hush? Hush when this huge beast with the big teeth and even bigger ears was heading right for them? Hush, indeed. He barked again before settling back into a low warning growl.

"It's okay, Tiger, really, it is okay," Sadie assured him as she took a firm grip on his collar. "Please don't scare it away."

"Actually," Lila said. "Tiger should be in the car. Donkeys do not like dogs."

"Well, this dog doesn't seem to like donkeys either," Sadie said. She coaxed Tiger toward the car. It took a few minutes and, when Tiger was finally back in the car peering suspiciously out the driver's window, Sadie turned to find the donkey at the fence in front of Lila. It obviously liked the comforting clicks. Lila reached through the fence and scratched the donkey's shoulder. It liked that even better, shutting its large, limpid eyes and leaning into the fence.

"You surely have found a friend," Sadie said, rejoining Lila.

"What is this animal doing here?" Lila demanded.

"It's strange isn't it? Mike thought that it was supposed to eat the weeds, but could there be enough weeds for it here?"

"Weeds? I do not know. But friends there are not. Donkeys need friends. Being alone is not good. Why is this poor animal alone here?"

"I don't know. I really don't know anything about it."

"We must do something," Lila said. "It is not right. Do you not agree?"

"Yes, something … but what? I wonder if the Humane Society could help."

"This donkey needs help now. I think we should call your friend, the policeman," Lila said.

My friend, the policeman, Sadie thought. First he's going to arrest some guy for objecting to Lila's stopping traffic by standing in the middle of Arapahoe. Now, he's going to rescue the donkey.

Lila was still talking. "No, no, I think the newspaper. The students will read about the donkey in the newspaper and they…"

"The newspaper? That's a good idea. But I may have an even better idea. I know a news photographer. If he took a picture, I'm sure the *FITT Mustang* would use it. Maybe the *Boulder Star-Trumpet* would even be interested. And then, once the media are interested, something may get done," Sadie said.

The more she thought about it, the more she liked her idea. And she thought Lee Hong might like it as well. Besides which, she admitted to herself, it was an ideal excuse to call Lee Hong. After she'd given him this great photo tip, she could ask him what he was doing these days, besides saying he worked for her at the Institute.

Pondering possible scenarios with Lee Hong as they drove back to Boulder, Sadie was grateful for the lack of traffic. Fans going to the game had all gotten there and almost everyone else was watching the game on television. Sadie piloted the Mini Cooper straight down Arapahoe, again making the green wave of timed traffic lights.

Lila chattered on about donkeys. She seemed to know a great deal about them. Tiger, still pouting because Sadie had ignored his warnings about the strange beast, gazed stoically out the back window until they arrived in front of Flatirons Vista.

"Thank you so much, Lila," Sadie said handing over the car keys. "I think maybe I could actually learn to enjoy driving."

"You are welcome. And it was interesting. Such a nice don-key … she is very lonely, I think."

"How do you know it's lonely?" Sadie asked.

"She is not an 'it,' she is a 'she,'" Lila remonstrated. "You should not call animals 'it.' You do not call Tiger 'it,' do you?"

Chagrined, Sadie shook her head. "No, but I know he's not an it. Although, actually, he is."

Lila did not understand. Sadie explained. Lila did not approve.

I guess that's just one more thing Lila thinks Americans do wrong, Sadie thought as she waved goodbye.

Having had enough excitement for one day Tiger was ready to go inside. Spared the need for another walk, Sadie settled down in her pink recliner, phone in hand again. Should she call Lee Hong? Was she just being nosy? Nosy about the donkey? Nosy about Lee Hong? Well, yes. Yes, which? Yes, both, she admitted.

Her brief soul-searching complete, Sadie rummaged through her Day-Timer, looking for the number of Ming Fang Wang, Lee Hong's wife, and sister of the still-absent Ling.

She quickly punched in the number, not wanting to think about the wisdom of the call any longer. The phone rang and rang. Sadie was almost ready to hang up when a woman finally answered. "Hello, who is this?"

"It's Sadie Wagner. Is Lee Hong there, please?"

"Lee Hong?"

"Yes, is he there?"

"He is here."

"May I speak to him please?"

"No, not now. He is busy. I take message." The voice sounded familiar, too familiar.

"Is this Ming Fang?" Sadie asked.

The answer was slow in coming. "Ming Fang not here. Lee Hong busy. I take message."

"I'll call back," Sadie said shortly. She hung up and sat there, clutching the phone. The voice on the phone had been Ling's. She was sure of it. Ling, who supposedly hadn't yet come back from China. Ling, who hadn't yet come back to her job as Sadie's teaching assistant. As Sadie considered whether to call back, the phone rang.

"Yes?" she said.

"Professor Wagner?" It was Lee Hong.

"Yes," Sadie repeated.

"I am calling you back," he said.

As Sadie explained about the donkey and how it would make a poignant photograph, her mind ran on two tracks. While she talked about the donkey, she considered where to start her confrontation with him: about claiming her as his employer or about Ling. After a lengthy explanation of how to find the donkey's pond, Sadie made her decision. "Oh, Lee Hong, one other thing," she said. "My first class on Monday is at nine o'clock. Tell Ling I expect her to be there."

Seven

Saturday had been a long day, and Saturday night seemed even longer. FITT won their Homecoming game, and the streets were full of celebrating undergraduates. The noise from the outdoor Pearl Street Pedestrian Mall, Boulder's downtown gathering spot, ebbed and flowed in the early evening until it was punctuated with sirens at about 10 p.m. Sadie turned on the TV news and was treated to a shot of the tree-lined, brick-paved mall only two blocks away teeming with drunken revelers. Since the shot wasn't live, it offered no information on the reason for the sirens.

Whatever, Sadie thought. It doesn't seem like a good night to go for a stroll. Accordingly, Tiger had to make do with the small fenced area between her patio door and Arapahoe Avenue. He didn't like it, but he eventually gave up and anointed the tall wooden gate, now rarely opened since Mike had installed a complex lock. The gate opened onto the busy sidewalk along Arapahoe Avenue. Sadie saw the near-constant traffic as extra eyes and thus security. Mike saw it as a massive failing of her condo complex. Why have a locked lobby that required buzzing visitors in, yet gates onto Arapahoe that many residents didn't bother to lock? He hadn't liked her answer: residents often left the lobby door unlocked and many, as Mike knew first-hand, just gave lobby keys to frequent visitors.

Dating a cop certainly changes your perspective. It also often means spending Saturday night alone, Sadie thought, as she readied for bed early. Thoughts of the donkey's sad, dark eyes rimmed by fuzzy rings of gray fur accompanied her slow drift off to sleep and returned the instant she awakened to a pounding on the door. What time was it? Good grief! The clock showed 9:00. She'd slept almost twelve hours. Grabbing her robe and shoving her feet into her fluffy pink slippers, she headed for the door. A check of the peep hole revealed a disheveled Mike Robb, who yawned widely just as she opened the door.

"Oops, excuse me." He covered his mouth. "My mother really did teach me not to yawn in people's faces. You didn't answer your buzzer so I just used my lobby key."

"You look dreadful. Have you been up all night?"

"Essentially. Up all night … I don't know about the dreadful part."

"I'll make coffee," Sadie said as Mike stumbled into the kitchen.

"Actually, I'd rather just take a short nap, if you don't mind," he said stepping around Tiger and heading for the bedroom.

"Tiger, I bet you want out," Sadie said. "I'm surprised you let me sleep this long." The dog, who relished his dawn patrols of the garden, was usually a very good alarm clock. She let him out and waited for him to come back. Returning to the bedroom, she found Mike sound asleep. Well, best let him sleep, I guess, she thought, quietly shutting the bedroom door. There were always papers to grade. She eventually settled down at her desk in the living room and quietly read and commented on most of the week's assignments.

Four hours later, the bedroom door opened. "Wow, I'm great company. Sorry about that," Mike said. "I'm just getting too old to stay up all night."

"Are you okay now? Four hours isn't a lot of sleep."

"It's enough for now. I slept really well. Thank you!" He combed his fingers through his sandy hair. "Now, if I can just take a shower, I'll be a new man."

"I'm not sure I want a new man," she teased.

"Hmmm, there is that."

"There's also coffee."

"In a few minutes," Mike said, turning back to the bedroom and heading for its adjacent bathroom.

Sadie went into the kitchen to see what might be had for lunch. She heard the shower start. By the time it stopped, she still hadn't figured out what to fix for lunch. Mike came out of the bedroom wearing a towel around his midriff and drying his hair with a second towel. "You offered coffee?" he asked.

Sadie poured him a cup, which he took back to the bedroom. When he emerged again, he was dressed in the somewhat rumpled clothes in which he had arrived. "Now," he said, "lunch. Then what? What would you like to do? I've got the whole rest of the weekend off."

"Rest of the weekend? It's almost two o'clock on Sunday afternoon. There's not a lot of the weekend left."

"Yeah, well. Let's use what *is* left. So, lunch and then what?"

Then what? The donkey's sad eyes hovered in the back of Sadie's mind. "I'd like to go back out and see that donkey again," she said.

Mike wasn't enthusiastic but he agreed to go after lunch. They foraged lunch from the Wild Oats Market next door to Flatirons Vista. Over her bowl of mixed greens from the salad bar, Sadie told Mike about her visit to the donkey's pond with Lila. He was amused by Lila's traffic direction. He was not amused by Lila's assumption that he could just arrest anyone she would like to have arrested. "Who does she think I am?" he asked.

"Maybe the police in France are different," Sadie said.

"I'm sure they are, but not that different," Mike answered.

"Anyway," Sadie said. "I'd like you to really look at the conditions in which that donkey is living. I think they are inhumane."

"Donkeys aren't human."

"That's not what humane means."

"I know that."

"So?"

"Okay, so let's go," Mike said pushing back from the table. "But you have to drive, okay?"

"Sure," Sadie said more confidently than she felt.

Soon they were on their way out Arapahoe, and Mike started lecturing her about the green light wave. "You already told me that," she said testily.

"If you go this slow, you'll miss a light and then you'll probably miss more than one," Mike said.

"Okay," Sadie said as she pulled into the parking lot in front of the Humane Society Thrift Store. "You drive. I don't want you to keep harping at me." She slammed the seat back, got out, and stomped around to the passenger side, meeting Mike as he walked around to slide into the front seat behind the wheel.

Soon they were at the pond. Mike pulled up beside the fence. The donkey was nowhere to be seen. "She was hiding when Lila and I were here," Sadie said, "but Lila taught me how to call her."

"Useful lady, Lila," Mike muttered.

Ignoring his sarcasm, Sadie started to make a soft clicking sound when she reached the fence.

The trees at the far side of the pond remained still. Sadie continued the reassuring clicks as she tried to see into the dense thicket of Russian olives. Maybe there was a slight movement. Click, click, click. Yes, the donkey was there, but certainly unsure.

"It's gone," Mike said loudly—too loudly.

"Now you've scared her," Sadie said. "Be quiet. She'll come eventually." Sadie resumed her clicking and, indeed, the donkey did peek out from the cover of the trees. But she still didn't leave their sheltering shadows.

Sadie and Mike stood at the fence watching the animal, who continued to watch them. Finally, the donkey began to move out of the trees, stepping high as she did so. Avoiding direct eye contact with the donkey, Sadie continued her clicking call.

Mike wasn't looking at the donkey at all. Instead, he was staring intently at the obstacle the donkey had stepped over. "Uh oh," he said quietly to Sadie. "I think we have a major problem here."

"We certainly will if you keep scaring her," Sadie said as the donkey stopped to reassess the situation. "I think you should go back to the car."

"Actually, I need to go over this fence." Mike grabbed the top of the fence, put his right foot into the chain link, and swung easily over. As he dropped to his feet on the other side, the startled donkey whinnied and ran back into the trees.

"What are you doing?" Sadie was irate. "Now you've really scared her. We'll never get her to come to us."

"The donkey is the least of my worries," Mike said heading toward the trees.

Sadie watched Mike make his way around the pond to the trees. Stepping carefully on the grass, staying away from the muddy edge of the pond, he reached the trees and squatted on his heels. He pulled out his cell phone and punched in a number. "DB at Valmont and 63rd," he said crisply. "And," he added, "better send the equine unit from animal control as well. There's going to be a displaced donkey."

DB? What was that? What was going on? And who was going to displace the donkey?

Mike was coming back to the fence. "I'm sorry," he said. "You'd better go back to the car and wait. I guess you're involved in this but it isn't a very pretty sight."

"What isn't a very pretty sight? What are you talking about?"

"We're not the first visitors the donkey has had today. But it sure looks as though it didn't like the first one. I think the donkey kicked him in the head. And walked all over him besides."

"Kicked who in the head?"

"The man lying in the mud over there. He's dead."

Eight

"Who is it?" Sadie asked, her voice shaking.

"I don't know. He's face down in the mud with the back of his head smashed in. Looks like your poor, abused donkey had enough!"

"I don't believe that. She is so shy and gentle."

"Uh huh, shy and gentle. We'll see about that," Mike turned to consider the donkey, now huddled against the fence on the other side of the pond as far away from them as possible. "I wonder if the crime scene boys know how to match hoof prints to wounds."

Sadie's stomach lurched as a horrible thought suddenly occurred to her. "I told Lee Hong to come out here to photograph the donkey. Is it Lee Hong over there?"

"I don't think so, but I've only seen Lee Hong once and it was a long time ago. The body is face down in the mud, but it appears to be bigger than your average Chinese."

"Lee Hong isn't small. He is almost six feet tall."

"Then I don't know. Maybe. We'll have to wait and see," Mike said as an approaching siren sounded in the distance. "You need to wait for me in the car," Mike repeated.

The first patrol car was followed by another, and shortly thereafter an ambulance arrived quietly. No need for sirens and

39

speed, I guess, Sadie thought as she watched from the passenger seat where she had obediently retreated.

Soon the quiet, out-of-the-way pond was the scene of purposeful activity as vehicle after vehicle arrived. When Sadie lost sight of Mike in the growing knot of people at the other edge of the pond, she returned her attention to the donkey. Now thoroughly spooked by the activity in her meager compound, the donkey hugged the fence line across the pond from Sadie. Her feet almost in the water, she looked miserable.

Sadie got out of Mike's car and went around the outside of the fence to the donkey. Faced with choosing between Sadie and the men working around the body on the other side of the water, the donkey chose not to move as Sadie cautiously approached.

She extended her hand between the links of the fence and touched the animal's withers, speaking softly, interspersing her soothing words with reassuring clicks.

"There, there, little one. It'll be okay. In fact, I'm sure it will be better. The Humane Society even has a barnyard. You'll like it there."

Beyond them, behind the trees and invisible from the road where Sadie had been, a gate to the compound gaped open. Sadie and the donkey noticed this at the same time. Raising her head, interest piqued, the donkey saw a break for freedom. But to reach the gate, she would have to go back through the trees, very near the cluster of people. Sadie could almost hear the donkey's thoughts as the animal began to inch sideways. Maybe, maybe.

"No, no, little lady," Sadie spoke quietly but firmly. "You'll just get scared all over again. And it won't do you any good to be out on the road." She tried to grasp the flimsy halter the donkey wore. Was that there before? Sadie couldn't remember, but she thought not. The halter stretched as the donkey pulled against Sadie's grip. A halter that stretches? Weird. What kind of use is a halter that stretches?

"Mike!" Sadie called loudly. Mike turned to Sadie and raised an eyebrow. She gestured at him and he began to stomp around the muddy periphery of the pond, his annoyance evident in every step. The donkey shied away, backing into the fence and bending it outward toward Sadie as Mike neared.

"What?" he demanded when he reached them.

"Has someone called the Humane Society about this poor animal?" Sadie asked.

"I don't know, I suppose so."

"And," Sadie asked her second, much more urgent question: "Is it Lee Hong over there?"

"Apparently. At least that's what his ID says. And he looks like the picture on Lee Hong's driver's license. It was in his wallet."

Her heart plummeted. "My God, it's my fault. I sent him out here to be kicked to death!"

"Actually, I'm not sure about that."

"I did, I sent him out here. I told him it would be a great photo opportunity."

"I didn't mean that part; I meant the part about being kicked to death. I'm not sure your donkey is the culprit."

"No? What do you mean? And what will happen to her?"

Ignoring her first question, Mike chose to answer the second one. "You wanted someone to take care of it. I guess that's what will happen."

"Will you please quit calling her an it!"

"Huh?"

"The donkey is a female. She's not an it," Sadie realized she was testy and it probably wasn't really about the pronouns used to refer to the donkey. "When will the Humane Society get here?"

"I don't know. The donkey isn't really high on the priority list right now." Mike turned away and started back toward the now plastic-draped figure on the ground.

"Could you check? Or, better yet, can I do it?" she called after him. "And be sure they find Lee Hong's camera."

Mike turned back to her, a scowl on his face. "I don't think you need to tell us how to investigate a crime scene, Sadie."

"He would have had a camera, that's why he was here, to take photos of the donkey. I know that, but maybe those guys don't." She hadn't seen the crime scene techs pick up anything large. In fact, they seemed to be interested in tiny things. Two of them worked on their knees with tweezers and plastic bags.

"I'll tell them about the camera." Mike turned abruptly and hurried back to the other side of the pond, where Sadie saw him talking to one of the uniformed policemen. They both turned and looked at the donkey—or maybe at her? The policeman shrugged dismissively.

Sadie fumbled in her backpack. Aha, she did have her cell phone with her. Information worked as poorly as usual, and it took three calls to ascertain the number for the Humane Society. After another two calls, she got through to the correct number to report an animal emergency outside the City of Boulder but in Boulder County. It was the County Sheriff's Office and only a message phone. Hoping someone checked the phone recorder on Sunday, Sadie left a message.

"Abandoned donkey found at murder scene. Please rescue ASAP. She is at 63rd and Valmont Road. I'll stay with her until you come. Thank you." Sadie left her name and cell phone number.

"Okay, little lady, now we wait," she said reassuringly to the donkey, who hovered nearby, probably having decided that Sadie was the best port in an otherwise terrible storm.

They didn't have to wait long. In fact, it was less than ten minutes before a truck showed up towing a horse trailer. The young woman driver parked near the open gates. In deference to the chaos of the scene by the side of the pond, her uniformed passenger got out and walked around the outside of the fence toward Sadie.

"Hi, what's going on? Do you know?" she asked when she reached Sadie.

"Someone was killed over there," Sadie answered, pointing toward the group at the pond's edge. "They said the donkey kicked him in the head, but I doubt that. She's very gentle and scared. I'm impressed you got here so fast."

"Fast! We weren't fast at all. First, I had to replay the message five or six times before I could understand it. And then, when I finally did figure it out, it took awhile to get the horse van ready. It's probably been two hours since that guy left his message about the animal," the officer answered.

"Guy? What guy? I left a message, maybe fifteen minutes ago," Sadie said.

"Well, I didn't hear that one. I just heard the one from this guy who hardly spoke English. I could barely understand him. He kept saying we had to come rescue something … it sounded like bulloh. Finally we decided he meant burro. That's why we brought the Humane Society's horse trailer."

"Was he Chinese, do you think?" Sadie asked wondering if Lee Hong had made the call.

"No idea, but he wasn't American and he wasn't female, so I know he wasn't you."

So who called? Sadie puzzled over this as she watched the two women round up the donkey and gently prod her up the ramp into the horse trailer. Once inside, the donkey turned around and looked at Sadie with large, sad eyes that seemed to be pleading for help.

Feeling a mix of pity and helplessness, Sadie asked the animal control officer, "The donkey will be okay, won't she? What will happen to her?"

The answer sounded well rehearsed: "The Humane Society tries to reunite lost pets and their owners."

"You think this donkey is a lost pet?"

"Maybe not a pet exactly, but this donkey is not wild. It has a halter and it seems to be used to the horse trailer."

Not totally reassured, Sadie watched them put the tailgate up and drive off with the donkey. She wished she hadn't seen the recent TV news story about a wild horse roundup. Herds of healthy animals, run to ground by hovering helicopters, were hauled off to dog food factories. She shuddered.

"What's the matter?" Mike had come up behind her just in time to see the shudder.

"I was just wondering what would happen to the donkey now," Sadie answered.

"Worried about the donkey but not about your friend over there?"

Sadie's stomach went into free-fall. "If that really is Lee Hong," she started and lost her voice for a moment before starting over, "If that is Lee Hong, then it's my fault he's dead. How can I possibly deal with that?" The tears began to flow.

Mike pulled her into a comforting embrace. "We're not sure who it is yet. You know that."

"Yes, and whoever it is is beyond help now," she said. "But, you know what? The donkey isn't beyond help yet. So, yes, I am worried about the donkey."

Nine

The drive home was tense. Mike insisted on driving, and when Sadie again mentioned Lee Hong's missing camera, his response was curt. "Look, Sadie, I want you to stay out of this. Remember what happened the last time you meddled in a murder investigation?"

"Excuse me! If I remember correctly it was you who dragged me into the 'last time,' as you call it," Sadie replied. Last spring Mike had summoned her to the police station to "explain" why the man who had argued loudly with her in Atlanta while they were waiting to board a Denver flight was dead within two hours of arriving in Boulder. It was the first time she met Mike Robb and the "meddling" she did in his subsequent investigation was only to free herself from suspicion.

"Would you consider it meddling if I told you that a man called animal control hours before I did? And that he didn't speak English very well?"

"How do you know that?"

"The animal control officer told me. I thanked her for coming so fast for the donkey. She said it took several hours. They hadn't even gotten my call. They were responding to an earlier call. Do you think it could have been Lee Hong who called?"

"You think he called to report a lone donkey? Before he was killed?"

"You saw how scared the donkey was. Something awful happened out there."

Grim-faced, Mike didn't respond. They continued westward toward Boulder, successfully riding the wave of green lights until, at the corner of Arapahoe and Broadway, Mike's luck failed. The light changed and he braked hard.

"Now, if I had done that, you would have said I was driving too fast," Sadie said.

"No, I would have said you were driving distracted and not thinking ahead. Which is exactly what I was doing."

"Distracted? You? I don't think that's possible."

"I really don't want to argue with you. So I'll just ignore that remark." The light changed to green, and Mike drove past Wild Oats and turned left into the parking lot of Sadie's condo. The one and only guest parking spot was taken.

"I'll just hop out," Sadie offered. "Then you won't have to worry about finding a spot on the street."

"Nope, you're not getting away angry. I'll just park right here," he said, pulling into an empty slot designated for the condo manager. "Of course, we wouldn't have this problem if you'd just get a resident's parking permit and give it to me," he added.

"There's a problem there, and you know it."

"The good professor still has your parking permit? What does he use it for? Going to the library, I hope."

"I don't think he uses it for anything. I don't know that he even still has it. But the manager says I have to turn in my 'lost' permit before he can issue another one."

"That makes no sense. If it's lost, how can you turn it in?"

"I think he knows it's not exactly lost."

"So ask Simone for it," Mike said. "How hard is that?"

How hard was that? Good question. Sadie hadn't really talked to her former lover since he had moved in and out in a record twenty-four hours last May. That wasn't exactly true. They had talked. Just not about parking permits. And now, well now it was really too late—and way too awkward—to ask him for the parking permit he had undoubtedly long since tossed away.

"Okay, go ahead and park here, but I'm not responsible if the manager has your car towed," Sadie said, opening the car door.

"He knows better than to have my car towed. And if he doesn't, the towing company will know better than to tow a cop's car."

"Okay, okay ..."

The tense silence fell again as they walked from the car into the lobby, through the courtyard and around the corner to Sadie's door. Both silence and tension disappeared in the tumult of unrestrained joy that greeted them inside Sadie's door. Who could remain angry—or anything but amused—when faced with an 85-pound whirling dervish on four feet?

Tiger was enraptured. Sadie had come home. Mike had come too. This could only mean one thing: a long, satisfying exploration of the Boulder Creek Path! The excited dog twisted as he leaped in the air, yipping with joy.

"How about it, buddy? Want to go for a run?" Mike asked as he playfully cuffed the big dog. Tiger turned and grabbed his leash from its hook.

"I guess that means 'yes,'" Mike said. "How about it? You want to go too?" he asked Sadie.

"No, I'll just stay here, I think. You two can really run if I don't go along."

"What about it, Tiger? What do you think?" Mike asked the dog, who was waiting, excitement radiating from every move.

Not understanding the words but knowing they were addressed to him, Tiger wagged his tail even faster.

"He says 'Nope, we'll just walk,' so you can go too. You'll feel better, come on!"

"Well, Tiger is very smart, I'm sure he knows best," Sadie said. "Besides which, we can move your car then."

"Always a reason. You have to watch her, she always has a reason," Mike explained to Tiger as the trio headed out the door back toward his car.

"I guess it'll have to be campus. It's getting late and I can't think of anywhere else to walk Tiger in the dark," Mike said.

"Yes, that would probably be best. And parking won't be a problem on a Sunday night."

But parking was a problem. Even though the Homecoming football game had been over for more than a day, the Homecoming celebrations were continuing. At least the campus police had not yet reopened many of the parking lots closed to all but the influx of football fans.

Goodness knows, all those people who donate money to the athletic programs certainly need a convenient place to park when they come to see the results of their largess, Sadie thought.

Eventually, they found an open parking lot on the south end of campus far from the football stadium. The nearest building was the planetarium. Tiger enjoyed exploring the scale model of the Universe that stretched from the Sun in front of the planetarium to Pluto more than a quarter mile away almost to Colorado Boulevard. Separate concrete pedestals marked the relative locations of all the planets in between on a scale of 1 to 10 billion.

Tiger examined each of these pseudo-fire hydrants with extreme interest. Somewhere between Jupiter and Saturn his leg-lifting became pro forma. But, like the trooper he was, Tiger continued his attempts to leave a record of his visit long after he ran out of canine calling card "ink."

Laughing at Tiger's antics, they had a good time walking across campus and, in Mike's case, reminiscing about his undergraduate days at the Institute.

"Did I ever tell you that I wanted to be one of the FITT wranglers?" he asked as they passed Neptune at the Engineering Building and turned west. The newly constructed skyboxes at the stadium loomed in front of the mountain backdrop.

"You wanted to run around on the football field trying to hold onto a bucking mustang?" Sadie asked incredulously.

"You make it sound so stupid." He sounded irritated.

"Well, it is rather stupid, don't you think?"

"Maybe. I suppose someone could get hurt. Mustangs can be dangerous, especially with fifty thousand people screaming at them.

"So, you didn't get the job?" Sadie tucked her hand into the crook of his arm as they stopped for the light at Colorado Boulevard.

"Nope. Not well enough connected, I guess."

They had reached the stadium now, and Sadie marveled at the newly constructed skyboxes. The night lighting made their entrance hall look like something out of medieval times. No, Sadie thought. Not medieval times. Medieval times as done by Hollywood.

Tiger was not impressed with the skyboxes and, tugging at his leash, he urged Mike on down the hill toward Arapahoe and the busy shopping area there.

But Sadie wasn't finished with the skyboxes, and the athletic program and the whole football milieu. "What do you think of that monstrosity?" she asked.

"Monstrosity? The skyboxes? I guess I agree … they are an architectural monstrosity. But if someone offered me a warm, dry seat in one for Homecoming, I'd take it!" He shrugged.

"That's just the trouble with everything. We don't like it, but if it's going to be there anyway, we'll take it. You could say that about so many things. Football. Illegal immigration. Iraq."

"Iraq? How did we get from football to Iraq?"

"Actually, we've gotten to Frank Shorter, and I think it's time to turn around," Sadie said as Tiger sniffed the base of the statue erected to honor Boulder's famous Olympic gold medal marathoner, and founder of the annual Bolder Boulder 10K race.

"I thought we'd go down to McGuck's, get Tiger a chew bone, and stop for coffee at the Brewing Market," Mike said.

"And then walk back up this hill? In the dark?"

"Walking up hills is good for you. And this dark isn't very dark. We're on a busy street. Besides which, you have both your man and your dog with you. What more could you want?"

What more indeed, thought Sadie. Interesting pronoun—*your* man. Did that make her Mike's woman?

Deciding not to go there, Sadie tacitly agreed to go to the coffee shop. They continued to stroll down the hill, Tiger growing

more and more excited as they neared the busy intersection at
Arapahoe and Folsom.

It took two light cycles to cross both busy streets, but once
they were actually in the shopping center, it was clear that Tiger
knew where they were headed.

He strained at the leash, imploring them to hurry, hurry up to
McGuckin Hardware. Once a basic hardware store, now usually
called just McGuckin's, the store was a local shopping mecca.
Just about anything anyone needed could be found there. And
leashed dogs were welcome shoppers, especially in the dog sup-
ply section, where floor-level bins of interesting chew toys were
displayed unwrapped.

Tiger took his time making a careful selection from the bin.
The rawhide he finally chose was shaped like a bone. It wasn't the
biggest one there but it was the darkest one. "Probably drenched
in some chemicals that aren't good for you," Sadie said to the
pleased dog. Despite that, she let him carry his new chew toy up
to the register, where he refused to relinquish it to the clerk.

"I don't think it had a bar code anyway, did it?" Sadie asked
the young woman behind the counter.

"No. I guess it came from the large toy bin. Right?"

"Right," Mike said handing her a five-dollar bill. After he got
a few coins in change, the three of them left, Sadie and Tiger to
sit at a table on the Brewing Market patio next door and Mike
to stand in line at the counter. The barista impressively juggled
three orders at once, and Mike soon returned with a latte for
Sadie and a chai tea for himself. They sipped their hot drinks
while Tiger attacked his new toy under the table.

"So," Sadie said, returning to the fear that nagged at the edges
of her consciousness, "that was really Lee Hong at the pond?"

Mike put his cup down and sighed. "Sadie, I don't know who
it was, but since Lee Hong was supposed to be there and since
his ID was on the body, it's a good bet."

"If it was Lee Hong, his camera should have been there. You
didn't find a camera, did you?"

"No, but there didn't seem to be anything around. No camera, no weapon, that is, no weapon except maybe a donkey's hoof. There were muddy hoof prints on the guy's shirt. Two perfect ones right below his neck."

Sadie caught her breath. It wasn't possible. "But, you saw how the donkey avoided the body. She stepped over it, way over it."

"That time, yes. Who knows what she did before that. We'll figure it out, but right now, I don't know. And we're just speculating." He looked at his watch. "We've been here almost an hour; let's go."

Responding to the last two words, Tiger scrambled out from under the table. His enthusiastic response interrupted Sadie, and gave her time to think better of continuing her questions.

They started back up to campus. Tiger, proudly carrying his new chew toy, set a steady pace, and soon they were back at the car.

On the ride home, no one mentioned Lee Hong, his camera, or the donkey—at least not directly. However, as the car again pulled into the manager's parking space, Sadie did say, "Well, I guess my donkey rescue plans didn't work out quite the way I hoped."

Mike reached over her and shoved her door open. "I'll see you tomorrow," he said. Responding to this apparent brush-off, Sadie got out and pulled her seat forward so that Tiger could bound out of the back. They were almost to the lobby when Mike caught up to them.

"Wait a minute," he said, "Tiger forgot his chew toy and you forgot to kiss me good-night." He handed Tiger the now-slimy chew toy and gathered Sadie into a welcome embrace.

Ten

As Sadie got ready for bed, she encountered the unmistakable evidence of Mike's earlier presence. The more than usual disarray in the bathroom. The used bath towel, flung over the shower bar. And, of course, the still rumpled, unmade bed. All reminded her that it promised to be a lonely night.

It was. Sadie was still lying awake when the phone rang at midnight. It was Ling, who made no mention of her unexplained absence, but instead poured out her concern for Lee Hong.

"He went to see your donkey," she said. "He has not come home."

Why had the family not been notified? Sadie wondered. Was there a good reason? At least one good enough that Sadie probably shouldn't be the one to tell Ling that Lee Hong wasn't coming home. However, this might be the time to get more information. "What was he doing?" Sadie asked. "I mean besides taking pictures of the donkey?"

"He had many photo jobs," Ling answered.

"Like what?" Sadie pressed remembering, Commander Gross and his odd visit. "Who is he selling pictures to now?"

Ling became evasive. "Well, mostly newspapers, you know."

"National newspapers?"

"Maybe. No, now it is photo essay. He is not finished."

"Photo essay about what?"

"Mountain towns."

"Mountain towns? Towns? Not mountains? Ski towns, do you mean?" Sadie asked.

"No, not ski."

Why was it so hard to get information from Ling? Experience had taught Sadie that Chinese people rarely gossip. And they seem to consider any proffered information to be gossip. Or maybe it's that they don't gossip with Americans. Still hoping to get some information, Sadie began to ask a series of carefully honed questions.

"Lee Hong is working on a photo essay?"

"Yes."

"He has a market for this?"

"Market?"

"A place to sell the photos when he's done."

"Yes."

"What is this market?"

"Very good price."

"Yes, but what is it? Is it a national magazine again?"

"No, not a magazine."

"What then? A newspaper?"

"No, a report."

Aha, Sadie thought. It *is* for Gross. What could Lee Hong be photographing in mountain towns that the U.S. government would care about? Drugs sold under cover of the ski industry? Illegal immigrants working in luxury hotels? What?

"Which mountain towns?" she asked Ling. "And," remembering the ancient Yugo the extended Chinese family drove, "how did he get over the passes? I'm surprised the Yugo would make it to the Eisenhower Tunnel, let alone go over Vail Pass."

"Oh, no pass," Ling said.

"No pass?" What mountain town could be reached without going over a pass? There weren't many ski areas along the Front Range. Eldora was a short bus ride from Boulder, but the family ski resort near Nederland didn't seem like a place where drug trafficking could be of interest. Sadie couldn't think what to ask next when suddenly her mind zeroed in on a new idea: not drugs, maybe gambling!

"Do you mean Black Hawk?" she asked. Was Lee Hong doing a photo essay on gambling?

Ling's answer was slow in coming. "Yes, Black Hawk."

"So has Lee Hong been doing a photo essay on gambling in the mountain towns?"

"Maybe."

Interesting, Sadie thought. Usually a Chinese "maybe" means no. This time I think it may actually mean yes. She decided to try a direct question.

"So Lee Hong was taking pictures for the U.S. government?"

Ling's sharp intake of breath was audible over the phone. What did it mean? Ling was startled? Frightened? Sadie didn't know how to find out.

Ling abruptly changed the subject. "I am sorry I am so late back to school." The switch from Lee Hong's apparent disappearance to her own curious absence puzzled Sadie but she thought, I'll go with this flow.

"Yes," she said. "I don't understand why you are late. I do need an explanation, especially why you didn't let me know."

"Yes," Ling replied.

"And?"

Silence. "And?" Ling parroted quizzically.

"Yes, and. And what is your explanation?"

"I don't know."

"Oh, for heaven's sake. You must know where you've been. Have you been here all this time and just not coming to school? Or have you been in China all this time? Or what?" Sadie rattled on even though she knew she was probably talking too fast for Ling to follow her words over the phone.

"China, yes, China. I went to home," Ling said.

"When did you come back?"

"Last week. Really, last week."

"School started three weeks ago."

"Yes."

Exasperated, Sadie gave up. "So, I will see you tomorrow? At my nine o'clock class. Is that right? Do you know what it is? And where?"

"Yes, I know. I have your schedule but I think that tomorrow is already today and, first, first I must find Lee Hong."

Should she tell Ling? She hesitated. Unable to think of a good reason why the police had not notified the family, Sadie decided not to say anything. After all, maybe the body at the pond hadn't been Lee Hong after all. I need to find out for sure, she thought, as she said perfunctory good-byes to Ling.

Eleven

Morning came too soon. Tiger's gentle whimpers crescendoed into full-throated demands before Sadie struggled up from the depths of slumber. She peered at the bedside clock but couldn't make out the digital numbers. Surely it wasn't eight o'clock already? But that certainly seemed to be what the glowing red numbers said. In fact, it was 8:03. And, even more alarming, Sadie's first class was due to start in fifty-seven minutes!

"Omigod!" Sadie exclaimed as, finally fully awake, she threw the covers to the floor. She ran to the patio door, unlocked it, and slid it open. "Tiger, you'll have to settle for the garden," she told the dog, who was surveying the open door with distaste. Why on this morning of all mornings did Tiger suddenly disdain his dawn patrol? Maybe because it was past dawn, Sadie thought. Way past dawn.

"Out!" she commanded as she shoved the reluctant dog out the door. A quick stop in the kitchen got the coffee maker started making hot water, and she heard it begin to burble as she turned on the shower. No dawdling under the warm water, no time to try to straighten her unruly red curls. After a fast shower, Sadie wrapped one towel around her head and another around her body. As she headed back toward the kitchen, she glanced again at the clock; it showed 8:12.

What can I skip? Sadie was desperate as she poured a cup of water through the ground coffee she had dumped into the filter atop a cup. Well, breakfast. For sure, there's no time for breakfast. No time to pack a lunch either.

What to wear? Always a problem this time of year in Colorado. Was it going to be warm? Or might it snow? Sadie flicked on the TV as she headed back toward the patio door to let Tiger in.

Local weather wouldn't be on until 8:18. That was four minutes away, time enough to feed Tiger. Sadie rushed back to the kitchen, grabbed Tiger's dish, filled it with kibbles from the cupboard, and topped them off with two spoonfuls of vanilla yogurt. She returned to the TV just as *Local on the Eights* proclaimed, "Today's high will be seventy-two degrees."

Okay, Sadie thought. Slacks, blouse, and blazer. No problem! No problem, except for finding clean, reasonably matching garments in her untidy closet. She couldn't find her blue slacks and her only really clean blazer was navy blue. The clock said 8:32. She grabbed her red slacks, still pristine in their plastic bag from the dry cleaner. It was 8:34 by the time Sadie had her slacks and shoes on. She began to contemplate her blouse collection. What went with red and blue? None of her patterned blouses, for sure. Well, white would do. It was 8:36 when Sadie rushed out of her bedroom, looking exceptionally patriotic but dressed and ready to go.

Except now Tiger was ready to go also. He was sitting beside the door with his leash in his mouth and his tail thumping the floor.

"Tiger, I can't. You've just got to go out into the garden again. And you have to do it in about ninety seconds. Can you do that?" she asked the startled dog as she pushed him out the patio door and shut it for the second time in an hour.

Tiger turned around, sat down, pressed his nose against the glass and looked mournful. But Sadie didn't have time to appreciate his sad-sack act. She was too busy at her desk, trying to shove everything she might need into her backpack.

Papers to return to her nine o'clock writing class, the syllabus for her eleven o'clock conversation class, notes for the discussion in her late afternoon seminar, and some still remaining papers to be read and graded, should she have a spare moment. What else? There was something else, but Sadie couldn't think what it was.

She opened the door to let Tiger in. "You didn't do anything did you? You just sat there pouting," she scolded the dog, who registered his disapproval by burrowing into his bed, tucked safely under Sadie's desk.

"May the Force be with you," Sadie said to Tiger as she headed for the front door. To the unhappy dog, this meant, "I'm going now but I will be back."

I sure need the Force to be with *me*, Sadie thought as she shut the door. It was 8:42, and she was going to be late to her first class.

Sadie hurried up Broadway toward campus. The fastest time she had ever made from her condo to her office in the Language Arts Building was sixteen minutes. But that was two years and two sprained ankles ago. Nonetheless, she held to the hope that she could make it to class with a minute or two to spare.

Of course, she didn't. The clock on the wall at the front of her ground floor classroom said 9:05 when Sadie pushed the door open. The room was quiet because twenty students were carefully copying down the three sentences Ling had written on the board.

All mammals are warm-blooded.
All whales are mammals.
Therefore, all whales are warm-blooded.

Although grateful that Ling was actually there, Sadie was decidedly curious why she had chosen to discuss the classical syllogism. She slid into a seat at the back of the room and listened.

"You agree with this conclusion?" Ling pointed to the last sentence:

All whales are warm-blooded.

There was no immediate response.

"You must agree, no?" Ling prodded.

"I know nothing about whales," someone ventured from near the front of the room. "They live in the sea, but they are warm-blooded. Is this true?"

"Of course it's true, look at this." Ling stabbed her finger into the board. "It says so right here."

She added letters to the sentences.

All mammals (B) are warm-blooded (A).
All whales (C) are mammals (B).
Therefore, all whales (C) are warm-blooded (A).

"So, you do not even have to know the words. All you have to know is this." Ling wrote three equations on the board under her sentences.

All B are A.
All C are B.
Therefore all C are A.

"If you can write a problem like this, you don't have to know anything. You can just tell is it true or is it not true. This is Western-style logic," Ling concluded with a sweeping gesture at the board.

Everyone nodded their heads but Ling had a shocker for them. "Actually, what I said is not right. Truth is not the question. Valid is the question. This is a valid argument. But we don't know for sure it is true." Ling folded her arms and leaned against the blackboard. "How would we know for sure it is true that whales are warm-blooded?"

No one answered. As the silence lengthened, more and more of the students seemed to notice that Sadie had arrived. Uneasy glances bounced from Sadie to Ling and back again but no one ventured a comment until Ling said, "This is one big problem for Chinese people. Valid does not mean true. Until you understand this, you will not understand how Western people think.

"I think Professor Wagner will explain more," Ling said, smiling at Sadie. She sat down in the front row as Sadie rose and carried her bulging backpack to the front of the room.

Valid, true. Great! Now I get to tackle Aristotle on top of a forced march up the hill, Sadie thought. Considering the limited options Ling had left her, Sadie decided to address her last challenge: the difference between valid and true.

"Ling asked how you know if a valid conclusion is also a true conclusion. The answer to Ling's question is easy. She scanned the room, making eye contact with a number of the students before answering the question. "If we know that both premises are true, then we know that the conclusion is also true—both valid and true. Okay?"

Most of the students nodded and Sadie decided to segue from logic into writing: the purpose of the class. "Ling," she asked, "why is logic important in a writing class? Why does logic matter?"

Ling answered promptly. "Because when we write in English, mostly we must argue. And to argue well, we must be logical. We cannot just say this is true, we must show that it is true. To do this, we must understand Western logic."

"Indeed," Sadie agreed. "Logic isn't measurable like light or heat. Logic is a cultural concept. What we call logical is what conforms to Aristotle's ideas of good argument, logical reasoning. Just this sort of thing." She pointed back to the blackboard. "FITT offers semester-long courses in logic. This was only a really brief overview."

"Different from Confucius," Ling observed in a quiet aside that Sadie ignored.

Sadie opened her backpack and pulled out the pile of papers she had graded Sunday afternoon. "So, let's look at what you wrote last time. Remember the topic was American TV. Do you learn anything from American TV? Almost all of you had one problem or another with the way you presented your argument for whether or not you find American TV worth watching."

As she passed the papers back, she continued, "I'd like you to pair up and look at each other's papers. See if you can identify exactly what is wrong with your arguments in each case."

"You want us to fix it?" a student asked.

"Eventually," Sadie answered. "But first I want you to identify your problem. Be sure you understand what was wrong.

Then, once you understand the problem, we can try to find the solution."

As her students busied themselves reading and discussing her comments with their partners, Sadie circulated around the room, eavesdropping and occasionally interrupting a discussion.

Although most of the students had concluded that American TV wasn't worth watching, their arguments supporting this conclusion were unstructured, weak, and sometimes even wrong.

As she listened to their conversations, a thought occurred to Sadie: Maybe she too had come to a wrong conclusion. Maybe it wasn't the donkey's eyes that had flashed in the headlights. But, if not, what *was* it?

Twelve

She was still mulling over her question about the donkey when the students started to pack up and drift out the door.

"Lee Hong still not home." Ling's voice startled her out of her reverie. "Can you ask your policeman friend what we should do?"

"I think so," Sadie answered. "I will call him."

"When?"

"Ummm, right now, I think."

"I will come also."

Oops, Sadie thought, that could be a problem. If Ling hears my conversation with Mike, she is going to know that I knew about Lee Hong. She won't understand why I didn't tell her sooner.

Sadie gathered her materials off the lecturer's desk as Ling waited, exhibiting extreme patience that she probably didn't feel. As they left the classroom and started up the stairs, Sadie continued to stew about what to tell Ling. Well, she thought, I don't really know for sure that the body at the pond was Lee Hong. No, not for sure, but still I think Ling will wonder why I didn't tell her if it does turn out to be Lee Hong.

In the midst of this conundrum, she remembered that she had a major grievance with Ling. Aha, she thought, attack first!

"So, Ling," she asked as they reached the doorway into the fourth floor corridor. "Why were you so late getting back to classes this semester?"

"Yes," Ling answered. "I was late. I was very late."

"Indeed. And why?" Sadie unlocked the door to her office.

"It was hard to come back," Ling said. "I was in Mexico many days."

"Mexico?" Sadie asked as she settled into her desk chair.

"Yes." Ling sank down on the blue plastic chair next to Sadie's desk.

"Why Mexico?"

"First to Mexico, then to America."

"You flew from China to Mexico to Colorado?"

"No. From China to Los Angeles. Then Lee Hong drives to Mexico."

Sadie's eyes widened. She now understood that Ling and Lee Hong had gone to Mexico and applied for political asylum. Sometimes Chinese students, tired of the ongoing hassles of re-newing student visas and ready to make new lives in the United States, simply went to Mexico, declared themselves political refugees and applied for permission to enter the United States permanently. It usually worked for those who were well edu-cated. After all, the United States is the land of opportunity, Sadie thought, somewhat cynically.

"So," she said to Ling, "you went to the American Embassy in Mexico to apply for asylum. Is that what you did?"

Ling looked at the floor and said something so softly that Sadie could not hear her. She remained head down, sitting very still.

"I didn't hear you," Sadie said.

Finally Ling replied, still quietly but a bit louder, "Yes."

"And that's why you are late. It took longer than you ex-pected for you to get your paperwork?"

Ling still looked at the floor. Finally she said, "No."

Now Sadie was confounded. "No? It didn't take longer? What do you mean?"

"We all went," Ling said. "Whole family. Lee Hong is okay right away. And Ming Fang also. Because she is wife of Lee Hong, she gets papers right away also. And the two little girls," Ling said.

"So now everyone in the whole family is a political refugee. Is that right?"

"No," Ling replied. "Not me. Lee Hong and Ming Fang came back without me. I waited."

"So," Sadie said, putting words in Ling's mouth. "That's why you were so late. You were waiting for them to process your new entry papers."

"Yes."

"I think we'll have to talk to Human Resources about this," Sadie said. "They will want to have a copy of your current papers. I hope it won't be a problem to keep you as my teaching assistant." Sadie was so busy contemplating the possible problems of suddenly having no TA, no one to help grade the deluge of papers, no one to cover for her when she was late to class, that she almost missed Ling's response.

"No papers."

"Maybe it would be best to talk to someone in the department office first…. Wait, what did you say? No papers? The U.S. didn't give you asylum? But, didn't you have to give up your student visa when you went to Mexico?"

"Yes."

A horrible possibility occurred to Sadie. "You gave up your student visa, you applied for political asylum, you did not get political asylum, but you are here. How did you get back?"

"Lee Hong called someone to help me. Now I must call someone to help him. Please can we call your policeman friend? Now?" The tears that had been welling in Ling's eyes began to flow down her cheeks.

Sadie's heart sank. She was only making things worse. When Ling found out that she knew about Lee Hong, she would undoubtedly never trust her again. Steeling herself for the coming unpleasantness, Sadie turned, sat down at her desk, and drew the phone toward her.

"I'll call him now," she said reassuringly to Ling.

She slowly dialed Mike's direct number as she tried to think how to word her question with Ling listening.

"Robb here." Mike's response was clipped.

"Hi," Sadie responded. "It's me. I have Ling here with me in the office. She is very concerned about the fact that Lee Hong has apparently disappeared."

Mike either didn't pick up on Sadie's problem or chose to ignore it. "He didn't disappear. You know where he is," he replied.

Ling, her shoulders slumped, eyes downcast, looked the picture of grief.

I think she knows, Sadie thought. But what does she know?

Throwing her previous caution away, Sadie asked Mike, "You weren't sure before. Are you sure it is Lee Hong? And if so, why haven't you told his family?"

Ling's head snapped up. She leaned forward. If she was trying to hear Mike's answer, it wasn't too hard. Mike was nearly shouting.

"We'd love to inform his family. We can't figure out who that would be. I know Ling is family. But she's not next-of-kin. We have combed the Ponderosa Apartments and talked to every Hong over there. None of them is Lee Hong's wife. We're trying to locate her through the Institute now. But ..."

"Wait," Sadie interrupted. "You're looking for a woman named Hong? If you find one, she won't be Lee Hong's wife. His wife is Ming Fang Wang. You know that. Or, if you didn't remember, you could have asked me."

"His wife doesn't have the same last name?"

Sadie didn't have time to cope with Mike's cultural ignorance because Ling was coming apart in front of her eyes. She fell to her knees wailing. The heart-wrenching sound gave Sadie goose bumps.

"No, no, noooooo," Ling sobbed as she grasped at Sadie. "Why, why? Why does he want Ming Fang? Where is Lee Hong? Is he hurt? No, noooooo...."

"You hear that?" Sadie demanded of Mike. "Ling thinks Lee Hong is injured. What do you want me to do?"

"Don't tell her anything. Give me his wife's name," Mike ordered.

"I just did." Sadie was angry now. "It's Ming Fang Wang. This is absurd!"

Sadie slammed the phone down and tried to coax Ling up from her knees. Unsuccessful, she squatted beside her and hugged the younger woman. "I'm so sorry, Ling," she said, "but the news is really bad. Lee Hong isn't just hurt, he's dead."

Ling stared at Sadie. "Dead?" she whispered. "Dead! It cannot be. How can he be dead? Not now."

Sadie had no idea what Ling was talking about. And that didn't matter anyway.

What mattered was Ling's increasingly deliquescent state. The young Chinese woman seemed to be shrinking as she clasped herself, rocked on the floor at Sadie's feet, and continued to sob quietly.

"I think we should get you home," Sadie said gently. "Ming Fang is going to need you. But, first, I think you'll feel better if you wash your face."

Ling nodded and, sniffling, stood up and headed for the restroom across the hall. Sadie heard her lock the restroom door before she picked up the phone. Midway through dialing Mike's number again, Sadie thought better of it, stopped, and hung up.

Maybe Mike wasn't the best person to ask to give Ling a ride home. He'd probably just interrogate her. But if not Mike, who?

Sadie considered her limited options. Who did she know who had a car on campus? Who could leave right now? And not ask a lot of questions?

The simple answer was no one. First, most of her friends didn't drive to campus. They walked or took the bus. Second, most of them had eleven o'clock classes. Everyone she could think of would soon be in class or preparing to be in one.

What about people who don't teach? Who? Rick Baines, Dan's good friend, was a researcher. He didn't have classes, but as Sadie reached for the phone to call Rick, she glanced out the window and saw him bounce down the stairs of the Animal Husbandry Labs and head up the street toward the library.

So, not Rick. There's always Dan, she thought reluctantly. He doesn't drive to campus but his house is close. Maybe Lila is home.

Sadie dialed Dan's familiar number. Just as Ling came out of the restroom, Lila answered. "Allo?" she said, in her lilting style.

"Lila," Sadie said quickly. "I need a really big favor. Could you please come over to the Language Arts Building and take my TA, Ling, to her home? It's the Ponderosa Apartments across 28th Street from campus. It won't take you long, and she really needs a ride."

Silence. Lila was obviously waiting for more explanation. When it wasn't forthcoming, she said, somewhat hesitantly, "Right now?"

"Yes, right now."

"I guess so. Do I know Ling?"

"I don't think so. But Dan does. I can explain later, but right now could you come and meet us at the front door of the building, the one on Colorado? I'll be there with Ling.

"What do you think?" Sadie asked as she glanced at the clock. "Do you think you could be here in ten minutes?"

"I can be there in five minutes if it is really important."

"It is," Sadie said gratefully. "We'll be waiting. Thank you, Lila."

Sadie hung up, stood, and put her arm around the disconsolate Ling. "Lila will take you home," she explained. "She's meeting us downstairs in a few minutes."

The two women headed out the door and down the stairs. They reached ground level and emerged into the crowded main hall. Sadie kept her gaze lowered, avoiding eye contact with several of her colleagues who were gossiping near the faculty mailboxes. Sadie and Ling reached the street just as Dan's red Mini Cooper swung into view.

Moments later, as Sadie watched Lila drive off with Ling, she realized that she now had an additional unsolved problem: What exactly was Ling's status? Had she really given up her student visa?

Emotionally exhausted, Sadie faced the fact that she had more classes to teach today. After that, she could worry about donkey's eyes and surrendered visas.

Sadie returned to her office in a hurry to pick up the syllabus for her eleven o'clock class. She tucked the backpack Ling had left behind beneath her desk for safekeeping. At the elevator, she grabbed a handful of copies of the *FITT Mustang* to use in class. The campus newspaper was free and always offered timely conversation topics if she needed them.

Thirteen

Advanced ESL Conversation was an easygoing class. The students all seemed to relish the opportunity to practice their growing English fluency. They were long past the traditional discussions of the weather. Recent news was always a favorite topic, especially when it offered the opportunity to criticize the United States. Sadie rarely had to do more than start the conversational ball rolling.

Her prepared syllabus let students review vocabulary related to the day's topic. "Sports" was the scheduled topic today, so she started by handing out the *FITT Mustang* with its Homecoming headlines.

"Do you know who won the Homecoming game on Saturday?"

"FITT," the class responded in unison. They didn't need the newspaper after all.

"Did anyone go to the game?" she continued.

"Yes," a few answered. One hand waved in the back of the room. Sadie acknowledged Gizella Polgar, a Hungarian student who had recently become very interested in selecting exactly the precise word to describe an action.

"If *working* there, is that same as *going* there?" she asked.

"Do you mean you worked at the game?"

"Yes, selling hot dogs. I work for food service."

"Hmmmm," Sadie responded. "Well, you were there. I think that is going to the game."

"But I did not see the game. I see only the hot dogs ... and the money. So, if I did not see the game, how can I say I go to it?"

As she contemplated her options, Sadie thought: This day started off badly and is only getting worse. After a few more seconds of thought, she decided to try to end the discussion with a definite answer. "If you want to be really correct, you should say you went to the game to work."

Gizella seemed satisfied that her question had been answered. Howard Feng, a Taiwanese computer science major, wasn't so sure.

"What if I am photographer?" he asked. "Photographer for newspaper? Then I am working at the game. And I really see the game because I am looking at the game, not ...," he added turning from his front row seat to look meaningfully at Gizella in the back of the room, "not looking at hot dogs and money."

"Then," he said turning back to Sadie, "I think you can say I go to the game because I see the game through my camera."

Opting for her usual way to gain time to think, Sadie responded by throwing the question back to the class. "What do the rest of you think?" she asked.

Apparently not much. Fifteen pairs of eyes stared at her. Howard looked amused, the rest looked a bit bored.

Sadie's mind was scrambling around various ways to rise above nit-picking the semantics of single words and get to expanded conversation. Unfortunately, Howard's photographer example had brought back her guilt about Lee Hong. The feeling of dread that had been hovering in the back of her mind became a stomach-churning wave. Concern about Ling followed in the backwash. Sadie decided to re-channel the conversation.

"If you sell hot dogs or take photographs at the game, you are working. So you must have the correct visa. Let's talk about visas."

The new topic interested the students. Sadie wondered briefly whether it was visas per se or the abrupt topic switch that was of interest. But she didn't care. This might kill the proverbial two birds with one stone: start the class conversation rolling again and get her some much-needed information.

"Tell me about your visa, Howard. Is it a student visa? Or can you work?"

"It is called F-1. Visa to study."

"And you, Gizella?" Sadie asked. "Is your visa an F-1 also?"

"No," Gizella answered, sounding pleased. "I have a green card!"

"Green card! That's wonderful," Henri Mathieu, a visiting Belgian scientist, chimed in. "How did you get that?"

"I have been here a long time," Gizella answered. "I do much work."

"Yes, but still. Your husband—is he American?"

"Yes, but I still must qualify."

"Well, being married to an American sure helps," Henri said waving a hand dismissively.

Gizella seemed offended. "No, no, it does not help. I still must be someone America wants!"

"Just be glad you are not from Taiwan," Howard said. "America only wants our money. Not our people. No one from Taiwan can get a green card. Anyone from China can get one."

China! That's what Sadie wanted to hear about. "Does it really matter where you are from as to what sort of visa you can get? What kinds of visas are there, anyway?"

Shan Lau, a Chinese physics student, grinning as he relished the opportunity to teach the teacher, said, "There are three kinds: F, H, and J. And each kind has more."

"More?" Sadie asked, seeking clarification.

"Yes, there is F-1, H-1B; stuffs like that."

Conversation class or not, Sadie couldn't let "stuffs" go by unremarked. She turned to the board and wrote *stuff*. "Is this a count noun?" she asked.

"No," the class chorused.

"So, if it's not a count noun, we don't add an 's'. What is the plural of stuff?"

"Stuff." Again a group answer.

"Yes, sorry," Shan Lau responded. "I forget. Anyway, I make list of visas." He strode to the board and wrote.

F-1 Student

H-1B Scholar

J-1 Visitor

As Shan Lau returned to his seat, Howard said, "Don't forget L. There is L visa also. But," he added "of course, not for Taiwan people. Not so many choices for old U.S. friends. Lots of choices for new friends...."

"What is an L visa?" Sadie asked as much to change the subject from new and old friends as to find out about L visas. She added L to the list on the board.

Many students answered at once. Migrant or immigrant seemed to be the consensus.

"So, does anyone have an L visa?"

No one responded.

"Okay, let's look at Shan Lau's list," Sadie said. "Who has an F visa?"

Seven students raised their hands.

"J?" Sadie asked. Five students raised their hands.

"And Gizella has a green card. That leaves two of you. What visa do you hold, Henri?" Sadie asked.

"I am H-1B," he said. "Visiting scientist. Meteorological Service of Belgium sends me to learn weather forecasts. I want to improve my English so I come to this class also."

"I see. What about you, Andrei?" she asked Andrei Cherkesov, a tall, blond Russian who rarely spoke unless Sadie asked him a direct question.

"I am J-1," he answered.

"Who sends you?" Henri asked.

"Fulbright Exchange," Andrei answered. "I come here, American teacher goes there."

This was news to Sadie. Andrei was a teacher? "What do you teach, Andrei?" she asked.

"English."

The murmur from the class was audible. Howard, ever the outspoken extrovert, put the general dismay into words. "So, if you are English teacher, how come you take this English class?"

Andrei looked decidedly uncomfortable as he answered. "I … I want talking practice."

"But you never talk!" Howard responded.

My sentiments exactly, Sadie thought as she waited for Andrei's response. He reddened and looked down at his clasped hands, but he said nothing. The silence lengthened uncomfortably until Sadie relented and ended it.

"So, back to visas," she said cheerfully. "I think there are many other kinds. Does anyone know about any others?"

"Famous opera star? What about them?" Henri asked.

"They get P visa," someone said.

"No, Q visa," Howard said firmly.

"Q is a fancy kind of J visa," Andrei said. "When I came, they thought maybe Q, but J is better. Q is for famous visitors, J is for not so famous."

Andrei and Howard continued their discussion. Letters ping-ponged back and forth.

"Just like my advisor is O-scholar. And Henri is H-1B scholar. Is it same?" Howard asked.

"Is what the same?" Sadie asked.

"O and H-1B are same as Q and J?"

"Sure," Andrei responded.

Sadie started to add the new visas to the list Shan Lau had put on the board. As she did so, Howard said, "Don't forget, put Q with J."

"Also, there is R," Gizella said.

"R?" Sadie asked.

"Religion," Gizella answered. "If you are here to teach about your religion, you get R."

R was news to Sadie, but it made sense. She added R to the growing list on the board just as Howard added another of his overly pithy observations.

"H-1B is scholar. H-2B is pea picker. Very similar!"

Those who appreciated his humor laughed. Only Gizella disagreed. "It is not H-2B, it is H-2A," she said firmly.

"How do you happen to know that?" Sadie asked.

"Because at home in Hungary I am a nurse."

"And?"

"And nothing. I am a nurse."

"Yes, but because you are a nurse, why do you know the visa of a pea picker?" Sadie asked. Giggles reverberated in the classroom as the students found this exchange at least as amusing as Howard's sarcasm.

"H seems like visa for worker. I look at all H visas. Nurse is H-1C," Gizella said. "And," she added, "I do not think it said pea picker anywhere."

"No? Maybe farm laborer?" Sadie suggested.

"Maybe," Gizella agreed. "But it is strange. Scholar, farmer, nurse, everything all one, all H. I wonder why?"

"Because any H visa lets you try for the green card," Andrei answered. "That's why H visa is so important. But do you think pea pickers and physics teachers really have equal chance for the green card?"

Finally, Andrei starts talking, Sadie thought. He had made a careful study of the U.S. visa morass. This thought was confirmed by Andrei's next statement.

"Also, there is E visa. That is if you have money. If you invest in America, you can come. No need to be tired and poor."

"Does everyone know what Andrei is referring to?" Sadie asked. "What does he mean by 'tired and poor'?"

"Statue of Liberty!" Shan Lau said triumphantly.

"Right, what does it say? Does anyone know exactly?" The minute she said this, Sadie thought oops, I sure hope so, because I don't … not exactly. Something about tired and hungry and storm tossed.

Both Shan Lau and Howard had opened their laptops. As they tried to Google the poem on the Statue of Liberty, Gizella made an attempt to quote it.

"Give to me your tired, your poor, your wanting to be free …
I have my light here on the golden shore," she said.

"Close! Close but not correct," Howard pronounced as he
read from the screen of his laptop.

> *Give me your tired, your poor,*
> *Your huddled masses yearning to breathe free,*
> *The wretched refuse of your teeming shore,*
> *Send these, the homeless, tempest-tossed to me,*
> *I lift my lamp beside the golden door.*

Writing quickly, Sadie tried to copy the poem onto the board.
She had to ask Howard to repeat the last sentence. Finally, she
had it all.

"Well," she said surveying the famous poem. "I think Gizella
did very well from memory."

They all looked at the poem. "Do you know all these words?"
Sadie asked. "What about refuse? Teeming? Tempest-tossed?" She
circled each word as she said it.

Refuse caused some problems. Most of the students thought
it was the verb "refuse." They questioned how the teeming shore
would refuse anything. For that matter, Andrei admitted, "teeming" itself was confusing.

But "homeless" got the most attention. "Men on street cor-
ners, homeless people. Do you say they are tempest-tossed?"
Shan Lau asked.

"Metaphorically speaking, maybe," Sadie answered, trying to
avoid a lengthy discussion of homelessness. But it didn't work.
The students were on the topic en masse.

"Why do they not work?" demanded a young woman who
rarely said anything. "I see signs every day. Help wanted. At
McDonald's. At Institute Grill. Everywhere. They can work."

"Not necessary," another woman said. "In America, not necessary to work."

"But why?" the first woman repeated.

Sadie let the homeless conversation follow its all too predict-
able path while she scanned the visa list again. It had grown
considerably.

E Investor
F-1 Student
H-1C Nurse
H-1B Scholar
H-2A Farm worker
J Visitor
L
Q Cultural exchange/like J
R Religious worker

Ling was a graduate student. A graduate student with a visa, eligible for student employment. What visa had she held? F or J, surely. But Sadie wasn't certain. What visa did Ling hold now? If any?

The list had a noticeable gap at L. Why had no one said anything more about L? Sadie started to ask about L but noticed the clock at the back of the classroom. Only two more minutes. Time to wrap up.

"Okay," she said. "You did a good job today. Our conversation started with sports and wound up with the poem on the Statue of Liberty. What about vocabulary? Did you learn any new words today?

"Yes, refuse. Refuse is leftover *stuff*." Howard smiled. "It is not you won't do something."

"Well, the verb means you won't do something," Sadie said copying Howard's syntax. "But the noun is really a synonym for trash."

"Not garbage?"

"Maybe garbage. Look it up in your dictionary. That would be a good exercise for you. It will help you remember it," Sadie answered. "Now, any other words?"

The class brainstormed words and Sadie wound up with a short list on the board. Mostly words from the poem, probably not very useful words. Still, they stretched the boundaries of the students' vocabularies.

"I'll see you Friday," she said as the clock reached 11:50. Most of the students left promptly and, always a thoughtful colleague, Sadie began to erase the board for the next professor. When she turned back to gather her materials from the teacher's desk, Andrei Cherkesov was waiting to speak with her.

He was so tall that Sadie had to look almost straight up to see his face. As she did so, sunlight lit his crystal-clear blue eyes in a way that made her a bit weak in the knees. His words, however, immediately destroyed the sexy effect of his eyes.

"You know," he said, "you must have H visa if you want to stay here. But, if you start with J visa, you must go home for two years. You can never change from J to H unless you go home. So, J is not so good. Maybe you should know this."

Sadie didn't respond. Was he talking about Ling? She wasn't sure Andrei even knew Ling, let alone knew about her recent excursion to Mexico. While she was trying to decide what to say, Andrei turned abruptly and left the room. Only Howard was left. He was making very slow progress in getting his laptop into his backpack. Sadie picked up her materials and fled.

Fourteen

Refuse? Is refuse garbage? Or is it just trash? Sadie thought as she waited for the elevator. What's the difference? Garbage can be wet. Is refuse always dry? Is that the basic difference? She doubted it was that simple.

She was still contemplating the difference between refuse and garbage when the elevator arrived. She got in and punched the fourth floor button.

"You might say hello," said a voice behind her. It was Rick Baines, Dan's best friend. Carrying a hefty lunch bag, Rick was on his way to the faculty lounge on the twelfth floor.

"I'm sorry, Rick, I guess I was in a fog," Sadie answered.

"Thinking too hard? About what?"

"Garbage, if you must know."

"Really, what kind of garbage? Freshman writing? Pornography?" Rick's chiseled good looks took on an unpleasant leer.

"No, the wet kind. That is, can it be called refuse if it's wet?"

Rick looked puzzled and then said, "That sounds like a Daniel question. You both talk about language in really peculiar ways."

"Not peculiar. Just trying to understand how to explain subtle differences to nonnative speakers. Refuse came up in my last class. Actually, what came up was the 'refuse of your teeming shore.' And it was sort of downhill from there," Sadie concluded with a laugh.

"Thanks for enlightening me. You coming up for lunch?"

"Actually, I didn't have time to pack my lunch this morning so I guess I have to scramble over to the food court at the student center," Sadie said as the elevator arrived at her floor. The door opened and she stepped out.

"I've got plenty if you want to share," Rick offered, putting his foot in front of the elevator door. "We had quite a meal last night. I can offer small portions of leftover ratatouille, chicken breast with parmesan and portabellas, a side salad, and brown rice."

"All in that lunch bag?"

"Yep, and more than enough for two. How about it?"

The elevator complained about Rick holding the door open too long. "Okay." She got back on the elevator and the annoying mechanical squawk stopped when Rick let the door close again.

The elevator continued upward. As they passed the ninth floor, Rick said, "We'll eat it all. Serves Daniel right for standing me up!"

"That's why you have so much food? Dan was coming over here for lunch?"

"Usually we meet at the Faculty Club, but he came over for dinner last night and there was so much left over, we decided to finish it today. I was elected to carry it in so I got to choose the place. But Daniel had an unexpected meeting."

Sadie felt oddly uncomfortable and a slow blush crept up her cheeks. Why? Why should she care about Daniel anymore? After all, she had thrown him out. But apparently she did care. She tried to ignore her burning cheeks, but Rick's next comment only made the situation worse.

"So," he gloated, "I'll feed you instead of him. Delicious. I love it!"

The elevator doors opened and Sadie headed for the ladies' room, saying, "I'll be back in a minute" over her shoulder to Rick.

Once inside the closet-sized room, Sadie stood and looked at herself in the mirror over the tiny sink. The unbecoming flush highlighted the freckles across her nose. Leaning over, she turned on the faucet and splashed cold water on her face. It felt good. Getting away from Rick felt good, too.

I have to figure out what's going on with me, Sadie thought ruefully. I for sure need to quit overreacting every time someone mentions Dan. She dried her face, took a brush out of her backpack, pulled it through her unruly curls, and, finally, left the restroom.

The lounge was getting crowded and there was quite a line waiting to use the lone microwave. Rick was putting in a small blue container and the people in line behind him were restive.

"He's not even in this department," a woman at the back of the line complained to no one in particular. She was Cheryl Reichard, the department secretary, who rarely had anything good to say about anyone.

"Who is he, anyway?" Cheryl demanded when Sadie stopped at the end of the line.

"He's a biologist from the research campus," Sadie answered.

"Don't they have their own lunchroom?"

Regretting that she had gotten into a conversation with Cheryl, Sadie just shrugged in response. A man, further ahead in the line, answered, "Yeah, but have you ever been there? Smells like an Animal Husbandry lunchroom."

"What do you mean?" Cheryl asked.

"You don't want to know," the man answered, before telling her anyway. "Remember all those rats that got loose last spring?"

"Yeech," Cheryl exclaimed. "Oh, good grief! He's got another container. Will he never be done?"

Oblivious to the discontent behind him, Rick had removed the blue container and was now selecting the proper time for the clear container he had carefully centered in the oven.

As the microwave began its cycle, Rick turned, saw Sadie, and said, "Come get some of this, Sadie," gesturing to a row of plastic boxes on the table beside the microwave.

"He's with you?" Cheryl accused in her overbearing manner. "Hurry him up, will you? Some of us have a limited lunch hour."

"Most of us have a limited lunch hour," Sadie answered as she went around Cheryl toward the head of the line.

"You don't have to punch a time clock." Cheryl sneered.

She's in fine form today, Sadie thought. No one has to punch a time clock around here. Granted, Cheryl should reopen the main office at one, but she didn't need to punch a time clock to do so. Remembering her own harried attempt to be on time a few hours ago, Sadie said, "You know, Cheryl, I pretty much have to punch a time clock every time I have a class. That's not just once a day after lunch, that's several times a day, every day, at different times. No one waits for me if I'm late, and I can't just call and say I'm going to be late either."

Everyone in line was staring at Sadie. Maybe they were thinking her tirade hadn't been called for. Then again, she thought, maybe they were wishing they had said the same thing. Sadie found it curious that she was not discomfited by their attention. She was not, in fact, discomfited at all until Rick spoke again, "Sadie, if you want any of this luscious lunch, you do really have to come help."

Walking quickly to the front of the line, Sadie grabbed the two containers Rick was holding out to her. She headed for a small table in the western corner of the lounge and sat down. What is it? she thought. What bugs me about this man?

There was no time to dwell on that question. Rick had arrived at the table with three more containers and several paper towels. He sat down and began to unpack the rest of his elaborate lunch bag. It yielded black paper plates, stainless utensils, cloth napkins and even two small glasses.

"I freeze water in a plastic bottle," he explained. "Then it keeps everything cold until lunch, and it's ready to drink as well." He poured the chilled water into the glasses.

"Let's see, now," he continued. "Mix the zucchini into the mushrooms and put it all on the chicken. There, you'll love this."

He carefully spooned brown rice onto Sadie's plate. The chicken breast was next. Then he topped it all off with the mixed vegetables.

"Then ratatouille on the side," his grin was infectious as Sadie's stomach let out an embarrassing rumble. "Hungry, are we?" he asked, heaping more gleaming eggplant and tomato on her plate.

"Yes, I guess so. And it certainly does look good. But why did you have so many containers?"

"You can't heat everything together. The mushrooms would be pure mush and the chicken would be like leather."

Thinking how many times she had heated many more things than mushrooms and chicken together, Sadie didn't comment.

They ate in silence. "You really are a wonderful cook," Sadie said to Rick. "I suppose everyone tells you you'll make some woman a wonderful husband someday?"

"That's a bit of an old saw," Rick replied, grimacing.

As she chewed a bite of tender chicken breast, Sadie thought about what she had just said. Not only had Rick never been married, it seemed he didn't even date. Belying his youthful demeanor, Rick was almost as old as Dan. Certainly at least forty-five. And Dan had been married for years before he was widowed. Probably Rick was just too set in his own ways.

"Ready for salad?" Rick interrupted her speculations about him.

"Salad? More food?"

"Indeed, salad to clear your palate. Unfortunately, I don't have anything worth clearing your palate for. No dessert today," Rick said glancing at his watch. "I'd like to get back and call Daniel. Can't wait to tell him who got to eat his gourmet lunch."

It was almost 12:45. Sadie's next class wasn't until 5:30, so she wasn't in any particular hurry. Except she did have some things to find out about. Questions about Ling's visa were fresh in her mind. But right behind them was a growing list of more uncomfortable questions. Was she responsible for Lee Hong's death? Where was Lee Hong's camera? What would happen to the donkey? What had she seen last Friday night if it wasn't the donkey's eyes?

Aha! Eyes! "Rick," Sadie said, "Can you tell me anything about animal eyes?"

"Huh? What eyes? What animal?" Rick was on his feet busily putting his food containers away. Sadie noticed that he even had a small plastic holder for the dirty silverware.

"A donkey, specifically. Would a donkey's eyes shine in headlights? You know how cats' eyes look green when they glow in the dark?"

"I don't think so. Intense eyeshine is indicative of an animal that has to see in the dark. Predators. Donkeys aren't predators, they're more likely prey. I'm not even sure donkeys have eyeshine, but if they do, it's not much."

"So, if I saw a donkey's eyes shining in the dark, then that's not what I saw. Is that right?"

Rick sat down again. "Okay, first it's dry garbage and now it's donkey's eyes. Is this an ESL question too?"

"No, no, I'm just wondering about something I saw. I thought it was a donkey's eyes shining in the headlights but now I'm not so sure?"

"Did you see a donkey?"

"Yes."

"Where?"

Sadie didn't want to get into specifics with Rick. "I was just wondering," she said. "So, do only predators have eyes that glow in the dark?"

"No, all species probably have some eyeshine. But predators have the most. That includes alligators, wolf spiders, owls, toads, even some fish, I think, but this isn't my field exactly."

"Maybe not, but you must know more about it than I do," Sadie answered.

"I'm not sure that's saying much," Rick said. "But let me show you how it works." He smoothed out one of the unused paper towels on the table and started drawing on it.

"You see, it's a matter of the physics of light and the structure of the eye."

A tall, gangly man stopped beside the table and surveyed Rick's sketch. "You are teaching physics? What is this Institute coming to?"

The newcomer was wearing a dark-blue Irish knit sweater and similarly colored Dockers. Handsome features were marred by a squint and near-constant blink. A telltale glint of contacts shone as he turned his head. The overhead fluorescent lights installed everywhere to save energy didn't improve his pallid complexion, and his graying hair did nothing to brighten his appearance. He didn't attempt a smile but merely nodded his head slightly when Rick introduced him to Sadie. "This is Georges LeBourne, the revolutionary computer jock from CEDEX, the one hauling FITT into the quantum computing universe at warp speed."

The revolutionary computer jock apparently did not believe in a daily shower, Sadie noticed. His rank body odor was more than distinct as LeBourne shifted from foot to foot, listening to Rick extol the promise of quantum computing.

"It's the next big thing in computing. Chips that use quantum properties. Chips that will be used in computers that will change the world. But meantime, there is the physics of the eye. It won't be changing anytime soon," Rick said. "I'm sure you agree I'm competent to discuss that, don't you, LeBourne?"

The man pulled out the extra chair at the table and sat down. "Maybe I can even learn something. The person I want to see isn't here anyway."

"You both know what a retina is, right?" Rick pointed to the back of the sketchy eye he had drawn on the napkin. Sadie nodded and Rick continued, "Predators have something called a tapetum lucidum in the back of their eyes. It's a specialized layer of the retina that acts sort of like a mirror. Light coming into the eye bounces off it at different angles."

He worked on his drawing for a minute and then turned the sketch toward Sadie. "See, the bouncing around concentrates the light. So the animal's vision is enhanced. For example, I've heard that cats see six times better than we do in the dark."

"And all this makes for shiny eyes?" Sadie asked.

"Exactly. It's called eyeshine. The color of the eyeshine is distinctive. That is, you can tell what kind of animal it is. When I was in Australia last year, the nighttime rain forest was alive with pink eyes. Possums have pink eyes. Really spooky. Back here most animals have red or green eyes."

"What animals have green eyeshine?" she asked Rick.

"Hmm, let's see. Cats and dogs, I think. Except maybe not Siamese cats. I'm not sure why I know that, so it may not be right. And ferrets. One of my colleagues has been working over near Dinosaur National Monument. They're trying to reintroduce the endangered black-footed ferret over there. She says the ferret's eyeshine is an unearthly emerald green."

Rick jumped to his feet. "I've really got to go. If you want to know more about eyeshine, I'll see what I can find out."

"No, this is interesting but all I really needed to know was whether or not a donkey's eyes would shine in the dark."

"Donkey's eyes?" LeBourne asked. "You have a donkey also?"

"No, no, I don't have a donkey. It's a long story."

"I like long stories," LeBourne said with a rabbit-like grin. "And I like donkeys. My family has a watch donkey to protect our horses. She watches out for coyotes."

Unable to think of any polite response that would not encourage LeBourne to keep talking, Sadie stood up. "It was nice meeting you, Professor LeBourne. My lunch hour is over."

"Mine, too," Rick chimed in. "What are you doing over here anyway, LeBourne? I didn't think you guys ever left the engineering center."

"I am looking for Dan Simone's sister."

"Lila?" Sadie asked. "You are a friend of Lila's?"

"Indeed, I know Lila and I hope soon to be a very good friend of the lovely Mademoiselle Simone." LeBourne raised his eyebrows in a suggestive manner.

Odd, Sadie thought. Lila has never mentioned this guy.

LeBourne continued, "We Frenchmen get lonely for a familiar accent you know. Simone thought his sister might be over here for lunch, but I guess not, so I'll go back to my engineering monastery." He too rose, and they headed toward the bank of elevators where Cheryl Reichard was standing.

"Goodness, Professor Wagner," she said with her usual false obsequiousness as the elevator arrived, "wherever are you going? You don't have to punch in for your next class until after five."

"Odd you know my schedule so well, Cheryl."

"Oh, not so odd. I looked it up just before lunch."

"Really? Why?"

"Some guy was looking for you."

"You give faculty schedules out to just anybody?"

"Oh, he wasn't just anybody. He showed me his identification. Naval Intelligence, I think it said."

The elevator arrived. Cheryl, Rick, and LeBourne got on. Sadie sought refuge in the ladies' room yet again.

Fifteen

Sadie returned to her office by way of the stairs. The enclosed, gray concrete staircase spiraled around the elevator bank, and she usually found it rather forbidding. Today, its cold isolation felt oddly secure and reassuring as she went down eight flights without encountering a single person.

Emerging in her own hallway on the fourth floor, she didn't waste any time getting into her office and shutting the door. Sunlight streamed through her west-facing window, giving more than enough illumination to see without the overhead lights.

Cheryl's revelation that Commander Gross was looking for her again had been the final straw. The butterflies in her stomach now fluttered against an ominous background of unease. She had to deal with her emotions explicitly.

Plunking down at her desk, Sadie picked up a pen. Writing always cleared her head. As she stared out her window toward the Animal Husbandry Labs, she became less and less aware of the bustling activity outside her window and more and more aware of the chaos churning inside her brain.

She wrote. *Ling? I'm annoyed with Ling.* No, she thought, I'm more than annoyed. I'm angry. As she wrote *angry,* she added *and worried.*

Yes, Sadie acknowledged, I am worried. And, with that thought, another emotion surfaced. Guilt! Sadie began to scribble frantically.

I feel incredibly guilty about Lee Hong. I sent him to the pond. If he hadn't been there, he wouldn't be dead now.

There it was, in black and white. She knew Lee Hong's death was her fault. That was why she felt so terrible.

Sighing, Sadie settled back into her chair and resumed her vigil gazing out the window. Having identified the root cause of her despair, she now needed to decide what to do about it. What could she do to ease her guilt? Again, she picked up her pen and started writing.

Help the family

As she wrote these words, a deluge of questions suddenly fought for her attention. There was so much she didn't know. Ming Fang was certainly Lee Hong's dependent. If he is dead, his dependents might be in visa limbo. But one of their little girls was born in the U.S. That makes her a citizen. Can the whole family stay if one child is a U.S. citizen?

And what about Ling? She isn't Lee Hong's dependent. She's here on her own visa. Or is she here on any visa at all? Sadie began to explore the possible implications of Ling's evasiveness about her re-entry into the United States without addressing the ominous feeling hovering on the edge of her consciousness.

Ling's visa—or lack of one—could be a major problem. But unlike her feelings of guilt over Lee Hong, the visa was a problem Sadie thought she could perhaps help solve. Before she could tackle Ling's status with the Institute's Human Resources Office, however, she had to know when Ling went to Mexico and what sort of visa she actually had now. Then she could find out if Ling still had student status. If not, was she still eligible for Institute employment? Was her TA status secure?

She had narrowed her concerns about Ling down to the issue of her status. Sadie put aside her scribbled writing and started on a new piece of paper.

Writing *To Do* at the top, she felt relief wash through her. Now she was getting it together. Generating a list of things to do always gave her a comfortable feeling of control.

Below *To Do*, she wrote:

Check Ling's visa with HR
Then she added details.
Ask HR for specific visa info
Call Ling; get copy of visa
Understand visas

Sadie turned and tapped her computer keypad. When the icons obediently appeared, she asked for Google. Her first set of words—visa student—yielded thousands of hits, but after selecting some more keywords from the offered list, useful information began to flow.

She reconstructed the list Shan Lau had put on the board and, with the help of on-line information, fleshed it out. Soon, she had a page full of handwritten notes about visas.

B-Tourist
B-2 Medical patient
E Investor
F-1 Student
H-1B Scholar
H-1C Nurse
H-2A Farm worker
H-2B Entertainer
H-3 Company training
J Visitor
L Immigrant
O Person of extraordinary ability
Q Cultural exchange/like J
R Religious worker
TN Professional from Canada or Mexico

Now that she had a better handle on the myriad types of visas, Sadie felt ready to ask Human Resources a few pointed questions. She opened her desk drawer to look for the campus phonebook just as someone knocked on her door.

Sadie froze. Was it Commander Gross? Could she avoid him? Did he know she was in? Probably not, because she had not turned on her overhead light. She sat unmoving, considering what to do. Another knock. Then a voice.

"Sadie, Sadie, are you in there?" It was Lila.

Relieved, Sadie pushed her chair back, rose, and hurried over to open the door. "Sorry, Lila, I guess I was napping," she lied.

"Napping? You are so tired?"

"Actually, it's more like a pounding headache."

"Headache? I think maybe heartache," Lila pushed past Sadie and dropped into the blue chair by her desk. "Do you think our donkey killed someone? This is not possible, I think."

"I'm afraid it is possible," Sadie said shutting the door. "And, Lila, could you please talk more quietly?"

"Why? You are avoiding the students? You are in here with the lights out? Why?"

"I told you, I have a headache," Sadie lied again.

"Okay, sorry," Lila said quietly. "But our donkey, she did not kill anyone. What happened?"

Sadie tried to explain. She told Lila about going back to the pond with Mike. About finding Lee Hong dead with a donkey's hoof prints on his back.

"What was this Chinese man doing there? Was he hurting the donkey?" Lila demanded.

"No, I'm sure not. He went to take pictures. In fact, I suggested it to him. He is … was … a photographer. I thought the donkey would be a poignant subject."

"So the donkey, she kicked him while he was taking a picture of her? I don't think so," Lila said. "Your head is better?"

"I guess so, why?"

"You brightened up."

"Oh, well…"

"Of course, you didn't really have a headache, did you? Who are you avoiding? I hope it is not my baby brother?"

"No, I'm not avoiding him. I even ate his lunch. It's this guy from the Navy; I'd rather not see him." But, even as she said it, Sadie knew she wouldn't be able to avoid Commander Gross.

"Please? What does this mean? 'Ate his lunch.' Is this some idiom?" Lila queried.

"No, in this case it means I really ate his lunch. Dan was supposed to eat with Rick Baines today, but he had a last-minute meeting. So Rick fed me instead. However," Sadie added, "you are right, 'ate his lunch' could be an idiom, sort of like 'cleaned his clock.'"

Lila considered this mini idiom lesson. "So," she finally said, "is clean a clock also real? I mean if you say that, could you maybe really be cleaning a clock?"

"I don't think so. I think that would always be an idiom."

"Meaning what?"

"Meaning ..." Sadie was interrupted by an abrupt knock. She rose and opened the door to find Sam Gross standing there.

"Professor Wagner," he said pulling out his wallet and opening it to his ID. "You remember me, I'm sure."

"Yes, of course I do," Sadie answered before gesturing at Lila. "This is Lila Simone, she was just leaving."

Lila did not take the hint. Instead, she leaned back in the visitor chair, crossed her legs, and said, "No, actually, I just arrived. Professor Wagner has a bad headache, and I am waiting until she feels better."

"Headache, huh? Well, I just need to ask Professor Wagner a few questions. Then you two can go back to discussing her headache," Gross said. "And, if you're going to be here, I'll need to see your ID. Do you work here too?"

"No." Lila waited. "I do not work here. I am the sister of Professor Daniel Simone. He teaches here. In the French Department."

"So you are a friend of Professor Wagner's?"

"Yes, I am her friend. Even if she is no longer my brother's friend."

Sam Gross waited. Both he and Sadie were still standing. Lila looked up at them and added, "Actually she is a very wise woman."

Ignoring this remark, Sam Gross said, "Professor Wagner, I need to talk to you today. Alone. We can do it now, or we can do it later. It's up to you."

"Later," Sadie answered promptly.

"When?" Sam Gross pulled a Day-Timer out of the breast pocket in his suit coat.

"My classes are over at six-thirty. I can be home right after that," Sadie said, thinking it couldn't last too long, since Mike usually showed up about seven.

"Fine. I'll see you just after six-thirty." Sam Gross turned and headed out the door toward the staircase.

"Unpleasant man," Lila said. "Also he didn't take the elevator. So no one can hear him coming."

"Everything about him is a bit unpleasant," Sadie answered.

"So, Sadie, can we clean his clock?" Lila asked with a grin.

Sixteen

Unease about Commander Gross lurked in the background for the rest of the day. Sadie left her last class promptly at 6:30 p.m. to find Lila waiting outside the doorway of her ground-floor classroom.

"Why are you still on campus?" Sadie asked.

"I was visiting another friend and time flew away."

"Would that be Georges LeBourne? At the Engineering Center? He doesn't look like anyone that could make time fly. Especially not for you."

Lila rolled her eyes. "I didn't know you knew Georges. He is really very funny."

"Funny? He also has kids. So he's probably married. You know that, don't you?"

"Daniel says his wife does not come with him."

"Oh?"

"Indeed." Lila looked down at the straps of her multi-colored sandals. "Indeed, I know it could be a problem, but he reminds me of home."

"Are you seeing him?" Sadie was being nosy, but she couldn't believe Lila hadn't mentioned this. After all, Lila seemed to think nothing of quizzing her in detail about Mike.

"Seeing him? This means what?"

"Oh never mind. Just be careful." Sadie started down the hall toward the elevators.

"Yes, I think so. I am careful. Especially, I am careful of me," Lila said as she fell into step beside her. "I am careful of me, of you, and of creatures who need care. For example, I've been thinking about our donkey. I'm sure she is innocent. Do you know where she is?"

"No ... well, maybe ... yes. The Humane Society picked her up on Sunday. Probably she's there in their barnyard. At least I hope that's where she is."

"Let's go to see her."

"Okay, when?"

"Tomorrow morning? Can you go tomorrow morning?"

"Actually, yes. I don't have any classes on Tuesday or Thursday, unless someone talks me into covering for them," Sadie answered remembering her rash promise to help out a colleague on Thursday.

They had reached the elevator and Sadie punched the call button. Lila didn't board the elevator with Sadie when it came. Instead, she said, "Okay, I will come to your house at nine in the morning."

"Okay," Sadie agreed as the elevator door closed, cutting off further conversation.

In her office, Sadie gathered up papers to grade and crammed them into her backpack. She checked her office. The window was firmly shut, the coffeepot was off, and ... and there was Ling's backpack, left behind in the emotional turmoil of her frenzied departure from Sadie's office, still stuffed under her desk.

She picked up the scuffed brown pack. It had a luggage tag. One side was covered with small, concise Chinese characters. The other side said *Ling Yang, Foothills Institute of Technology and Telecommunications, Language Arts, Room 426.*

Well, Ling would probably know where it was. Sadie put the pack under her desk, snapped off her office lights, and walked out, hearing the door click shut behind her. It was almost dusk when she left the Language Arts Building. Across the street in the

Animal Husbandry Laboratories, a few lights shone in the offices above the animal labs.

Trudging across campus toward home, Sadie revisited the distinction between validity and truth, a distinction she was sure still confounded many of her students. If she were to plan a discussion of formal logic, it would be wise to use a trait more familiar than warm-blooded. Maybe she could use something from Rick's mini-lesson on eyeshine. Surely all her students had seen a cat's eyes glowing in the dark.

Sadie walked along, trying to form a sensible syllogism. Something like "The eyes of predators glow in the dark. Cats' eyes glow in the dark. Therefore, cats are predators." No, not the right placement of A, B, and C.

As she considered how to get her new syllogism in order, she remembered her lunchtime talk with Rick. Donkeys aren't predators. So those eyes shining in the headlights probably weren't the donkey's. Whose were they?

But she didn't have time to dwell on this because not only Commander Gross but also Mike were waiting at her kitchen doorstep in a somber Saturday morning redux. Mike, showing up early, must have used his lobby key and let Commander Gross in with him. Or maybe Commander Gross came complete with skeleton keys. Whatever—a too-familiar dread grabbed at Sadie's stomach.

From just inside her door, alternating between threatening growls and plaintive whines, Tiger was mixing watchdog duties with invitations to play. It had been a long day, and this scene didn't promise to be short. Sadie suddenly felt very tired. Maybe she did have a headache after all.

"Once again, we congregate," Sam Gross said in a sarcastic tone of voice.

Sadie pushed past both of them to unlock her door. Tiger rushed out to greet Mike as Sadie went in. Sam Gross followed her and tried to shut the door. But Mike and Tiger were too fast for him. They both pushed through the closing door into Sadie's condo.

"And this time we really do congregate," Mike said. "You're in the midst of a homicide investigation now. No more private conversations about Lee Hong."

"Lee Hong is a murder suspect?" Sam Gross asked.

"No, Lee Hong is a murder victim."

This was obviously news to Sam Gross. He stared at Mike for a long moment before demanding, "Details! Where? When? How?"

"Not why?" Mike said. "You don't want to know why Lee Hong was murdered? Why not? Do you already know why?"

Sadie watched as the two men bristled at each other. Their animosity was so palpable that Tiger growled.

"Of course I don't know why." Sam Gross glared at Mike. "But I sure would like the details, Lieutenant!"

Changing the subject, Mike said, "What do you want with Professor Wagner? Get that out of the way and then we can talk about Lee Hong at the station if you like."

"I'm not sure I need to talk to Professor Wagner anymore."

Sadie waited. Sam Gross and Mike continued to glare at each other. Mercifully, the phone rang.

Although she could have picked it up there in the kitchen, Sadie chose to answer the phone in the living room, away from the three males squared off in her kitchen. Tiger was the only one who acknowledged her exit, but after briefly following her, he turned and took up a threatening stance in the doorway between the kitchen and the living room.

Sadie grabbed the phone on the third ring. "Hello?"

"Mrs. Wagner?"

"This is Sadie Wagner, yes."

"Well, Mrs. Wagner, this is Tiffany from the *Boulder Star-Trumpet*. We're returning your call about an incorrect ad." Sadie remembered what she had forgotten in her morning rush. The paper with the incorrect camper ad. It was a welcome interruption. Anything that would keep her away from the rising tide of testosterone in the kitchen.

"Oh yes. There is an ad for a camper that has my phone number but it's not my camper."

"So you want to cancel your ad?"

"It's not my ad. I want you to correct someone else's ad."

"You cannot change someone else's ad."

"But this ad gives my phone number. It's wrong. People are calling me."

Tiffany hesitated. "Maybe I can do that. What should the phone number be?"

"That's the problem. I don't know the correct phone number. You are using my phone number in the ad. And that is incorrect."

"If you don't have the correct phone number, I can't look up the ad. We file the ads by phone number."

"I can tell you which ad it is," Sadie said fumbling on the shelf under the phone for Saturday's classified section. "Here it is, it's on page 16G of Saturday's paper."

"And what phone number does it have?"

"Mine, but that's wrong."

"Yes, I understand. I will try to correct it, but first I need the phone number you used when you placed the ad."

A surge of annoyance washed over Sadie. "I told you I did not place the ad. So I don't have the phone number!" She was almost screaming. Tiger responded with a nervous glance but did not leave his self-imposed post at the door to the kitchen.

"Do you want to cancel the ad?"

"Yes, just cancel it."

Tiffany had managed to find the ad—at least Sadie heard a lot of computer keys clicking as she waited on the phone line. Eventually, Tiffany said, "Okay, where shall I send your refund?"

"I don't get a refund. It's not my ad."

"Look, ma'm, you paid for this ad in cash. I have to give you your money back."

"It's not my money. Don't you have a record of who paid for this ad? Because it wasn't me."

"We only get names when we have to collect money. When you pay in cash, we just take the money and put your ad in." Tiffany was now speaking very slowly, sounding as though she were trying to explain something to a very dense child.

Sadie decided to treat Tiffany the same way. "So, you have for sure taken this ad out?"

"Yes."

"Well, then, why don't you send the money to the Boulder County Humane Society?"

"Fine, and what is that phone number?"

Having given up all hope of getting Tiffany to engage her brain, Sadie pulled out the phone book and looked up the phone number of the Humane Society. After she read the number to Tiffany, she asked, "Don't you want their mailing address as well?"

"Oh, no. Our database is all phone numbers. I'll get it from there. Have a nice day!" Tiffany chirped before she disconnected.

Sure, Sadie thought, have a nice day. Reluctant to return to the two men in her kitchen, she sank into the pink recliner. The terse voices coming from the kitchen were too low for effective eavesdropping. Finally, Mike came to the doorway and said, "Sadie, Commander Gross and I are going over to the station. I'll get back to you later."

Tiger waited until the kitchen door slammed before trotting into the living room. He sidled up to Sadie's chair and put his head across her knees.

"Whew, Tiger. What a day," she said scratching his ears. "I guess we should go for a quick walk. Want to do that?"

Silly question! At the mere mention of the word "walk," Tiger was up and heading for the door. Sadie followed him, took his leash down from its hook by the door, snapped it onto his collar, and opened the door.

Soon they were marching along the Boulder Creek Path, Tiger with head and tail up, Sadie with head and spirits down.

Seventeen

The next morning, Sadie, still in a funk, poured water into her coffee maker before she contemplated the breakfast options in her refrigerator. They weren't very good: a too-old bagel, garlic and herb cream cheese, dry cereal, one egg, no milk, no fruit.

Wild Oats, just next door, carried a wealth of muffins, breads, and spreads. But next door seemed too far to go. Knowing she wouldn't feel better unless she ate something, Sadie jerked open the freezer compartment. There, in a wadded-up plastic bag encased in the ice that was overtaking the freezer, were perhaps a dozen frozen blueberries.

After prying the package out of its ice chrysalis, Sadie poured a cup of hot water and plunged the wizened blueberries into it. While the berries thawed and swelled, she fed chunks of the bagel into her blender. The resulting bagel crumbs, combined with the drained blueberries and the egg, produced a batter that was a very unappetizing purple. Hoping the color would fade as the mixture cooked, she spooned it into a skillet.

Solving culinary conundrums always gets me going, she thought as she watched her ersatz blueberry pancake simmer into crisp brownness.

Tiger lay under the table, not complaining but casting occasional baleful glances at Sadie. When the buzzer sounded from the condo lobby, he jumped up and raced to the door.

"Yes?" Sadie pushed the intercom button.

"It is I!" Lila's voice stressed the correct pronoun.

Sadie laughed. "Come on in." She pushed the door release button and walked across the kitchen to set her door ajar.

Moments later, Lila entered, wearing a stylishly cut two-piece gray suit with a powder blue silk blouse. A large gold and glass bob dangled from her neck.

Sadie felt Lila's eyes scanning her frumpy pink chenille bathrobe. Should she explain? Not that she had forgotten Lila was coming over; she would have remembered that eventually. Maybe it isn't necessary to explain, she thought as Lila stood in her kitchen, looking her up and down.

"So, Lila, are you just giving me the French once-over? Or are you really trying to be rude?"

"French once-over? I don't know what you mean. I was just looking. But," transferring her disapproval from Sadie to the skillet on the stove, Lila's carefully plucked eyebrows arched over her violet eyes, "what are you making? Why is it such a terrible color? Is this for Tiger, I hope?"

Tiger responded to his name by rushing over to Lila and sitting at her feet.

"He'd love to have it, of course," Sadie answered. "But, to answer your question, it's my breakfast. I call it ..." What could she call it? Sadie fumbled for a name for her concoction before announcing, "I call it Bagel and Blueberry Biscuit. Triple B, for short."

"Biscuit? I don't think it looks like a biscuit."

"I think a biscuit can be any sort of flat, bread-like thing," Sadie said.

"Ha! A biscuit is big and flaky, and you hold it in your fingers to eat it. I think you made this whole thing up."

That being exactly what she had done, Sadie quipped, "Never mind. It's nutritious and that's all that matters." She put her Triple B on a plate and carried it to the small table. "Want some coffee? It's there." She pointed at the coffee maker on the sink.

Triple B
(a.k.a. Bagel and Blueberry Blender Pancake ... sort of)

Leftover bagel
Handful of blueberries
1 egg
dash of sugar or sweetener

Grind up bagel in blender. Mix
resulting crumbs with other ingredients. Stir. Scrape into Teflon
skillet. Cook a few minutes, turn
pancake over. If not brown on
bottom, turn again. Keep doing
this until both sides are brown
and inside isn't runny.

Sadie's note:

If you don't have a leftover bagel,
use any dried-out bread product.
Graham crackers work, too.

"Where?" Lila said standing in front of the coffee maker. "There is only water in here."

"Yes, use the hot water to make coffee. There's instant on the shelf or, if you want, you can drip a cup. The Brewing Market coffee is on the shelf there also. Do you see it?" Not bothering to get up, Sadie pointed repeatedly as she directed Lila.

Avoiding the jar of instant coffee as though it were poison, Lila got a cup, found a filter, filled it from the Brewing Market bag, and started the hot water dripping through the coffee grounds.

"Why do you have jarred coffee?" Lila inquired as she opened the refrigerator.

Ignoring the question, Sadie asked, "What do you need?"

"Cream."

"I don't have any cream."

"Milk?"

"Nope."

"What did you put in your coffee?"

"Just coffee."

"I thought you liked milk in your coffee."

"Well, I do. But there isn't any milk this morning."

"Right next door there is a huge store. It has milk."

"Yes, but…."

"I'll go. Then I will not have to watch you eat that purple mess. What else do you need?"

"Nothing."

Lila opened the refrigerator and rummaged through the sparse contents. "We'll see about that. I'll be back in half an hour." Lila marched out the door leaving her cup of black coffee steaming beneath its filter on the counter.

Relieved to have her kitchen to herself, Sadie continued to chew her newly named Triple B. Actually, she thought, this is pretty good. The berries puckered with juice and squirted through the crisp bagel dough around them as she chewed.

She had finished her breakfast and Tiger was crunching his when Lila returned, laden with two large grocery sacks from Wild Oats.

"I found lots of good things," Lila enthused as she began to unload the sacks. "First, milk! Second, cream!" she said, putting the two cartons into the refrigerator. "Then, some fruit." She put a bunch of bananas, two mangoes, and an entire pineapple on the table.

Turning to the second bag, Lila took out a loaf of Rudi's Sunflower Whole Wheat Bread, two croissants, and, from the bottom of the sack, a container of sun-dried tomato and basil hummus and a jar of Newman's peach salsa.

"What more could you want?" she demanded spreading her arms wide.

"Nothing, I guess ... but a whole pineapple? What will I do with a whole pineapple?"

"We'll put it on the fish."

"Fish?"

"Yes, I am to pick it up after noon. They are expecting some fresh tilapia. Do you have any coconut? I forgot to ask."

Pineapple? Tilapia? Coconut? What's going on? Sadie thought. I just got her brother to move out—I don't need Lila moving in. She tried to think of a way to broach this subject, but Lila was on to other plans.

"Did you call the Humane Society? Is our donkey still there? Is she okay?"

"I didn't call. The phone book said they don't open until eleven o'clock so we're not in a hurry."

"Let us find out. I am concerned about her. Where is your phone book?" She was opening drawers in the kitchen as she fired off questions.

"Not in here, it's in the living room. In the cabinet under the phone."

Lila went into the living room, found the phone book and started paging through it. Sadie cleared the table, put her dirty dishes in the sink, and headed to the bathroom.

Thirty minutes later, she emerged dressed in a red denim skirt, a white tee, and her most comfortable Birkenstock sandals.

She felt ready to face the day. Tiger was ready, too. He greeted her with an anxious whine.

"I know, I know. We haven't been for a walk. But we're going right now," she reassured the now-excited dog.

"I told them we were on our way," Lila interjected.

"Told who?"

Lila cocked her eyebrow again. "Who? Should that not be *whom*, Miss English Teacher?"

Sadie blushed. "Well, yes it should be *whom*. But no one says that anymore. We usually just say 'who,' but we write 'whom.'"

"Indeed? That is sloppy, I think. But we must go. I told the Humane Society we would come. The large animal person is waiting for us."

"Well, he'll have to wait a little longer; I have a small animal here that needs attention first."

Sadie clipped Tiger's leash on and headed for the door. Lila followed them through the kitchen and out the door. She caught up as Sadie and Tiger reached the lobby entrance. "So, you didn't tell me about the jarred coffee."

The threesome stopped at the entrance to the Creek Path as Tiger explored myriad new smells in the grass.

"Some people prefer instant."

"Impossible!"

Sadie shrugged.

"Who? Who could possibly prefer jarred coffee?"

"I guess people who drink a lot of it at work."

"Who? Ah, your policeman friend? The one on your answering machine? You keep jarred coffee for him." Lila shook her head sadly.

Apparently chastened into silence by the thought of instant coffee, Lila walked along quietly beside Sadie as Tiger rushed from one side of the path to the other in his quest to know everything about everything as quickly as possible. He was thwarted when Sadie turned around fifteen minutes later. "We've got some things to do this morning, Tiger," she explained. "And I think you'll be much happier if you stay home while we do them."

Tiger didn't look as though he agreed with this concept when Sadie opened the condo door and ushered him in. Getting a dog biscuit from the cupboard, Sadie handed it to the dejected dog and said, "May the Force be with you."

Tiger took the treat, turned, and headed for his bed by the window. After all, Sadie had said the magic words. That meant not only that she was leaving but, more important, that she was coming back. He settled into his bed looking a little sad, but not worried, as Sadie and Lila left.

Sadie thought Lila had been exaggerating but, when they got to the Humane Society, the large animal person was indeed waiting for them.

"Mrs. Donkey is sure popular today," the young man said as he greeted them in the barnyard behind the main shelter building. "I waited out here in the barnyard with her because we hope you can help us. I'm Doug Ridlin." He extended his hand to Lila.

"This is Professor Wagner," Lila responded pushing Sadie forward instead of taking the young man's grimy hand herself.

"You're in the Animal Husbandry Department?" he asked Sadie after they shook hands.

Lila jumped in just as Sadie began her denial. "Professor Wagner is the person who called about the donkey. She is very worried about her. Is she okay?"

"She's okay, but we can't find her owner. No one seems to know where she came from or why she was fenced in at the Institute pond. The other guy thought it might be his kid's pet, but it wasn't."

"His kid's pet? What would a pet donkey be doing out there? Who was this person?" Sadie asked.

"The guy who was here when you called." He looked at Lila as they walked through the barn. "At least, it sounded like you. When I got back to the stall, the guy said it was a mistake. It wasn't his kid's donkey. In fact, if you hadn't called, I wouldn't have left him back here alone with the donkey. She was so scared of him it was pathetic."

He swung open the door to a horse-sized stall. There, huddled in the back by the manger, was the donkey.

"Isn't that unusual?" Sadie asked. "Or is she afraid of everyone since she's in a strange place?"

"She's not afraid of me." Lila strode into the stall clicking her comforting call to the donkey. A friendly whinny was her reward as the donkey stepped gingerly through the straw toward Lila. Soon, the donkey was leaning on Lila, relaxing as Lila scratched her.

"Wow," Doug said. "She really likes you. Maybe she's French too." He laughed.

Lila turned a frown on him. "Of course, she is not French. But she is smart. And she knows who cares about her. What will happen to her? Will she stay here?"

"No, she won't stay here," Doug answered. "If we can't find her owner, we'll try to find her a new home. That's why I was glad the Animal Husbandry Department was interested. I thought maybe she could go live there or something."

Sadie needed time to think. Why had Lila said she was with the Animal Husbandry Department? What should she say to this young man?

"Scratch right here." Lila pointed to a spot between the donkey's ears. "She will love that."

Sadie tentatively reached out. The donkey's hair was softer than she remembered. And just like Tiger, the donkey showed her appreciation by leaning into Sadie as she started scratching. Scratching and thinking. Who would be interested in adopting a donkey? Or at least helping to find someone who would adopt a donkey? Should I tell this young man that I am not who he thinks I am? As she puzzled, she scratched. And as she scratched, she bumped into the donkey's halter. It didn't move. In fact, it seemed exceptionally snug. Sadie tried to move it and it wouldn't budge. The donkey shied away.

"Doug, this halter seems to be too tight," Sadie said. "It's almost cutting into her head."

"Naw, that can't be. It's so loose it hardly stays on," the young man answered coming into the stall and reaching for the halter. "Good golly, you're right. What happened here? I don't understand. Just this morning, when I tried to lead her out to clean the stall, the halter was so loose it almost came off." He knelt down and unsnapped the halter under the donkey's chin. When it fell away, there were deep creases down the animal's face where the halter had bitten into her flesh. Doug was examining the halter carefully. "This isn't the same halter," he said. "This is leather, and it's too small for her. It isn't the same halter. I don't understand."

"I'm afraid I'm beginning to understand a lot of things," Sadie said. "Tell me more about the first visitor who came today."

Eighteen

"He didn't speak English very well," Doug said. "But his name is Wayne. How could somebody named Wayne not speak English? I didn't understand that at all."

"He told you his name was Wayne?" Sadie asked.

"No, that's what he put on his form."

"Form?" Sadie wondered why it was so difficult to extract information from this young man.

"Yes, you have to fill out a form before you can visit with one of the animals," Doug explained. "You know, the same form you filled out."

Lila's lilting French accent chimed in: "We had no form. We just walked around the building and came back here to the stable. Now tell us about Wayne's form, please."

It was like turning on an information faucet. Doug began to talk. "He wrote Wayne Chen on his form, but when I checked it with his driver's license, it didn't agree.

He got pretty testy when I pointed out that he'd used the wrong name. Said it wasn't wrong, it was just his American name. But I told him that the form has to be correct. I mean, we can't let just anybody in here to claim an animal. If we don't know who the people are, how could we know if the animal was really theirs? They could be going to feed it to their pet snake or something."

"A snake can eat a donkey?" Lila asked in a digression that made Sadie impatient.

"Well, no, that's what can happen to kittens and bunnies. But bad things can happen to a donkey, too. They could become dog food, for example," Doug said.

"So what happened?" Sadie wrenched the conversation back to the donkey's visitor. "Why did you let him see the donkey if he gave you the wrong name?"

"Well, everything else was correct; his address was right—one of those county roads, up in the mountains, near Black Hawk. I guess you might have a pet donkey up there. So I let him change the name on his form."

"And what was his real name?" Sadie asked.

"I don't remember, something Chinese," Doug said going to a clipboard that was hanging on the wall by the door of the stable. He took it off the hook and read from the top piece of paper. "Shan Chen, don't know how to pronounce it, really."

"Could we get a copy of that?" Sadie pointed at the form in Doug's hand.

"Of course not," he replied, clutching the clipboard to his chest. "This is private Humane Society business. Especially since the guy lied about his name. Even when he put his right name he insisted on putting Wayne after it." Doug waved the clipboard in front of him. "Look at that," he said. "He put AKA Wayne Chen. Used up almost the whole line with this silliness. What's AKA anyway, the Chinese way to say Mister or something?"

As Sadie struggled to think of a reply that wouldn't betray her astonishment at Doug's ignorance, Lila stepped in. "Let me see that, Doug," she cooed, slipping the clipboard out of his grasp. "It is so confusing, is it not? All the ways different people talk. I am puzzled often, but we can figure this out, I think, you and I." She smiled at Doug, who quickly mirrored her smile.

"Hmmmm, I think I have it," Lila said as she studied the form. "I think this is an abbreviation for something." She handed the clipboard to Sadie. "Maybe if you look at it, you will be able to figure out what it is, since you are an American and I think this must be an American abbreviation."

Sly Lila, Sadie thought as she scanned the information on the form. "Hmmm, let's see. I wonder ..." she muttered as she tried to commit an important detail to memory: Chen's address was 13684 County Line Road 52, Nederland.

Just as Doug started to reach for the clipboard, seemingly nervous about relinquishing the form, Sadie said, "I've got it. It *is* an abbreviation—it must mean 'also known as.' He added 'AKA Wayne Chen' because he wanted to say 'also known as Wayne Chen.' That must be it. What do you know? Learn something new every day."

She handed the clipboard back to Doug and motioned to Lila. "Let's go, we've taken enough of this young man's time."

She struggled to keep the address in her memory while Lila said a long good-bye to the donkey before following Sadie from the barn. When they walked around the kennel building, the hopeful dogs inside sent up a howling chorus. It made Sadie's heart ache, all those dogs hoping someone had come to take them home. Their excitement escalated when Sadie stopped behind the building to jot down 13684 County Line Road 52 on a scrap of paper from her pocket.

Lila shouted over the barking, "Why would that man lie about his name?"

Sadie shrugged and turned toward the parking lot. When they reached a quieter area, she explained. "He didn't lie. He probably really does have an American name. Not an official one, just one he uses to make it easier for Americans to talk to him." Thinking about her students, Sadie added, "Actually, it probably means he's from Taiwan, not China. The Taiwanese almost always pick out an American name. People from China rarely do."

"Why?" Lila asked in a puzzled voice.

"Why what?"

"Why do Taiwan people do that and not Chinese people?"

"I don't know, really, maybe just because the Taiwanese try hard to fit in. I'm not sure the Chinese do so much. But it may not be that simple. After all," Sadie said, "think about it. Giving up your name could feel like giving up a big part of yourself. If you had to pick a new name, what would you choose?"

"An American name, you mean?"

"Yes."

"Like Brittany or Abigail or Emma?"

"I guess."

"I do not know. I would want something like my real name. Something short, something that sounds the same almost."

"How about Lucy?"

"That does not sound much like Lila."

"Lizzie? Leslie?"

She grimaced. "I think I will just keep Lila, if you do not mind."

They had reached the car when Sadie remembered the halter. "What did you think about that halter, Lila? It didn't fit the donkey, and it certainly was not the one she had on Sunday at the pond."

Lila settled into the passenger seat. As she buckled her seat belt, her eyes darkened with suspicion. "Obviously," she said, "Mr. Chinese Wayne changed the halter. He brought one with him that didn't fit and took away the old one."

"Yes, obviously, but why? Why did he do that?"

"Because he wanted the old halter."

"And he didn't want anyone to know it, so he brought a replacement," Sadie said thoughtfully. "He didn't want the donkey at all, he just wanted the halter."

"You get the cigar!" Lila announced.

Now it was Sadie's turn to be puzzled. "What are you talking about?" she asked Lila.

"You know: Close but no cigar! You are not just close, you are correct. So you get the cigar."

"I see. Have you been studying English idioms again?"

"Not studying, just noticing. Rick says this all the time. I asked him what it means. It is stupid but so are many idioms." Lila's tone of voice said that was all there was to be said about cigars and maybe even about idioms in general. She leaned forward and turned on the car radio. Classical strains from Sirius Satellite Radio filled the little car, and Lila settled back to listen as Sadie piloted them back toward downtown and her condo.

Relieved of Lila's chatter, Sadie mulled over the morning's events as she drove. She wanted to tell Mike about the missing halter. And about the Chinese man. But how? He'd think she was interfering and probably get mad all over again. She puzzled over this until she pulled into a parking space in her lot and turned the engine off. Lila emerged from her music-induced reverie. "Remember to pick up the fish I ordered," she said. "If you do not know what to do with it, call me. I will be home." She opened the passenger door.

"Lila, I really don't fix fish often." Sadie pursed her lips before adding, "Can't you use it yourself? And the pineapple as well?"

Lila's eyes lit up. "Sure I can use it. I need a reason to call Georges. He will like a French home-cooked meal."

"I didn't realize you knew Georges LeBourne so well." Sadie was curious, and Lila's answer did little to satisfy her curiosity.

"Oh, not so well." Lila swung her legs out of the car and stood up.

Sadie got out also, and they met behind the car where Sadie handed Lila the car keys. "Thank you so much for going with me. And, of course, for letting me drive."

"No problem ... well, no problem for me. Maybe for you and for sure for the donkey."

"Yes," Sadie agreed.

"Are you going to tell your policeman? About the Chinaman and the halter?"

"Yes, I think I have to," Sadie replied. And that's just what she tried to do. Right after she greeted Tiger, she dialed Mike's number. After all, she reasoned, it was Tuesday and the start of Mike's usual "weekend." An invitation to a picnic in the mountains would be perfectly normal, especially on such a beautiful day.

Nineteen

"I'd rather not go until later. Let's go this evening and listen to the elk bugle," Mike said when Sadie called to propose a picnic in the mountains. Neither of them mentioned the disagreements of the previous day as they sparred about how best to spend their one free weekday afternoon together.

"To hear the elk, we'd have to go north, up to Estes. I want to go south, around Eldora, maybe down to Black Hawk," Sadie argued. "And besides, Tiger doesn't like elk bugling. I think it's too much male dominance competition for him."

"Tiger's going on this excursion?"

"Sure."

"I guess I should have known that," Mike said. "Okay, what time should I pick you up?"

Arrangements made, Sadie turned on her computer, logged into MapQuest, and keyed in the address Wayne Chen had given to the Humane Society. The best MapQuest could manage was a rather general overview of seemingly undeveloped land south of Nederland and north of Black Hawk, west of Highway 119. Zooming in and out didn't produce any more useful information and cost Sadie too much time. Mike was due in 15 minutes.

She dashed over to Wild Oats to pick up carry-out. She'd offered a picnic. She hadn't, however, said she was preparing the food. As usual, Wild Oats offered a plethora of ready-to-eat goodies. Sadie remembered the tub of sun-dried tomato hummus Lila had put in her refrigerator and selected a package of sliced provolone to go with it. From the deli she got generous servings of spicy tofu and vegetables and curried turkey salad. Her last stop, the bakery section, yielded a baguette fresh from the oven.

Sadie was home and transferring her purchases to a picnic cooler when Mike arrived. Soon they were on their way up Boulder Canyon. The aspen were all they should be. Glistening and shimmering in a gentle fall breeze, the willowy trees offered an occasional golden counterpoint on the rocky, steep sides of the canyon.

After the road climbed nearly three thousand feet from Boulder's already more than mile-high location, it reached the mountain town of Nederland, where Mike turned south on 119 toward Black Hawk. At this altitude, the aspen were truly in their glory. Waves of bright golden leaves crested in a sea of forest green pine trees. Sadie relaxed, reveling in the crisp fall air and the stunning countryside.

As they rounded a steep curve, the ambiance was shattered by a giant billboard.

On this site. The new Vail.
Coming soon. Stop, look, invest.

"Geez," Mike said. "What is that about? New Vail, indeed."

They didn't have to wait long to find out what it was about. Billboard after billboard told the story: a new development to be devoted to cross-country skiing. Homes spread along the trails. A ground-floor opportunity to invest in this daring new concept. Five-acre home sites. National forest land, newly purchased from the government.

"Curious, that last one," Sadie said. "National forest land? Newly purchased from the government? How did that happen? I thought developers weren't supposed to get any of the federal land that this Administration sold. But that may explain why MapQuest didn't really display this area."

"MapQuest? You looked up this new Vail on MapQuest?"

"Not exactly. I was trying to find an address around here."

"Whose address?"

"I was curious about the Chinese guy who visited the donkey this morning. He gave the Humane Society a mountain address. It was somewhere between Nederland and Black Hawk. I was just wondering …"

Mike's face turned red as he clamped his mouth shut. Clearly trying to contain his rage, he spoke slowly but deliberately. "I told you to stay out of this investigation. And you invite me on a picnic to see where this guy lives. What in the Sam Hill do you think you're doing? This is absolutely none of your business. Have I not made myself perfectly clear?" His knuckles turned white as he gripped the steering wheel.

"The donkey is my business."

"Why?"

"Because she's a victim. No one is looking out for her. If I don't, who will?"

"The donkey is not your problem. The Chinese man who visited the donkey is not your problem. Nor, for that matter, are either of them my problem."

Sadie's anger rose to counter Mike's. "They are too your problem. That man switched the donkey's halter. Don't you care why?"

"It would be police business if the Humane Society reported a theft. And it probably wouldn't be much of a theft if they did. What's a used halter worth?"

"It's not a theft," Sadie struggled to make Mike understand. "It was a swap. He took one halter and left another. So why? Why did he want that halter? Why did he bring another to swap with it? He didn't want the donkey, he wanted the halter. Why?"

Sadie lurched against the seat belt as Mike swung the car to an abrupt halt on the side of the road. Tiger rolled across the back seat and onto the floor, paws flailing as he scrambled to stay upright.

"Look, Sadie," Mike said turning to face her. "You simply have to stop obsessing about this. The donkey has nothing to do with anything. I'll grant you that the donkey probably didn't kill Lee Hong. It certainly at least witnessed his murder, but it can't tell us what happened. Or help us find the culprit, missing halter or not."

Sadie drummed her fists on the dashboard, punctuating her words with her frustration. "Not missing—swapped. And the Chinese guy must have done it. Why? And that's not all. Did Lee Hong call the Humane Society about the donkey? Or was it this guy? And where is Lee Hong's camera? And why won't you listen to me?"

Tiger responded with distressed whimpers as he cringed on the back seat. Mike looked thunderous and sat staring at Sadie until the demanding squeal of his cell phone pierced the heavy silence in the car.

He flipped the phone open, sighed, and keyed the answer button. His side of the conversation was monosyllabic.

"Yeah?"

"Where?"

"Who?"

"Coming." He wheeled the Honda into a tight U-turn and gunned the engine as they headed back toward Nederland.

"Now what?" Sadie asked.

"Well, it seems you asked at least one good question. Lee Hong's camera has been found."

"Where?"

"In Sam Gross's briefcase."

Sadie absorbed this information. Sam Gross had Lee Hong's camera? Lee Hong certainly had his camera at the donkey pond, where he was killed. "So," she said, "that must mean that Sam Gross killed Lee Hong."

"Hard to say," Mike answered as they turned into Boulder Canyon and started the 14-mile descent to Boulder.

Glad that Mike was at least talking to her, Sadie pressed on. "I wonder if he knows about the halter."

"Hard to say," Mike repeated.

"Maybe you can ask him."

"Nope."

"Why not?" Sadie's temper was rising all over again.

"They just fished his body out of Boulder Creek ... along with his briefcase and a digital camera."

Twenty

"You and Tiger can walk home from here," Mike said pulling into a No Parking slot in front of the library. He was halfway across the parking lot before Sadie was able to get Tiger's leash clipped. Although home was just across the street, she had no intention of going there. Instead, she guided the dog toward the edge of the crowd milling around the northern edge of the library parking lot by a branch of Boulder Creek. Mike had already shoved his way through the crowd and ducked under the yellow crime-scene tape that stretched from the parking lot to the Boulder Creek Path on the other side of the rushing, rock-strewn water. Four members of a crime scene investigation team were on their knees near the creek.

Street people, displaced from their usual loitering spots on the banks of the creek, worked the crowd that clustered behind the tape. Kids and dogs added a festive air as more and more city workers, senior citizens, and library patrons stopped to gawk. The growing crowd spilled into the parking lot, impeding incoming traffic and compromising the already crowded parking situation even more.

Unable to see what was happening down the steep slope, Sadie asked the woman next to her, "What's going on?"

"Somebody drowned," the woman answered. "They already took him away. I don't know what they're doing now."

119

"Was he tubing?" a burly young man with unkempt hair asked. "There's not enough water to tube. Dude should've known that."

"He wasn't a tuber. No way, man. Guy was a suit if I ever saw one," another young man offered. This set off a chorus of conversation in the crowd.

"What was he doing in the creek if he was a suit?"

"Just wading, probably."

"You nuts, guy? No one wades in that water."

"Dogs do, they like it right there."

The speculation continued in the parking lot as the activity diminished at the creek's edge. Mike came up the slope carrying an evidence bag. It looked too big to hold a camera, Sadie thought, but maybe it was Sam Gross's briefcase. She stepped behind the burly young man. Mike thought she'd gone home, and she preferred he continue to think so. The crowd parted as Mike, looking straight ahead, avoided eye contact with anyone. He strode over to his car, put the evidence bag in the back, climbed in, backed out, and drove off.

"Interesting. I wonder what that dude had."

"I wonder more why the guy was in the creek." The discussion veered back to speculation, and Sadie decided it was time to go. Tiger, who had been quietly sitting by her side, leaped to his feet and set off, tugging Sadie toward Arapahoe and home. Like the well-trained dog he was, Tiger stopped tugging as they reached the busy street. He sat and waited for Sadie to tell him when it was safe to cross.

Traffic on Arapahoe was complicated by the swelling exodus from the library parking lot. Trying to look both ways on the street and behind her at the stream of cars waiting to emerge from the library parking lot, Sadie was startled by a soft voice at her side. "Professor Wagner?"

She turned to find a worried-looking Ling. High cheekbones emphasized the shadows under her black, almond-shaped eyes. "I must ask help," she said, stress and sorrow roughening her usually lilting voice. "We have many problems."

Yes, I'm sure you do, Sadie thought. "Come home with me. We'll talk." She reached out to hug the distressed young woman and, arm in arm, they crossed the street.

Once on the other side, Ling pulled away. "Not home, your office. Can we go to your office?"

"My office? Why there? Home is right here." They were almost at the lobby door to Flatirons Vista.

"Yes, but I need backpack."

"You have a key. You can get your backpack later."

"I mean I need backpack and you."

Sadie didn't understand but decided to humor Ling. "Okay, but Tiger can't go. I have to take him home first. Do you want to come in?"

"No, I wait here. It is okay?"

"Sure, I'll be right back." Sadie hurried through the door and into her condo complex.

Being shoved into Sadie's condo, unleashed and left behind, wasn't what Tiger had expected. At least that's how Sadie interpreted his heart-rending wail as she hurried back out to the street to find Ling.

The two women were quiet as they hiked up the hill toward campus. Sadie marveled at her own ability to keep quiet while her thoughts tumbled through recent events. Lee Hong's death, the donkey's switched halter, Ling's immigration woes, Sam Gross fished out of Boulder Creek. Sam Gross? Why had Lee Hong told him he worked for Sadie? How did all this tie together? As they reached the Language Arts Building, Sadie sighed in frustration, earning a speculative glance from Ling.

"You are okay?" the Chinese woman asked.

"As okay as I can be under the circumstances." Sadie saw no point in sharing her thoughts with the uncommunicative Ling, who was now standing beside Sadie's office door, waiting for her to open it.

"Did you lose your key?" Sadie asked.

"No."

"Then open the door."

"Not lose. Not have."

"Oh for pity's sake!" Sadie flung her purse off her shoulder, popped it open, and starting rummaging in its depths. Unsuccessful at locating her keys, she shook the purse vigorously until a telltale jingle gave away their location.

Retrieving the keys, Sadie opened the door and flicked on the lights. The backpack was still there, under Sadie's desk.

Ling picked it up, unzipped it, and took out a large brown envelope. "This is it," she said. "We want to sell this." She handed Sadie the envelope. It felt like a manuscript.

"Sell this? What is it?"

"Please," Ling tapped the envelope. "Please, we need help."

Struck by Ling's supplication, Sadie sat down and opened the envelope. A number of eight-by-ten photographs spilled out. Ling perched in the blue plastic chair beside the desk as Sadie began to leaf through the photographs.

The photos seemed to be workplace portraits. Each featured a different Chinese man doing some sort of seemingly menial job. In the top photo, a man with round cheeks and round glasses, his mouth pursed into yet more roundness, glanced at the camera as he plunged his hands into a deep vat of soapy water. Behind him were piles of soiled pots and pans. Another photo featured a hawk-faced Chinese, eyes sternly avoiding the camera as he pushed a large broom across a tile floor. Still another showed a tall, thin man wrestling a bulging sack into a dumpster labeled Black Hawk Municipal Waste. Mountains loomed in the background darkness.

On and on the photos went. Sadie shuffled back through them. They were all different people. No one appeared twice, she was sure of it.

"Who are these people, Ling?"

"Chinese people."

No kidding, Sadie thought. "Do you think these people will buy their photos?" she asked stabbing her index finger at the round face of the dishwasher. "Why would they buy these pictures?"

"Not them. The government. We hope, the government."

"The government? Our government? I mean, the U.S. government? Is that what you mean?"

"Yes. Lee Hong made photos for U.S. government. Now Lee Hong is dead, but we hope they still want photos. We put ad in paper, just like last time. Pictures are ready, even if Lee Hong is dead, government will still buy the pictures? Yes?"

"Lee Hong took these for the U.S. government? Why?" Sadie felt her pulse quicken. Of course, Sam Gross said they had bought photos from Lee Hong. And they didn't want to buy any more until they were sure of his agenda. His "agenda" appeared to be that Chinese people were good janitors and dishwashers. What kind of agenda could that be? Or, for that matter, why would Sam Gross want pictures like this?

Ling interrupted her thoughts. "Can you help us sell them? My sister needs money. Very much. Lee Hong did the work. When he finishes we put the ad in paper but no one calls. Now Ming Fang needs the money."

"Ling, I have no idea how to sell these pictures. Do you know why Lee Hong took them?"

"Commando asked him. Lee Hong was very proud that U.S. government wanted his photos. U.S. government helped us all."

This last statement reminded Sadie about the immigration issue. "Does that mean the U.S. government helped Lee Hong get a permanent visa? Maybe even asylum?"

"Maybe."

"And you, did the government help you also?"

"No."

"So, I do need to know about this. How did you get back into the United States? You went to Mexico, gave up your visa, and applied for asylum. Is that right?"

"Yes," the young woman said, refusing to meet Sadie's eyes.

"And what happened?"

"Nothing."

"Nothing? They didn't deny your request for asylum?"

"Yes."

"Yes, they did?"

"Yes."

"They denied you."

"Yes."

"Then what?"

"I call Lee Hong."

Sadie waited. Nothing more seemed to be forthcoming so she forged ahead. "And what did Lee Hong do?"

"He came."

"To Mexico?"

"To San Diego."

"So, you were in Mexico and Lee Hong was in San Diego. How did you get back to Boulder?"

"Lee Hong sends commando for me."

Sadie threw her hands up in exasperation. "Commando! I don't think so. What are you talking about."

"Yes, Commando. His name was Commando. He brings me visa and we meet Lee Hong in San Diego."

"He brought you a visa? In Mexico?"

"Yes," Ling nodded. "And he promises to buy photos."

Understanding dawning, Sadie said, "Commander Gross. Not commando, commander. Is that who it was? Commander Gross?"

"Yes, yes," Ling nodded quickly. "My mistake. Commander is not commando?"

Sadie picked up the photos and tapped them on the desk to align them. How to tell Ling? Should she tell Ling? As she thought, the questions continued. Are these the photos Gross wanted? And, if so, why? And how could he get Ling a visa so quickly? She had many questions and no answers. Meanwhile, Ling was waiting for one answer: How to sell the photos. That was one answer Sadie did have. The photos seemed to be totally worthless.

"Ling, I cannot imagine that these photos are worth anything. If they are, the reason is not apparent. I suppose you could try to contact Naval Intelligence and see if they want these photos. But I don't know how to do that."

"Naval Intelligence is not necessary. Just Mr. Commander. He always comes quickly. The first day Lee Hong has his ad."

"Lee Hong advertises his photos?" Sadie asked.

"No, he writes little ad for something else. Something no one wants. Then Mr. Commander knows photos are ready. "

"Something like what?" Faint bells were ringing in Sadie's head.

"Nothing. Old camera, used shoes, old car, used camper, nothing anyone wants."

"Used camper? Was that the last ad?"

"Yes, Ming Fang made the ad but Mr. Commander did not call."

"On the contrary," Sadie said, "he did call. Many other people called, too. But they called me because the ad had my home phone number."

"No, not your home number. We always use office number." She gestured at the phone on Sadie's desk. "And I was here waiting to answer Mr. Commander. But he did not call."

"No," Sadie repeated, "you used my home phone number. And more than twenty people called—including Commander Gross. But, Ling, you shouldn't use either of my phone numbers this way."

Ling paled. "Ming Fang must have used wrong number." The Chinese woman spoke softly, head down. "I am so sorry. We are much trouble for you. But," she brightened, "if Mr. Commander called, maybe we can call him back now."

"That won't work," Sadie said. "Commander Gross is dead."

Ling seemed to shrink in the chair, fright etched in her face. She sputtered as she tried to find words. "But ... but ... not possible. We need ... He said ... When? When did he die?"

"I'm not sure about when. I guess I don't even know how. I just know that he was found in Boulder Creek this afternoon."

"Accident?"

"I don't know. I doubt it."

Ling jumped up, grabbed the photos out of Sadie's hands, and stuffed them into her backpack. Distress magnified in her haste, Ling barely turned to say "I'm sorry" before she rushed out the door.

Stunned, Sadie tried to collect her thoughts. As she often did, she turned to her west-facing window. Usually she found the snowy mountain peaks in the distance mesmerizing, but today she was more interested in the street. There, she saw Ling running, trying to catch a departing bus. The bus gathered speed, leaving Ling behind. Despair evident in every step, Ling turned and headed toward east campus. As her plodding figure disappeared from sight, Sadie felt overwhelmed by the woman's evident grief. What could she do to help Ling?

The phone jangled her out of her contemplation. It was Mike.

"Hi," he said, "I've got some photos I'd like you to look at."

"Why?" Sadie asked, still thinking about Ling's problems and Lee Hong's photos.

"Just want to see if you recognize any of them. Specifically, we think maybe one of them is Lee Hong. But it's hard to tell. He wasn't in the greatest shape when we found him. And ...," Mike faltered, "you know how it is...."

"No, I don't. How what is?"

Mike changed the subject. "Are you going to be there very long? I can bring the pictures to your office."

"Right now?"

"Sure."

"You must really be in a hurry. Okay," Sadie agreed. "I have papers to grade. I can work on them until you get here."

She didn't get very far on grading papers, however. She decided to stew about Mike's Anglo-centric attitude. He'd come very close to saying, "All Chinese look alike to me." But, Sadie thought, he didn't. He's trying. Too bad he has to try so hard.

She had talked herself into a snarky mood by the time Mike arrived less than fifteen minutes later. "Hey," he called, as he rapped on her door. "I know you're busy, so would you just look through these and tell me if any of these guys are Lee Hong?"

For the second time in an hour, Sadie was handed a pile of photos of Chinese men. But these photos weren't posed. They were just mug shots. Mug shots attached to immigration forms. Edges curled, some were even slightly damp.

"Where are these from?" she asked.

"Doesn't matter." Mike sat down and crossed an ankle over a knee. His typical male sprawl challenged Sadie's smallish plastic student chair.

"Where?" she repeated.

"Sam Gross's briefcase, if you must know."

Somewhat mollified, Sadie looked through the pile of photos. None of them were Lee Hong, but a sense of *deja vu* nagged at her consciousness as she turned page after page and examined the photos stapled to them. It wasn't until she got to the last page that Sadie understood. There, looking severely at the camera, was the same round-faced man she had last seen elbow-deep in soap suds in one of Lee Hong's photos.

Twenty-One

"Who are these guys?" Sadie asked Mike.

"We don't know." A terse, unhelpful answer.

Sadie thumbed a photo up and looked at the paper underneath. It was an application for a visa. No, it was more than that. It was an approved application for a visa, an E-2 visa.

"They all seem to have names," she said.

"Knowing their names doesn't mean we know who they are." Mike shrugged his shoulders.

"Or why their visas were in Commander Gross's briefcase. Is that what you mean?"

"Something like that."

Struggling to remember the particulars of E-2's, all Sadie could recall for sure was that they involved money. A lot of money. Didn't E-2's require a huge investment in a business in the United States?

"Why would you think Lee Hong might have an E-2 visa?" she asked.

"We don't necessarily. We're just trying to connect the dots."

Putting the photos down, Sadie opened the bottom drawer of her desk. There, on top, was the list of visa types she had compiled yesterday. Mike leaned forward to look in the drawer. "What's that?" he asked.

She pulled the list from the drawer. "Just some information from the Web." She slipped the list under the stack of papers and photos Mike had given her and riffled through them again. This time, she lifted each photo and confirmed that the attached paper was, in fact, an approved application for an E-2 visa. When she was finished, she handed Mike her visa list.

"Look, all these guys have E-2 visas. That means each of them brought at least half a million dollars with them when they came to the United States."

"That's a lot of money." Mike read the list slowly. "Why do you happen to have this list of visa types so handy?"

"It all started as a class exercise. We were talking about the different kinds of visas and I discovered I didn't know much about them. So I looked it up."

"Your students have E-2 visas?"

"No, of course not."

"Then why ...?" Mike waved the list at her.

"It just came up. And I remembered it when I saw these visa applications. Are all these men here in Colorado?"

"No idea. All we know for sure is that their pictures, and their visa applications, were in Sam Gross's briefcase. And ... and we want to find out as much as we can before the feds arrive and take this case away from us."

"That will happen soon?"

"It's already happening. Naval Investigators don't wind up shot without exciting a lot of people. We've heard from the FBI, the Navy, and even Homeland Security. There's going to be a huge turf battle when they all get here."

Sadie didn't care about turf battles. She was stuck on the first thing Mike said. "Shot? I thought he drowned."

"Nope, shot and apparently fell into the creek. We found the spot where he was shot. It was under the Ninth Street Bridge, just where the creek branches to flow behind your condo."

Still digesting that news, Sadie went back to one of her original questions. "You said Gross had Lee Hong's camera. Did it have pictures from the donkey pond? Will it tell you anything useful?"

"The memory chip was missing. All we have is the camera—the camera and these." Mike reached over and took the packet of photos and paper from Sadie. "Now I guess the feds will have to start looking for all of these guys."

"I wonder ..." Sadie stopped when Mike raised an eyebrow at her.

"You wonder what?"

"Well, I just wonder if one of these guys was at the Humane Society this morning. Could we take these photos and show them to Doug? The donkey wrangler at the Humane Society? Do you think that would be a good idea?"

"Didn't the guy have a driver's license? And a name? We could just check the names. What was his name? Do you remember?" Mike pulled the stack of photos toward him.

"Chen, I think. Wayne Chen, but he's from Taiwan. These folks are all from China, aren't they? See ..." Sadie picked up the photos one by one and pointed to Country of Origin. "See: China, China, China. No one is from Taiwan. Come to think of it, we probably don't give E-2 visas to Taiwanese anyway."

"Why not?"

"We don't treat Taiwan as a nation. The U.S. pretends that we believe Taiwan is a Chinese state."

"I don't understand. Didn't Taiwan secede from China?"

"Not exactly. It's complicated. But if we think it's complicated, imagine what people from Taiwan think. They have an army, a navy, an air force, and everything else most governments have, but hardly any countries recognize them as a nation. It makes it very hard in lots of ways. Even hard for individuals to travel."

"I remember that now. Didn't we refuse to let the president of Taiwan land in Alaska or something?"

"I think we let his plane land. We just didn't let him get off the plane. And it's not just the United States. It's most of the world. The president of Taiwan had to go way out of his way to get from Taiwan to Paraguay a few years ago. No one wanted to let his official plane land. That way they could keep pretending that Taiwan doesn't exist. And, more important, they didn't offend China."

"All of which has nothing to do with the problem at hand," Mike said.

"No, I suppose not. Except that none of these guys is Taiwanese. So none of them is the mysterious donkey visitor. And, to answer your original question, none of them is Lee Hong, either."

"Yeah, well, I'll just be taking these now," Mike said gathering up the photos in front of Sadie and standing up. "You'll be grading papers all afternoon? I'm afraid I'll be tied up with the Sam Gross investigation the rest of the day and probably this evening as well."

"Any idea what he was doing by the creek?"

"Well, I don't think he was sunbathing. But there isn't any official word yet."

"Why would he have Lee Hong's camera? Especially with no images? Or memory chip?"

"We have a lot of questions about Commander Gross. Questions we've asked Naval Intelligence. Starting with why he was vetting foreign nationals as potential employees."

"I'm not sure he was," Sadie said. "I think he just made that up to have a reason to talk to me."

"You've lost me." Mike sat down again, waiting for an explanation.

Sadie explained to Mike and, as she did so, some things became clearer to her. Sam Gross *had* called her number when he found Lee Hong's ad. He expected to be told where to pick up the photos, but Sadie's curt response told him not only that there was some sort of mistake, but also that she had received a lot of calls about the camper.

Needing to unsnarl the confusion, Gross had to talk to Sadie. Gross wanted to see what Sadie knew about Lee Hong and he wanted to do it fast. So, he made up the story about Lee Hong applying for a job and saying he worked for Sadie. Once he got into Sadie's condo, Gross must have realized that she knew nothing about the photos, but Mike's presence probably forced him to continue with the putative vetting process.

"So Lee Hong and Gross were using classified ads to arrange their meetings? That's like something out of the Cold War," Mike said. "What could Lee Hong be photographing that warranted such behavior?"

Should she tell Mike about Lee Hong's photos? Maybe. Why not? She plunged into the subject without thinking further.

"Ling seems to have a lot of Lee Hong's recent photos. She was just here to see if I could help her collect money from Gross for the photos. It seems he commissioned Lee Hong to take them."

Mike sat down. "Photos of what?"

"People, Chinese people, Chinese people working."

"Working? Here?"

"Actually, I'm not sure where the photos were taken. Probably in Black Hawk. In casinos maybe. I think so, but I'm not sure."

"Why did Gross want the pictures?"

"I don't know. I think I've told you more than I know about the pictures."

"You're telling me more than you know?" Mike grinned. "It's great to hear you admit that. I thought you usually know more than you tell."

"That too, sometimes. But not this time. I don't know anything." But, a caveat surfaced in her head, that's not true. I know that at least one of the guys in Sam Gross's pictures is also in Lee Hong's photos. Were there others? Remembering her vague unease as she looked through the photos Mike brought, Sadie thought that probably there were more matches between the two sets of photos.

"Mike," she began tentatively. "Maybe Ling would recognize some of those guys. Can I make copies of the photos before you take them?"

"How are you going to copy photos?"

"Just a copier. They won't be great but they should be recognizable. Would that be okay?"

"I don't think so, actually. These are part of an active investigation," Mike gripped the photos firmly and stood up. "No, Sadie. I think you should stay out of this. And that means Ling should stay out of it also. I'd best get going."

He turned at the door and added, "After all, I have to get this wrapped up in time to celebrate your birthday tomorrow. Tiger and I have made a lot of plans."

"You remember my birthday? Wow, I'm impressed. How did you do that?"

"Electronic memory. Not very romantic, but quite functional. I'll call you later. Meantime, just grade papers and try to stay out of trouble, okay?" His words were light and joking but the expression on his face was stern and serious. "I mean that. Please let me deal with the Chinese and visas and missing photos."

His words were forgotten as soon as he shut her office door. She couldn't get the image of the round-faced dishwasher out of her head. Why would an E-2 visa holder be washing dishes? And in a Black Hawk casino kitchen? Were Lee Hong's photos only of the men whose visas were in Gross's briefcase? Or might his photos include other Chinese around Black Hawk? Other Chinese such as Wayne Chen? Sadie thought it was a good idea to find out more about Wayne Chen. A photo would be really helpful. If not from Sam Gross's photo collection, then maybe from Lee Hong's. She picked up the phone and dialed Ling's phone number. It rang and rang. No one answered. No answering machine, either. Odd, Sadie thought, Ling should be home by now, even though she missed the bus. It wasn't more than a mile walk.

Twenty-Two

Sadie weighed her options. Ling wasn't home. Mike was not going to be around for the evening. It was less than an hour's drive to Black Hawk. Why not go there for dinner? The sun still shone brightly in the blue Colorado sky but it was approaching the mountains. When it got there, dusk would descend quickly. If she wanted to avoid driving the canyon in the dark, she had best leave soon.

With whom? Tiger was waiting at home, possibly still miffed about the fast brush-off he'd received earlier. Why not Lila? Sadie picked up the phone and punched in the familiar number.

"Simone here," Daniel answered. Sadie's stomach lurched. She stuttered, "Oh … ah … hi, Dan. Is Lila around?"

"Sadieee," Dan drew the vowels out in the quiet, sexy way he always did. "I am so glad to hear your voice again. How are you? And Tiger? How is the beastly beast?"

"We're fine. I just need to talk to Lila, please," Sadie said, wondering why she had to be so rude. No answer to that—she just didn't trust herself to talk to Dan. The smooth-talking Frenchman had always bested her in any discussion. That is, until the last discussion months ago, when she had resolutely held her ground and evicted him from her condo and, she hoped, her life.

"My big sister? Ah, yes. I know she enjoys your company. We both do … or did." He chuckled softly.

I will not ask for Lila again, Sadie thought as she bit her lower lip to keep from speaking while a knot began to form in her stomach.

After what felt like an interminably awkward silence, Dan relented. "I'll call Lila."

"Thank you," Sadie said.

"Oh … and Sadie?"

"Yes."

"*Joyeux anniversaire.*"

Startled, Sadie replied, "Thank you." After Dan put the phone down, she wondered how he remembered that her birthday was on the horizon. For sure, Dan didn't use an electronic memory. He had enough trouble logging into email. None of the new-fangled electronics for him. It was somehow unsettling that he remembered, but also flattering.

She heard Lila clatter to the phone. "Sadie?" Lila said. "How are you? I got the fish and made a wonderful lunch for Georges. It was tilapia, pineapple, many things. Georges said he could feel the Sun of Provence." Lila giggled.

Maybe Lila was too full of fish—or Georges LeBourne—to be interested in dinner, but Sadie asked anyway. "I was hoping you'd go up to Black Hawk with me for dinner."

"Black Hawk? Where do you eat in Black Hawk?"

"All the casinos have restaurants. Some of them are even good. There are some outstanding restaurants, like the Black Forest Inn," Sadie said more confidently than she felt. Had the Black Forest Inn survived the influx of legal gambling, casinos, and tourist buses that now swamped what had once been a sleepy mountain town?

"I have to drive, yes?" Lila said.

"Well, yes. I'm afraid so."

"Let me ask Daniel."

Sadie heard Lila and Dan talking but couldn't pick up the content of the fast-flowing French. Dan sounded amused. Maybe he was teasing Lila, as he had been teasing Sadie. Maybe he had other plans for his car. Sadie waited.

"It is okay. Daniel decided he does not want to go."

Lila's Fish

1 stalk of celery, chopped
1 T fresh ginger, chopped
1 t cumin
1/2 t cayenne
1/2 pineapple, chunked
5 oz of flaked coconut
1/2 pound of Tilapia

Preheat oven to 400°.

Cover cookie sheet with aluminum foil. Pat water on it. Put Tilapia on sheet. Set aside.

On top of stove, in pan, heat olive oil over medium heat. Cook celery 1-2 minutes, add ginger. Sprinkle the celery and ginger with cayenne and cumin.

Put pineapple in bowl. Add contents of pan and coconut. Mix.

Cover Tilapia with mix from bowl.

Bake about 15 minutes.

"Good, but I don't want to keep Dan from doing something he wanted to do," Sadie answered.

"Oh, he had no plans. He just does not want to go to Black Hawk with us."

He wasn't invited, Sadie thought. But of course, since his car was a necessary part of her proposed expedition, perhaps he was *de facto* "invited." The knot in her stomach relaxed. She was glad he didn't want to go.

"So," she said, "we should probably go soon. What do you think?"

"I can be at your house in thirty minutes," Lila answered.

"Great!" Sadie hung up, stacked the papers she had been grading neatly in the center of her desk, hurriedly locked her office door, and left.

When she arrived home, Tiger was delighted. Wiggling from nose to tail, he fetched his leash and brought it to Sadie.

"Is there time? I wonder. Let's try it," Sadie agreed as she clipped on the leash and ushered the dog out the door. They were barely on the sidewalk in front of the condo complex when Lila pulled up in Dan's red Mini Cooper. So much for Tiger's walk.

"Tiger is going?" Lila asked.

"Is that okay? He's been alone all day ... well, almost all day."

"Okay with me. Is it okay with the casino?"

"No, but he won't mind waiting in the car. It will be cool by the time we get there," Sadie said, opening the passenger door and urging Tiger into the back. Always ready for a walk, Tiger was even more ready for a ride. Rides were rare events. He clambered in happily and sat down, staring intently out the side window.

As soon as Sadie settled in the passenger seat, Lila peeled away from the curb, executed a smooth but too fast U-turn in front of the library, and headed west on Arapahoe. Tiger crouched on the seat to protect himself from the unexpected centrifugal force and Sadie, flung into the car door, managed to collect herself and get her seat belt fastened before they got to the mouth of Boulder Canyon.

"Good grief, Lila," she said. "You aren't supposed to make a U-turn back there. And for sure you did it too fast."

"Too fast? If slow, no one will stop," Lila answered. "Besides, we are friends of the police, no?"

"No, probably not. At least not that way," Sadie answered. "Mike really can't keep you from getting a traffic ticket."

"No?"

"No."

Lila slowed down. The drive up the canyon, Sadie's second of the day, became very sedate. Tiger risked sitting up again and nuzzled Sadie's neck. She reached back and scratched his ears. The threesome was quiet, watching the rugged scenery twist by as the car wound around and up on the two-lane road in the canyon.

Half an hour later, they emerged from Boulder Canyon, and Lila turned left, to drive through the small mountain town of Nederland. The first sign appeared just south of the city limits.

Open House. Nordic Wonderland. Stop and Visit.

Is that sign new since this afternoon? Sadie wondered. Or did I just miss it earlier?

"Nordic Wonderland? What does this mean?" Lila queried. "Is it big Wagnerian heroes with spears?"

Sadie laughed. "No, I don't think so. It's Nordic skiing. You know cross-country. Not downhill."

"And Wonderland?"

"Just advertising."

"Do we want to see Wonderland?" Lila asked, as they passed the thicket of signs.

Next Right! Open House! The New Vail! Stop Here!

"It's late. Probably they're closed," Sadie answered but, as Lila slowed, Tiger added his opinion. The pleading whimper from the back seat strongly suggested it was time to stop. Lila swung the car onto a well-manicured dirt road. As they drove down the one-lane road, the pine forest seemed to close in.

"I'm sure they're not open," Sadie repeated as they approached a gatehouse. In fact, a man dressed in golfing togs was just locking the door. He waved them to a stop and approached the driver's side. Lila lowered her window to hear him say, "We're just closing, can you come back tomorrow?"

"Oooh, my. No, we cannot," Lila replied, gracing him with a pouty but pleasant look that complimented her French accent very well.

It worked. He hesitated. "Maybe we can make an exception. I think my colleague is still in the showroom. Let me check." He unhooked a cell phone from his belt. As he waited for an answer, he said, "Are you a tourist? Or do you live in the States?"

Strange question, Sadie thought, but Lila answered it. In detail. "I visit my baby brother," she said. "He is a professor of French at the Institute. Maybe I will stay here, but it is maybe not possible. Immigration does not care about brothers. Only husbands."

The coquettish look Lila bestowed on the salesman embarrassed Sadie. She squirmed in her seat and looked out the passenger window. Lila didn't seem to be able to talk to a man without lacing the conversation with enticing innuendo. Sadie tried to pretend this wasn't happening.

The salesman didn't seem put off. However, his colleague answered before he could respond to Lila. "Hey, Wayne," he said. "There's a lady from France here who's interested in seeing the development. I'd like to send her on up."

His colleague must have objected, because the salesman glanced at his watch and said, "It's only a few minutes after closing. And, like I said, this lady is from France. She may not be back this way. But she'd like to be—immigration problems, you know."

Odd, decidedly odd, Sadie thought.

"Right, her English is good. I'm not sure about her friend though. I'll send them right up," he said snapping his phone shut.

Sadie thought that, since she hadn't spoken, the salesman must have assumed she was French also. Monolingual French at that. Maybe that was good. Sadie could just keep her mouth shut and watch Lila's antics.

Lila steered the car around a bend in the road and into a parking lot. As soon as she braked and turned the ignition off, Tiger was on his feet, yowling and pacing on the back seat. Keeping his mouth shut was not in his immediate plans.

"Okay, okay. We're going," Sadie murmured. She opened the door and let him out. He didn't get very far. At the end of his eight-foot leash, he posed on three legs to drain his overfull bladder.

When Tiger finished and began to explore the new territory, Sadie looked around. The sales hut was rustic but upscale. Three steps edged by a sturdy pine banister ended at leaded double doors. One door opened and a short, stocky Chinese man emerged to greet Lila. His smile, highlighted by a gleaming gold incisor, seemed too wide for his face.

"Hi," he said, extending his hand in the classic salesman manner. "I'm Wayne Chen. I'm glad we were still here. You are ...?"

"Lila, Lila Simone." She avoided his hand and bobbed her head instead. "That is my friend, Sadie." Lila gestured at Sadie, still in the parking lot, holding Tiger's leash.

Wayne Chen? Did Lila recognize the name? Maybe not. Sadie couldn't tell. But here was the man who had visited the donkey, the man who said he was looking for his son's donkey. And the man who must have switched halters at the Humane Society. Here was the man she had hoped to find. Right here, greeting Lila effusively. Sadie's hands began to shake. Sensing her excitement, Tiger rushed back to Sadie's feet, the hair on his back standing up as he tried to identify the source of Sadie's concern.

"Come in, come in, Madame," Wayne Chen said, opening the door wider. "And your friend can bring her dog, too." He waved at Sadie, urging her forward. She smiled back and gestured helplessly at Tiger.

"The dog is okay, Madame, come, come," Wayne Chen repeated, again waving his hand in welcome.

Trying to smile shyly, Sadie nudged Tiger forward. They climbed the steps, and Sadie nodded at Wayne Chen. He was all smiles. Sadie avoided eye contact and focused instead on Tiger. His "anger ruff" was softening but still present as he eyed Wayne Chen somewhat belligerently.

"Now, ladies," Chen said, "let me show you the development." He gestured toward a large table in the middle of the room. They all moved to it, and Sadie saw a scale model. "We are here," Chen said, pointing to the circular parking lot they had just left. A forest of tiny pine trees continued beyond the parking lot and up the mountain rise behind it. Trails were etched through the forest and occasional Monopoly-style green houses dotted the model.

"This is the Chalet," Chen said pointing toward a chunky red block. Even a Monopoly-style hotel, Sadie thought. "The Chalet will be available to all homeowners. There will be a gym, a pool, meeting rooms, a spa—everything anyone would want after a hard day of skiing." Again the toothy smile. Chen produced a brochure. "This tells you all about the project," he said. "It has model styles, options, building schedules, dates, maps—almost everything you need to know. I say almost everything because there is one thing it doesn't mention. And this might be very important to you, Madame Simone."

"Oh, yes?" Lila answered.

"Yes. You see, there are two ways to invest in property here. One is to build your own house. That's what this brochure explains," he said, tapping the brochure now in Lila's hands. "The other way is to join us in developing the entire resort."

"I do not understand."

"It is what we call a limited partnership," Chen seemed to be hitting a typical salesman stride now. He was talking only to Lila, either assuming that Sadie couldn't understand him or sensing that Lila was the more likely prospect.

"Limited partnership means everyone's money is all in one pot. We work together to build the project. Each partner benefits equally. There is much less risk than there would be if you bought an individual property. And here is the really, really important part. If you are a limited partner, you are an investor. And in the United States, if you are an investor, you are a welcome citizen."

"Oh, yes?" Lila repeated.

"Yes, indeed. You can come to the United States. You can come immediately. You can get a special visa. No problem."

"Oh, yes?" Lila was beginning to sound like a broken record.

"Yes, it is no problem. You can stay with your brother forever. It is no problem."

Lila finally found her voice. "How much is this limited partnership?" she asked.

"Only five hundred thousand dollars," Chen replied.

Lila looked at him, her violet eyes wide. "Five hundred thousand dollars! That is half a million dollars. Who has that?"

"No problem," Chen said. "We can arrange financing. All you have to do is apply for the visa."

"Oh, yes?" Lila was back to her mainstay. Sadie waited breathlessly for one or the other of them to blink.

Chen blinked first. "Yes," he said. "We'll even help you apply. It's called an E-2 visa."

Twenty-Three

Sadie regretted her earlier subterfuge. She had so many questions, but she couldn't ask them because Wayne Chen thought she didn't speak English. As he continued to press Lila for information, he offered very little himself. Lila finally escaped from his super-salesmanship but only after relinquishing Daniel's phone number and promising to attend a sales seminar someday ... someday soon.

As they drove back toward Highway 119, Sadie said, "You know that was the guy who switched the donkey's halter, don't you?"

"Yes, strange is it not? That we would just meet him so easily. Or, was it strange?" Lila cast a sideways look at Sadie.

"Who knows." Sadie shrugged. It's a good thing you didn't have your passport with you. He'd have had you applying for a visa tonight."

"Oh, yes. I have my passport. But I do not need a different visa," Lila said.

"Maybe you do."

"No, I do not think so. Where are we now?"

"Turn right," Sadie said. "It's just a few miles to Black Hawk."

She dismissed further thoughts about Mr. Chen as Lila steered the car through increasing traffic on the winding mountain highway. Beside precipitous drop-offs, tall, straight pine trees crowd-ed the road. Marching upward, the dense trees melded on the distant slopes into a fabric of forest resting below bare, soaring granite peaks. Shadows of passing clouds added to the illusion of undulating green velvet slopes.

Tail high, feet churning, a tiny critter skittered across the road in front of them. Lila braked to give it time to cross.

Speeding through Rollinsville, they passed the road to the Moffit Tunnel, an eight-mile-long passage torn through the mountain in 1926 to get the railroad track across the Continental Divide at a reasonable altitude. Tilted sandstone now dominated the cliffs above the highway. On the left, a single peak was topped by a square fenced area. It was Fritz Peak, site of an early meteorological observatory.

Dipping into a shallow valley, they sped across Missouri Creek and passed the Gilpin County School, a modern edifice financed no doubt by the county's gaming windfalls. Looming on the right side of the highway, the school's design mimicked the faux gold mine architecture of the modern casinos that would soon appear in abundance. But, before that, they passed the remains of a real mine. The Golden Gilpin Mill stood in stark testament to the past. A past preserved in some way, according to the sign noting that Black Hawk is a National Historic District.

Hard to believe, Sadie thought as they rounded the final bend in the highway before the gaming district came into view. The city-limits sign heralded Black Hawk's elevation above sea level: 8056 feet.

"That is always funny," Lila said.

"What?"

"For Colorado cities, they always say how high, not how many people. Very funny."

"I don't think very many people actually live here."

"But there are many people here; look at that." Lila pointed toward the solid stream of cars coming toward them, northward from Denver. Most turned off into the parking lot of one of the huge casinos that dominated the mountainsides beside one of the few traffic lights in town.

Black Hawk was a surreal blemish packed tightly along the creek. New, wide streets with hanging baskets of flowers funneled traffic past parking areas built into the mountainsides. Signs on the five- and six-story parking garages offered places near the elevators for "elite" gamers and valet parking for others.

On the right, the green, peaked roof of The Riviera seemed more evocative of a chalet by Disney than the architecture reminiscent of mine shafts favored by most of the other casinos.

Sadie remembered the many ads she had seen for The Riviera. The largest casino in Black Hawk, it boasted almost one thousand slot machines, blackjack and poker tables, live music, a variety of food from pizza to fine dining, and, of course, free parking. A huge parking garage dominated the embankment behind the casino.

Lila pulled the car into the parking lot of the Silver Hawk, the first casino on their side of the road. A man dressed in scruffy denims like an old-time miner waved a cane wrapped in red, white, and blue bunting, signaling her to pull up to the valet parking station.

"Do you want to go here?" Lila asked Sadie.

"Let's just drive through town and look around first."

Lila backed out of the lot and turned up Gregory Street. Billboard notices were painted on most of the older, wooden buildings in contrast to the ultramodern video screens rolling on the sides of the new, multistoried, metal and glass casinos. A bucking mule graced the Sure Shot Casino, and Pot o' Gold promised "Hit a jackpot, eat for free on next visit."

Old mine tailings ringed the cliffs above the town, attesting to the nineteenth century designation of the richest square mile on earth. Beneath the probably unstable tailings, bolts dotted the mountainside, holding up massive steel restraining nets.

The roads were crowded with many people en route to try their luck on the gaming floor or to feast on the inexpensive food at the casino buffets. It was stop-and-go past the next few casinos, all of which appeared to occupy old storefronts. Their garish, come-on billboards promised the very loosest slots and a wide selection of low-bet video poker.

"Those places must be the mom-and-pop version of private enterprise," Sadie said.

"What does that mean?"

"If they don't have poker or blackjack, they don't need dealers. So a couple can run the casino pretty much by themselves. They probably don't even serve food."

This last observation was refuted moments later, as they passed the Whistle Stop Casino. Its billboard boasted "Deli Sandwiches, Daily Specials."

Sadie laughed. "So much for that idea. But that's not exactly fine dining, either."

They arrived at the second traffic light, and Lila turned right. Isle of Capri signs directed them toward another huge casino—actually, Sadie thought, maybe two other huge casinos. The Isle of Capri was linked to Colorado Central Station by an overhead pedestrian bridge that spanned the twisty, narrow street.

"I wonder if that's the biggest casino. I mean, if it's all one place. Or maybe it's two places with a bridge," Sadie mused.

"So, let's go see." Lila turned left onto the access road between the two giant casinos.

It was time to fill Lila in on their mission. "I need to explain to you what we're really doing here," Sadie said.

Lila slowed the car and glanced sideways at Sadie. "Not dinner? I'm hungry."

"Maybe dinner. But first, remember when you picked up Ling on campus Monday? When she was so upset? After she found out Lee Hong had been killed at the donkey's pond?"

Lila nodded.

"Later Ling brought me some of Lee Hong's pictures. It turns out that Lee Hong was taking very unusual pictures, pictures of Chinese men at work. Ling said the U.S. government had asked him to take these pictures. So Lee Hong's family wants to be paid for them."

"I don't understand." Lila was driving slowly behind a virulent green bus. It stopped and Lila pulled in behind it.

"I think these pictures were taken in Black Hawk and I'd like to see if we can find out exactly where."

"Do you have the pictures with you?"

Sadie sighed. "No, that would be too simple, wouldn't it?"

The green bus pulled out. Catching sight of the side panel, Sadie saw that the green color was actually paintings of money. Money adorned every square inch of the bus. "Follow the Money Bus," she suggested.

Lila did so, but the bus soon turned into a garage that advertised the biggest casino in Black Hawk.

"Do we want the biggest casino?"

"No, probably not. Lee Hong's pictures weren't taken in a glitzy, modern building. At least I don't think so."

Lila turned uphill. "So, where do you want to go? We are driving out of town already." The road steepened to begin the climb to Central City, 500 feet above Black Hawk.

"Did you recognize any place?" Lila asked as she downshifted.

"I'm not sure. The pictures were all so different. Only one was taken outside. That was by a dumpster. With a mountain in the background."

"There are mountains everywhere."

"Yes. But, you know, I think there was something else." Sadie tried to remember the startled man, his image captured as he hoisted a huge plastic bag over his head into a dumpster.

"Yes, I remember. There were boxes piled up beside the dumpster. And they didn't look like things a casino would use. Or a restaurant. They looked like things a grocery store would stock. I remember now. One was ramen noodles."

"So we look for a grocery store? I did not see any grocery store, did you?"

"No, but let's ask someone."

"Who?"

"How about that guy?" Sadie pointed to a man who was waving a flag, inviting them to park in his tiny parking lot. A sign explained the details: "Parking: Five Dollars. Free Shuttle to the Casinos."

Lila pulled in and lowered her window.

"Five dollars," the man said, holding out his hand.

"We do not park. But I do have a question," Lila said.

"Chamber of Commerce is just down there." He pointed down the hill.

"Can you tell me where is a grocery store, please?"

"Denver."

"No, I mean in Black Hawk."

"We don't have grocery stores. We have casinos and parking lots. This is a parking lot."

Sadie leaned across the car. "We just need to get a snack," she said. "Where do you go to buy something like ramen noodles?"

"Ladies, you are blocking my parking lot. Please either park or get back on the road."

"We'd be happy to leave but we don't know where to go. We just need some staples. You know—milk, bread, ramen noodles—that sort of stuff."

"Some of the casinos have convenience stores. Not the big ones, the little ones. Try that one down there. It looks like an old house. In fact, it was an old house before the Colorado voters opened up the town to gambling. It's a casino, but it just has machines, and, in the back, maybe even ramen noodles. Also, it has no parking, so do you want to park here or not?"

"I guess so," Sadie said. She found a five-dollar bill in her wallet and handed it across Lila and the steering wheel to the man.

After Lila parked the car, Sadie explained to a dejected Tiger that he had to wait in the car. With a parting "May the Force be with you" to Tiger, she joined Lila and headed downhill toward the Wild Card Saloon. The clapboard house was a stand-alone structure that promised to be different from the cookie-cutter casino mold. This promise was false, however. Just inside the door, they were enveloped in sensory overload. Mirrored balls spun from the ceiling, bolts of light bounced off red and black flocked wallpaper, bells chimed from the slots, rock music beat at a body-shaking volume, and clouds of cigarette smoke hung in the air.

Sadie led the way around the bank of slot machines that stretched across the building only a few feet from the entrance. Only two of them were in use, but farther back in the huge room, most of the machines were in play.

"What's wrong with those?" Lila asked, pointing to the machines near the door.

"I think they're just nickel slots. People like to play for more," Sadie explained. "They think they can win more if they bet five dollars instead of five cents."

Lila stopped behind a plump woman who was methodically pushing the buttons of a dollar machine. She pushed, waited, and pushed again. Six times, seven times, then, on the eighth push, she won. Bells clanged and dollar signs danced across the video screen. The woman squealed and punched out, grabbing the paper chit with her newly won bounty as if it were the dollars themselves.

"How much did she win?" Lila whispered to Sadie.

"That's not the right question."

"No?"

"How much did she lose—that's the question. And I need to find the ladies' room. Come on." They headed off in search of the restrooms. After some searching, Sadie finally found them, down a hallway in the back of the casino. When she came out, Lila was waiting in the hall outside the door.

"It is good air here," Lila explained. The hallway did have a refreshing absence of smoky air. Enough to tempt them out the door marked Exit at the far end.

They were in an unlit alley. Only a faint bulb glowed over the back door of the Wild Card Saloon.

"Is this safe?" Lila's voice had a slight quiver.

"I'm sure. Nothing bad can happen in Black Hawk. It wouldn't be good for business. Besides which, we're looking for a dumpster. And alleys are where dumpsters are."

Lila pursed her lips and scowled. Sadie started downhill toward the next casino, almost a block away. "Watch your step," she warned Lila as they negotiated the tire tracks in the dirt path down the alley. "It's hard to see."

A pool of light shone into the alley ahead of them. As they got closer to the next establishment, Sadie saw that the light was coming from a display window. "The Station Stop" was inked across the window in archaic print reminiscent of an old-time corner store. Across the alley, barely visible in the shadows, were three large dumpsters.

"Is this the place? Where Lee Hong took the picture of the dumpster?" Lila spoke in a hushed whisper.

"I'm not sure. I thought there was only one dumpster, not three. But maybe…. I wish I had the photo with me."

The Station Stop's door was ajar and a man backed out, pushing the door open as he came. The two large grocery sacks, one hanging from each hand, looked heavy.

"Sorry," he said, as he swung around and nearly collided with Sadie. "We ran out of milk and just about everything else. It's expensive to buy stuff here but it's sure better than driving to Denver."

Not waiting for a reply, he set off down the alley toward the cross street.

"So," Sadie said. "We've found a store. Let's look around." They went into The Station Stop and found a modern convenience store. Many things were on offer, including four or five varieties of ramen noodles.

"This must be the place." Lila was whispering again, and it made the proprietor nervous. "Can I help you ladies?" He came out from behind the counter.

"We were just looking," Sadie replied.

"For what? The Money Station is through there." He pointed at a bright green door beside the cooler that held a few gallons of milk. Two slot machines stood next to the milk cooler. According to the garish signs on them, one took nickels only and the other played quarters.

"I was just curious why your store is in an alley. You must not get much walk-in business."

"I don't need walk-in business. I stock things for the people who live here. Not the people who drive up to play here."

"But I see you do have slot machines."

"Even the locals like to play an occasional slot." He raised both fists and planted them on his hips. Sadie decided to take the none-too-subtle hint.

"I guess we'll go back to the casino. I hope we didn't bother you." She turned and headed toward the green door, Lila following on her heels.

On the other side of the door, they entered a smoke-laden gaming fantasyland again. "Like day and night," Lila said.

"That's night and day."

"No, we left day, this is night."

Sadie laughed. "You aren't supposed to take idioms so literally. But, yes, you're right. This is night, maybe even a nightmare."

They worked their way through the crowd toward the front door. It wasn't easy. There was a solid line of people waiting for a table at the upstairs restaurant—and, of course, most were playing the conveniently located slot machines while they waited.

When Sadie finally made it through the crowd and arrived at the front door, she realized Lila was no longer behind her.

Twenty-Four

Where had Lila gone? Sadie stood by the front door, looking back into the darkened casino. No Lila.

Thinking perhaps Lila had decided to look for the ladies' room, Sadie headed back into the crowd. Just as she had the inconspicuous "Restrooms" sign in sight, she heard Lila squeal over a cascade of bells and bongs.

She was playing the slots. Lila had found a machine that still dealt in coins instead of the high-tech chits. Three bars had produced more quarters than Lila could cram into her tiny purse. She was standing up, stuffing quarters into the pockets of her sweater when Sadie arrived behind her.

"Good grief, you scared me, disappearing like that."

"Look at all this money! It's too much to carry. Can you take some?" Lila handed a fistful of quarters to Sadie.

"You need one of those plastic cups." Sadie looked around. There was a stack of yellow cups on a machine five stations away. "Over there," she pointed.

"Would you get one for me? I don't want to lose my machine." The machine continued to trill and bong, heralding its big payout.

Sadie shouted over the noise. "Your machine! Lila! Have you gone nuts? You just won a lot on this machine. It won't win again for ages and ages."

"Oh no? Maybe it is one of the loose ones. I will keep it. Get me a cup, please."

Sadie sidled through the people who had gathered to witness Lila's jackpot. The cups were in front of a man who worked like an automaton. His right hand shoved a quarter into the slot and his left hand pushed the button as his right hand dipped into his yellow cup to collect the next quarter and move back over to the slot long before the wheels stopped spinning in the window.

"Excuse me," Sadie said, brushing against his shoulder as she reached for a cup. He didn't acknowledge her apology and pushed the button again.

The crowd behind Lila had thinned, and Sadie had no trouble getting the cup to her. Lila stood and began to empty her pockets. Soon the cup was almost full of quarters.

"You know this would be a good time to stop, don't you?" Sadie asked.

"No, these are too much to carry."

"You can change them into paper money at the cashier's window."

"Maybe I will win more. This is a hot machine."

Sadie threw both hands up. "Lila, stop it. You know better than that. Let's go."

"Just a few more. Here, sit down." Lila patted the now-empty stool next to her. "That is not a good machine. Do not put anything in it."

"Don't worry." Sadie sat down and looked at her watch. "Five minutes, Lila. Five minutes and I'm leaving."

Eyes glued on the spinning wheels of her machine, Lila's response was to purse her lips in a classic Bardot expression.

"You do *la moue* better than Bardot herself." Sadie laughed.

Getting no response, Sadie gave up and began to look around. The line for the upstairs restaurant was long. But no one seemed to mind. Video poker and slot machines lined one side of the waiting area. She entertained herself trying to estimate how much money the house was making while customers who "only came in to eat" were waiting.

First she counted the machines. All twenty were in use. Next she tried to guess how many times each was fed a coin. It looked like at least three or four times a minute. Now, what coin? Quarters. Were they all quarters? No, there were several dollar slots. No nickels? Nope, a quarter was the lowest bet possible for anyone in the restaurant waiting line.

She was trying to juggle the arithmetic in her head when a flash of gold distracted her. A flash of gold in a familiar smile. It was Wayne Chen. Smiling and nodding, he slithered through the line of people waiting for a table at the upstairs restaurant.

When he arrived at the foot of the stairs and the hostess station, he pulled aside the green velvet cord that barred the stairway. No one in line seemed to mind. Maybe no one noticed that Wayne Chen had just cut in front of several dozen people.

Curiosity piqued, Sadie stood up.

"Not yet, not yet," Lila said. The quarter level in her cup was noticeably lower now.

"Okay not yet. You stay here. I'll be back in a minute."

Sadie set off and, like Chen, wiggled her way through the line of waiting people. "Excuse me," she said to the first person who objected, a woman whose husband was intently playing video poker.

"I have a reservation." Sadie lied.

"They don't take reservations."

"I just want to talk to the hostess." Sadie kept going despite the woman's hostile glare.

When she made it to the hostess, Sadie told the sleek young woman the truth. "I saw Mr. Chen go upstairs a minute ago. I just need to speak to him for a moment."

When the hostess hesitated, Sadie added, "I'm not eating and I won't take a table. I'll come right back down, I promise."

The "I promise" seemed to do the trick. The hostess pulled aside the velvet rope and Sadie hurried up the stairs.

The restaurant was a breath of fresh air in more ways than one. It was smoke-free, and large windows opened onto the moonlit mountains above the town.

A few people were at the double-sided buffet table that ran down the middle of the room, but most were seated at round wooden tables eating from overladen plates.

Wayne Chen wasn't at the buffet table nor, as far as Sadie could see, was he seated anywhere. She walked around the periphery of the room trying to look as though she had forgotten where she was sitting.

The modern design of the restaurant afforded a clear view of the kitchen through a window that ran the entire width of the room. The kitchen was a busy place, but Wayne Chen wasn't one of the people bustling about in it.

Chen wasn't in the restaurant. He wasn't in the kitchen. Where was he?

"Can I help you, miss?" a young woman in a cowgirl outfit asked. "Where are you sitting?"

"Nowhere, actually. I mean … is there some way out of here besides going back that way?" Sadie gestured at the stairway she had come up.

"There's a back door from the kitchen. It's just where we take the garbage out. No one can go that way. You have to pay over there, by the stairway, before you go down."

"Oh, of course. I wasn't trying to skip out on my bill. I didn't even eat. I just came up here to look for someone. And he's not here, so it was a mistake, I guess."

Sadie could feel the faux-cowgirl's eyes on her back as she walked over to the cashier's station. The cashier was easy. "Oh, yes, I saw you come up a minute ago. Did you find him?"

"No, how did you know I was looking for a him?"

"Oh, honey, why else does a good-looking woman come skulking up the stairs, not eat, and wander around checking everyone out? He may be stepping out on you, but maybe you don't want to know that. That's my advice, which, as you know, is worth exactly what you paid for it." She laughed, showing nicotine-stained teeth.

Sadie felt the blush begin below her collarbone. By the time she got down the stairs, she knew her entire face was probably beet red. But since she was back in the dimly lit, smoky casino, she hoped no one would notice.

Lila was at the same machine. Sadie tapped her on the shoulder, and Lila responded by rattling her cup. "See," she said, "only five quarters left. It won't be long."

"You're going to spend them all?"

"Bohff," Lila said raising her shoulders and tucking her upper lip under an outthrust lower lip in a classic Gallic denial of knowledge. "I guess. This machine must be about to hit again." Lila stuck in a quarter, and another and another before stopping to fish the last two coins out of her cup. "Might as well put them all in." She pushed the button.

The wheels spun. Sadie watched lemons and bars and cherries and sevens spin by. The first wheel stopped on a seven. "That's it. You only win on fruit. Let's go."

The second wheel stopped. Again on seven, one that matched the "decked out" first seven. Lila stood up and grinned sheepishly at Sadie. "It is fun, you know." The third wheel stopped. On another matching seven. The special effects erupted. Lights flashed, bells rang, the machine bonged, and quarters began to pour out of the machine.

A casino employee was among the first there. "Wow, you hit it. The machine doesn't have enough to pay you off. It will only give you five hundred quarters. Here's a chit for the rest." She took a receipt book from the pocket of her apron, wrote on it, tore a page off, and handed it to Lila, who was still collecting quarters in her cup, her purse, and her pockets.

"Where's the cashier?" Sadie asked.

The woman pointed toward the back of the casino. "See the gold bars back there? That's the cashier's cage."

"Let's go." Lila's eyes were huge. "I am ready to go, quickly, before I forget I am ready to go. Here, take this." She handed Sadie the slip of paper.

It took almost five minutes to get back to the cashier's cage. People kept stopping Lila to congratulate her, slap her on the back, and ask her questions.

"How long were you playing that machine?"

"Do you always play that one?"

"Have you won this big before?"

"Did you know it was about to pay off?"

Lila just nodded, murmured, "Thank you, thank you," and kept moving. "How much did I win?" she asked Sadie when they were in front of the cashier's cage.

"I don't know. The machine said it gave you five hundred quarters, so that's what? That's one hundred and twenty-five dollars, right? And then, whatever this is for." Sadie looked at the now-crumpled chit in her hand. It said $2375. "Wow," Sadie said. "You did win a lot. Two thousand five hundred dollars. That's amazing."

"No, the machine is not amazing. It is loose." Lila grinned as she pushed her chit under the grille to the cashier.

But, of course, it wasn't that simple. The casino would pay her but only after withholding appropriate income tax. For which they wanted a social security card. Which Lila, being a French citizen, didn't have.

More than an hour later, when they left The Money Station. Lila had a check for $1788.60. And two pockets and a purse full of quarters. The cashier had demanded the cupful to be tallied with Lila's total winnings, but no one mentioned the bulging pockets and purse.

"How do they know I have to pay five hundred eighty-five dollars and forty cents of tax? How do they know that?" Lila demanded.

"Just be glad you had your passport with you, otherwise you might not have gotten anything."

"They can do that?"

"I have no idea. In fact, I have no idea about a lot of things." The uphill slog was making Sadie a little breathless. Lila didn't seem to have any problem with the altitude. She kept up a running complaint about taxes all the way to the parking lot, where a very anxious Tiger waited in Daniel's car.

"Good boy. You are really a very, very good boy." Sadie spoke in the high, squeaky voice that Tiger loved. But, squeaky voice or not, he wanted to get out of the car.

Sadie looked around. The hawker with his colorful cane was gone. There was no one else in the lot or on the sidewalk and there was a tiny patch of grass across the street.

"We'll just run across the street." Sadie snapped the leash on Tiger's collar. Lila slipped into the driver's seat and began to unload quarters from her pockets into the glove compartment.

Across the street, Tiger sniffed and sniffed. He raised his head and looked at Sadie as if to say, "This is all I get? After waiting for hours and hours."

"Sorry, guy. This seems to be all there is. But maybe we can get a little exercise. Uphill first." She led the dog back to the broken sidewalk and they started up the hill at a rapid walk that didn't last long. The altitude was hampering Sadie, especially on top of the three-block hike up from The Money Station.

Well out of the lights flooding the parking lot, Sadie stopped and looked up. The mountain backdrop gleamed in the moonlight. Above the mountains, stars twinkled in more profusion than she'd seen in some time. "I guess we really do have a lot of light pollution in Boulder," she said to Tiger, who had stopped at her side. "Can we turn around now? And can you please find some place to your liking?"

Tiger complied, raising his leg against an aging mailbox. Sadie gazed up at the stars again until she heard a car racing down the street. Too fast, she thought, turning to look toward the oncoming car. And too dark. Only the parking lights were on. With no headlights to blind her, Sadie could see that the car was overfull. There were three people in the front and at least four in the back. As it sped past her, the driver looked at her. His smile glinted gold.

Twenty-Five

Back in the car, Lila raised the question of supper. "We came up here for dinner, no? Are we going to eat?"

Sadie wasn't particularly hungry, but that was beside the point. She had, after all, offered Lila dinner. "Let's go on up to Central City and eat there," she said.

"Why?"

"It's nicer, it's quieter, and I'm sure the food will be better. The restaurant next to the opera house is run by a famous chef."

"Sounds expensive to me, but maybe we can have just hors d'oeuvres." Lila started the car and swung it out of the parking lot. They drove uphill, past the old houses that lined the street between Black Hawk and Central City. Although most were now painted with bright, primary colors, they still looked like the miners' cabins they were, left over from an earlier era.

They passed the shuttered opera house and turned into an unattended parking lot. Tiger whined.

"He knows he's going to be stuck in the car again," Sadie said. "I hate to do that to him. Are you really very hungry?"

Lila tapped her manicured nails on the steering wheel. "Actually, no, I am not very hungry. A sandwich, perhaps. And a piece of fruit?"

Relieved, Sadie explained to Tiger that he had to wait, but not for very long. She could feel his accusing eyes following her as she and Lila walked downhill out of the parking lot toward the street.

They passed the opera house and moved into the pools of light spread by the streetlights illuminating the garden sheltered between the opera house and the Teller House next to it.

Posters next to the hotel door hawked the restaurants within and the famous bar, the one with the face originally painted on its floor in the heyday of the "Golden West" when Central City overflowed with gold dug out of the nearby hills.

"What is this face?" Lila asked Sadie.

"It's a painting of a woman," Sadie explained. "A man who couldn't pay for his drinks painted a portrait of the bargirl. There's a lot of myth and stories around it."

Asking for "just a sandwich," the upscale restaurant referred them to the bar. They each ordered a sandwich and iced tea. In addition, they were treated to the story of the face on the bar-room floor.

"It's an opera," the florid-faced bartender responded to Lila's query about the painting.

"It's a painting. How can it be an opera?" Lila smiled up at the bartender.

"It's an opera about the painting," he said. "The Central City Opera has put it on every year since 1978. That's when it was written. It's short but interesting.

"Interesting? Tell us please." Lila took a sip of her tea and made a face. "What is this? It's not tea."

"Sure it is, it's the special tea of the day. Mango peach, I think."

Sadie laughed as Lila pushed the offending tea aside and asked for a glass of water instead.

Their sandwiches appeared on the windowsill of the kitchen. The bartender brought them, along with Lila's water and their bill.

"You still want to know about the opera?" he asked.

"Yes, please." Sadie took a bite of her tuna fish sandwich. It was thick and chunky. It also promised to be messy as the filling oozed out from between the thick slices of bread.

"*The Face on the Barroom Floor* is really two stories in one. The time is different in the two stories but the people are the same."

Lila looked confused but didn't interrupt as the bartender continued.

"The story starts with the Central City Opera of today. Isabelle is one of the singers in the chorus. She has a boyfriend, Larry, but before that she had been the girlfriend of the bartender— the bartender of this very bar." He hit his finger on the bar for emphasis.

"So, she and Larry are in the bar, this bar, the one with the face painted on the floor." He pointed to the portrait on the floor.

He'd be a good ESL teacher, Sadie thought. He repeats everything and he points to what he's talking about.

"Larry asks about the face, just like you just did." He winked at Lila who was chewing an over-large bite of pastrami on rye.

"Voila! The bartender turns into a nineteenth century version of himself."

"Voila? What do you mean, voila?" Lila demanded.

"You know... voila ... like presto-change-o."

"I do not think that means voila."

"Well anyway, he changes into John, a frontier barman. Someone in the nineteenth century. And the bargirl is his girlfriend."

Lila looked skeptical. Sadie, nudged her with her elbow and said, "Let him tell the story." She was almost finished with her sandwich and Lila hadn't even started on the second half of hers.

"Okay, so now we're back in time. A time when the girls in bars were bargirls, not customers. So this bargirl, named Madelaine, welcomes a traveler who orders drinks for everyone in the bar. But he cannot pay for them. Instead he offers to paint a portrait of the woman he loves.

"He paints Madelaine. This infuriates the bartender, the two men fight, and Madelaine is killed when she tries to break up the fight."

Sadie, finished with her sandwich, emptied her glass of tea. The bartender was too busy story-telling to notice her empty glass so she rapped it lightly with her spoon.

"Sorry, I was transported there," he laughed. He refilled her glass.

"So, is that the whole story?" Lila asked.

"Nope, next we flip back to now again. The bartender—that would be me—forces Isabelle to dance with him. He tells Larry about Isabelle's past and says he still loves her. Then, guess what?" The bartender leaned over the bar putting his face in Lila's.

"She shoots him?"

He reared back. "No, of course not. She gets shot. Just the same way as Madelaine. Larry and the bartender fight, she tries to break it up, and she gets shot."

Lila folded her napkin, put it down, and picked up the bar bill.

"I invited you, remember?" Sadie reached for the bill.

"*Non,* I hit the jackpot." Lila laid a twenty-dollar bill on the bar and stood up. Sadie joined her.

"Thank you, ladies." The bartender picked up the bill and money. "Do you want change?"

"No, no change," Lila answered. "But ... next time, I think it would be better if she shoots him."

Sadie and the bartender both laughed at Lila. "That's not the way the story goes," Sadie explained as they left to head back to the car.

"I know, always the woman gets shot. It's tiresome."

"I know something else that's tiresome," Sadie said when they turned the corner into the parking lot. "Waiting in the car."

Tiger was so glad to see them coming, he set the Mini Cooper bouncing on its springs.

Soon they were on their way back down the mountain toward Highway 119, Nederland, and home. As Sadie gazed at the passing mountain landscape, a golden grin loomed in the back of her mind.

It returned later that night with a faint feeling of unease as she settled into bed, Tiger snuggled close beside her.

Pushing thoughts of Wayne Chen firmly aside, she fell asleep early. Tomorrow was not only her birthday but also her busiest day of the week.

Twenty-Six

There was a bit of everything in her Wednesday schedule, including the three-hour writing lab in the late afternoon. Her day started at 10 with a pronunciation lab in Hickory Hall. Ten minutes after that ended, Sadie had to be back in the Language Arts Building to teach ESL grammar. Then, before her one o'clock lunch break, she had a noon seminar for the ESL graduate students who were TAs, the teaching assistants who taught undergraduates. Since neither teaching experience nor language skills were a requirement for the TA jobs, courses such as Sadie's had been developed to combat the inevitable problems that arose when students could not understand their teachers.

The day dawned gloriously bright and sunny. Stretching in bed, Sadie thought, I'll be busy enough that I won't obsess about being a year older. "How old am I? Let's see, I was born in 1970. One good thing living with a dog," she said to Tiger. "You can always pretend you're talking to the dog." She giggled.

Determined to enjoy her birthday despite her packed schedule, Sadie gave some thought to her lunch. Blueberries, yogurt, Fiber 1 cereal, and, she giggled again, two chocolate cookies. Of course, she would have to find time to buy the chocolate cookies at Wild Oats before she left.

She found the time and was soon on her way up the Broadway hill toward campus. Singing softly to herself, she strode along the sidewalk in the midst of the student stampede. Ten o'clock was a popular class hour.

Ling met her on the steps of the Language Arts Building. "Happy birthday, Professor Wagner," she trilled, black eyes flashing. "Even though we are very sad at home, I know it is your special day. I have this for you." She handed Sadie a bright blue envelope.

Inside was a folded sheet of blue linen-like paper. Sadie unfolded it. *Year of the Dog* was embossed in silver print across the top. Beneath the title was the inevitable personality profile. Sadie read:

The Dog will never let you down. Born under this sign, you are honest and faithful to those you love. You are plagued by constant worry, a sharp tongue, and a tendency to be a fault-finder. You would make an excellent artist, businessperson, teacher, or secret agent.

"Very true," Ling pronounced, nodding her head. "Very true."

"Which part? The fault-finder? Or the sharp tongue?" Sadie asked.

"Maybe both, but also excellent teacher. Most excellent teacher."

"Hmmmm, thank you, … I think," Sadie answered. "And now, if I'm such an excellent teacher, we need to get busy. Do you want to work with the pronunciation lab today?"

"Okay," Ling said. "I am ready. We have an ancient saying in China. It's about the birds of sorrow. I cannot stop them from flying over my head, but I can stop them from building a nest in my hair. Both Ming Fang and I believe this. We sorrow for Lee Hong but we will have no nests.

"When I missed the bus to go home, I decided to take Lee Hong's pictures back to Ming Fang. In Lee Hong's desk she found an email address for Mr. Commander, so we wrote to that address. And we got an answer. Right away. We went to the post office and mailed the pictures. The government will pay us. So, no nests!"

Sadie had trouble believing what she was hearing but she certainly hoped it was true. Ling seemed to be almost back to her uberconfident self.

"Don't worry about pronunciation class," she assured Sadie. "We will talk about vowel space. And then they can work together. Just must mix up Chinese speakers and others. Maybe put the Russian with a Chinese man. That will be fun." Ling picked up the pronunciation book and consulted the table of contents.

"Okay, it is here," she said marking the place with her finger. "I will go. When will you come?"

"In about ten minutes; will you be okay with that?" Grateful that the young woman seemed to have recovered her usual ebullience, Sadie still worried that Ling was perhaps not yet very functional. When Sadie arrived at the language lab in Hickory, her headphoned class was busy listening to tapes and parroting the exercises. Some of them noticed her arrival. Most did not. Ling moved from student to student pausing to listen to their words. She corrected some but, Sadie noticed, only the Chinese. I'll have to ask her about that, she thought.

Throwing a switch on the lectern, Sadie interrupted her class. "Good morning," she greeted them. "Would you like to try a drill now?"

There was a general chorus of nods, so Sadie went ahead. "You've been working on the vowel space, the space in your mouth where you put your tongue to make different sounds. What else controls how you make a sound?"

"Your lips," several students answered promptly.

"Right. Your lips and the position of your tongue are both important. Now let's try a short drill." Sadie turned to the board and wrote three words: color, collar, and caller.

"I am going to say one of these words and I want you to write down which it is. I'll go through them several times and mix them up. Remember, you can't just watch my mouth. You also have to listen to the vowels. You have to be able to hear where my tongue is when I say the word. Ready?"

Most of the students nodded, all of them were poised with their pens, ready to write. Sadie started slowly. "Collar."

Most of the students wrote on their paper promptly. Ling continued to circulate, looking at their papers. She smiled at Sadie. They must have gotten it right.

"Color," Sadie said. Again, the class wrote. Again Ling nodded.

"Collar," Sadie repeated just to be sure they were really listening. Most of them apparently were not. Only three looked thoughtful. The others, expecting the third word in the series, simply wrote "caller" on their paper. Of the three thoughtful ones, only two believed their ears. The third guessed "caller," if Sadie was reading Ling's expression correctly.

"Okay, now I'm going to speed up," Sadie said. "Color, collar, caller, color, color, collar." Most of the students looked at her in exasperation.

"Too fast?" Sadie asked.

"Not fair," someone said.

"Not fair? Why not fair?"

"No one would say that. Not fair."

"Yes, that's true. No one would say that. But I did say that. Let me say it again."

She repeated the six words again, more slowly. All of them tried to hear the difference. Most of them tried to transcribe Sadie's words.

"That's better," Sadie said. "Now, please pair up and work with each other. You can use these words or try some others. How about ox, x, axe? That's important for those of you who teach undergraduate math. Your students need to know when you're talking about the x-axis."

The class continued in a cacophony of sound as the students struggled to differentiate the sets of similar-sounding words for each other. As they finished and filed out, Sadie rushed by the stragglers. She had a few blocks to go and only ten minutes to do it. Ling stayed behind to straighten up the lab, return the headphones to their hooks, and be sure the machines were switched off.

"Sadie, Sadie! Wait for me." She heard Dan's voice as she approached the crosswalk at 18th Street.

"I'm really rushed," she said, as Dan arrived at her side. "I have an eleven o'clock."

"I will rush with you," he said. "I'm on my way to see Rick anyway." They started across the pedestrian crosswalk and a truck actually stopped for them. "I need to talk to you," Dan added. "When would be a good time?"

"About what?"

"Just talk."

"Not today. Today's a nightmare."

"And it is your birthday."

"Yes, and it's my birthday."

"Your policeman? Does he know this? Will he make you happy today?"

"He knows it." Sadie was getting breathless trying to keep up with Dan's long strides. This is good, she thought, I need to walk faster.

"I hope you are happy, Sadie," Dan said, turning to look at her with his soft, doe-like eyes. "You are a good person. You should be happy. I did not make you happy. And that is what I want to talk about. Can I call you tomorrow?" They had reached the stairs to the Language Arts Building. Sadie glanced at her watch. It was two minutes before eleven.

"Dan I've really got to go. Yes, call me tomorrow. But please, don't …"

"Don't what?"

"Just don't worry. I'm okay."

"Maybe tomorrow," he said, turning to cross the street toward the Animal Husbandry Labs.

Sadie arrived at her classroom door at exactly eleven o'clock. Her students were all there, in their seats, waiting. How do they do that? Don't they have to come from somewhere else also? Maybe not as far away as she did.

She greeted the class, opened her backpack, pulled out the syllabus, found the right date, and said, "Okay, today is prepositions. Anybody have any questions about the reading?"

There were some questions, but not many. The main difficulty seemed to be with prepositions of location. "When do I say 'in,' and when do I say 'on'?" one Russian speaker asked. "I mean like for my address. Do I say I live on Robinson Hall?"

"No," Sadie said. "You live *in* Robinson Hall. Remember, it's increasing specificity." She turned and wrote on the board: *in, on, at.* "Each one is more specific than the previous one." She pointed to the word *in* and said, "I live in Colorado. Now," pointing to *on*, she added, "I live on Arapahoe Avenue, and," moving her chalk to *at*, she finished, "I live at 980. Is that clear?"

"Yes," said the Russian, "but I do not live in Robinson Hall, I live in Tall-Grass Hall." Sadie laughed with the class, but she was a tad annoyed. Big joke, she thought. Oh well.

The class continued without incident. Everyone had done the exercises at the end of the chapter, and they whipped through them, ending the class almost ten minutes early.

With time to grab a cup of coffee from the Faculty Lounge, Sadie felt luxuriously unrushed as she settled into the seminar room to meet the graduate student TAs.

Ling, who did not need this class but often sat in on it to observe how Sadie taught her fellow TAs, arrived just as class was ready to start. Joining Sadie at the front of the classroom, Ling rapped on the table where Sadie was sitting to command attention. "I have special announcement," she said. "Today is Professor Wagner's birthday. I think we should excuse her from class. Besides, she has important lunch date."

Sadie was startled. What was going on? Excused from class, indeed. Just as she stood up to respond, Mike walked in.

"Here he is," Ling said. "Important lunch date. Now everybody wish Professor Wagner Happy Birthday. If you have any big problems, see me. If not, see you next week, same time."

Her students were amused and, given the glorious weather, in agreement with canceling class. Two, however, did approach

Ling. Too bad, Sadie thought. Ling asked for it, so she could deal with their problems. She smiled at Mike, gathered her things, and walked out with him.

"Where are we going?" she asked.

"Wherever you want. It's your birthday."

"I thought we were going out tonight."

"That too. We can do that, but I'd sort of thought about staying in," he replied with a wink.

"Do you want to go to the Faculty Club?"

"Never been there. Is it good?"

"Not particularly."

"Let's go to Chautauqua then. You have time. Ling said you don't have to be back until two."

"Well, yes, I don't have to teach until then, but it wouldn't hurt to be back a bit earlier."

"Okay, let's go," Mike steered her out the door and toward the loading dock where he had illegally parked his car. He held the door for her. As he walked around the back of the car to get in himself, Sadie glanced up. Dan and Rick were standing across the street, watching.

Twenty-Seven

"This was a great idea," Sadie said, as they sat down at a table on the porch of the Chautauqua Dining Hall at the base of the Flatirons on Boulder's western edge.

"Always glad to have a great idea," Mike replied. "Especially since I didn't have time to even get you a birthday card."

"If it was to be anything like Ling's card, I can just as soon skip it," Sadie said.

"Oh, one of those nasty ones about being over the hill?"

"No, just a personality profile for dogs."

"Dogs?"

"People born in the Year of the Dog."

"And ...?"

"Dog people are great at finding fault. Or so it says."

"I've never found you to be much of a fault-finder. Maybe Ling got you the wrong horoscope."

"Nope, here it is," Sadie pulled Ling's card out of her backpack and handed it to Mike.

He started to read it just as the waitress showed up. "Hi, I'm Jenny, from Iowa City. What can I get you folks to drink?" she asked.

Mike frowned. "Just water for me. I guess we can't celebrate yet. I'm still on duty, and you've got to teach this afternoon, right?"

"Right, I'll just have hot tea," Sadie told the perky waitress.

"Would that be black tea or herb tea?"

"What kind of herb tea do you have?"

"Celestial Seasonings. We have chai, peppermint, Lemon Zinger, and some blends. I could just bring you the box."

"The box, please."

After the waitress went away, Sadie said, "It's getting really complicated. Too many things to choose from." She picked up the menu and was assaulted with a huge variety of options.

"At least they don't have as many teas as the Dushanbe Teahouse," Mike said.

"This isn't a teahouse, either."

Jenny was back. She recited a long list of specials. Sadie didn't really listen since she had already decided on the halibut. She always had herb-crusted halibut when it was on the menu. Mike opted for steak. The tea box came and, after fingering several of the colorful foil packets, Sadie selected Lemon Zinger. All difficult decisions made, she relaxed and watched the teabag steep. As she swirled her spoon through it, the warm liquid slowly turned to gold. Gold like the aspen. Gold like Mr. Chen's tooth.

She continued to stir as she debated whether to tell Mike about her excursion to the "new Vail." Something didn't feel right about Chen, starting with his intense interest in Lila. Why? Then, later in the casino, where did he disappear to? Lastly, why was he speeding out of Black Hawk with no headlights and so many people crammed into his car?

She needed to tell Mike not only about her excursion to Black Hawk but also about her questions. Maybe he'd be more interested in that than he was in the donkey. Her stomach lurched. That was another question—a big one. Why had Chen visited the donkey at the Humane Society? And so quickly after the donkey's rescue. How did he even know the animal was there? Too many questions. No answers. Not even a glimmer of a single answer. She sighed. She had to tell Mike, and sooner was probably better.

"Mike," she said, "Lila and I went back to the mountains yesterday."

"After I left you at the library?"

"Later. We decided to go to Black Hawk."

Their salads arrived; Mike picked up his fork and stabbed a piece of lettuce. A heavy cloud of silence hung over the table.

"You want pepper?" The waitress was back, wielding a huge pepper mill.

Mike nodded. She thrust the wooden mill over his salad and twisted. "Say when," she directed. Mike scowled at Sadie as the pepper continued to flow onto his salad.

"You really want that much pepper?" Sadie asked.

Looking down at his blackening salad, Mike said, "Enough!"

The waitress, grinning widely, started around the table. Sadie covered her salad with fluttering hands. "I can always use some of his," she joked, dismissing Jenny and her pepper mill.

"Maybe we should mix our salads and start over," Sadie said, looking at Mike's overly peppered greens.

"Maybe you should tell me why you went back up to Black Hawk. Or even why you decided to go back to the mountains," Mike said.

"Yes, I was just getting to that. Remember all those signs we saw about the new cross-country ski development? Just south of Nederland?"

Mike nodded. Sadie continued, "Lila got really interested so we decided to stop and take a quick look. It was almost five o'clock. In fact, the sales office was actually closing, but they stayed open just for us." Sadie speared a tomato and popped it into her mouth.

"You must have looked like really hot prospects." Mike had given up on his over-seasoned salad.

"At first, the guy said they were closed, but he changed his mind after Lila talked to him."

"And is Lila going to buy a house there?"

"I doubt it. The whole thing was really strange. The strangest thing is that the salesman is the same guy who visited the donkey at the Humane Society."

"Donkey!" Mike snorted. "How did we get back to that blasted donkey? How do you know it's the same guy? Did you go looking for him?"

"Not exactly. Well, I did want to see where he lived ... or at least if the address existed. But we weren't at that address. I'm telling you we were at the sales office for this huge new development. And there he was. With a name tag on: Wayne Chen. Right there in front of me."

"I suppose you demanded to know why he visited the donkey."

"No, I didn't say anything, actually."

"No?" Mike's eyebrows rose so high they nearly disappeared into his hairline. "I find that difficult to believe."

"I couldn't. He thought I didn't speak English."

Mike's eyebrows dropped into a puzzled scowl. "I don't get it. What were you masquerading as this time?"

Sadie's lips pursed. Why did Mike have to be so judgmental? How could she explain her unease about Wayne Chen if she had to be on the defensive all the time?

"Look, just listen to me, okay?" she said.

Mike's right hand made a "be my guest" gesture as he sat back in his chair, arms crossed. Despite his off-putting demeanor, Sadie began at the beginning, starting with the decision of the man at the gatehouse to call and ask Wayne Chen to keep the sales office open a few extra minutes. "I think he did that because Lila is French," she said.

"Since when are we doing favors for the French? I thought they were pretty *persona non grata* these days," Mike countered.

"Yes, except I think this resort really wants foreigners to buy in."

"So they won't show up often? Or why?"

"I'm not sure. It seems like a legitimate operation but Chen really wanted to sell Lila a partnership in the resort instead of a condo or a house. The sales office is set up to sell condos and home sites, but mostly he talked about limited partnerships. In fact, he was trying to get her to attend a special sales seminar about that this coming weekend."

"Why on earth would anyone think Lila could afford a partnership in a ski resort?"

"Exactly. Lila asked that question herself. Chen told her it wasn't a problem. They'd help her get the money. All she had to do was start the paperwork to get an E-2 visa."

That got Mike's attention. Staring at Sadie, he demanded, "E-2 visa? Lila has five hundred thousand dollars?"

"No, that's what I'm trying to tell you. She probably doesn't have anything like that. Wayne Chen didn't care. He said that all she had to do was get the visa. If she had the visa, he'd get the money for her. All she has to do was start the paperwork for the visa."

"Here we are," Jenny chirped as she put an elegantly arranged plate of halibut and vegetables in front of Sadie. "Mind the plate, it's hot," she cautioned Mike, putting a sizzling steak platter in front of him. Home fries spilled off the edge.

Mike stared at the steak, still scowling. "Is there a problem with your steak, sir?" Jenny asked.

"What? Oh, no. No, the steak's fine."

As Jenny scurried away, Mike added, "The steak's fine, it's the birthday girl cum Nancy Drew that's got a problem." He picked up the steak knife and attacked the meat on his plate.

"I don't have a problem, unless it's with you." Sadie put her fork down and leaned across the table toward Mike. "I'm just telling you what happened. I can't help it that Sam Gross had a briefcase full of photos from E-2 visa applications."

"Sam Gross? I was thinking this was all about Lee Hong."

"Maybe it is. Maybe it's about Sam Gross *and* Lee Hong, and maybe even Ling."

"Ling? Ling has an E-2 visa?"

"I don't know what Ling has. I only know that she went to Mexico with the rest of her family this summer. When she left the

States, her student visa was automatically revoked. Lee Hong and his family all got back in immediately as political refugees. Ling's application was denied and she was stuck in Mexico. Lee Hong and Sam Gross got her back into the U.S."

Mike stared at Sadie. "Lee Hong and Sam Gross? How long have you known this?"

"Not long. And I don't understand it."

"You don't have to understand it. I'll worry about understanding. You worry about staying out of this," he jammed a too-large piece of steak into his mouth.

"This is supposed to be a nice birthday lunch," Sadie said. "Now that I've told you all the news that's fit to tell, could we go back to celebrating?"

"Sure," Mike said. "But …"

"No buts," Sadie interrupted. "If you're going to get upset every time I tell you something, it makes it hard to tell you anything. Ever think about that?"

Mike went back to his steak. Sadie tried to enjoy her halibut as she pondered what to do. Should she tell Mike that at least one of the pictures in Sam Gross's briefcase of the E-2 visa holders was of a man Lee Hong had photographed in Black Hawk? Normally, she would have done so. But his edginess about her excursion with Lila suggested that she should save this bombshell for a later time.

She looked at the man across the table. He looked like nothing more than a man determined to eat too much food. As Mike continued to alternate chunks of steak with forkfuls of oversized home fries, Sadie continued to think about Lee Hong's photos.

Well, she decided, let's get all the unpleasantness over with at once. "There is one other thing," she started.

Mike's eyes narrowed, but his mouth was too full to reply.

"Remember the photos that Ling brought to me—photos that Lee Hong took? At least one of the men in the photos was the same as a man on the visa applications you found in Sam Gross's briefcase."

Mike swallowed and grabbed his water glass. After he'd gotten the meat down, he said, through almost clenched teeth, "So that's why you wanted to copy the photos from Gross's briefcase. You wanted to compare them to the photos Ling has. Is that correct?"

Sadie considered her answer. "Actually, I don't think that *is* correct. I told you that Ling had some photos she wanted to sell, photos that Lee Hong had taken. She says they were ordered by the government. I told you all that, didn't I?"

"Did you? I don't think so."

"Well, maybe not all at once like that but, yes, I did tell you."

"So Sam Gross ordered these photos?"

"I don't know. Ling just knows that the government ordered them. She and Ming Fang are actually expecting the government to pay for them. They had some cloak-and-dagger system to let Gross know when his pictures were ready. In fact, that's what the spurious ad about a used camper was—an ad that was so wacky no one would call except Commander Gross. Except they didn't make it wacky enough. A lot of people thought it sounded like a good deal and called."

"What sort of things had they used before?"

"I don't know. Ling said something about the newspaper refusing one of their ads because it was stupid. A used coffee pot or something like that. I don't really remember."

"And they used your phone number?"

"That was a mistake. Ming Fang placed the ad and she used my home phone number. Usually they used my office number, if you can believe that!" Sadie's disgust showed in her pursed lips and pinched forehead.

"These people abuse their privileges and maybe you as well, yet you still value Ling? I don't get it."

"They don't really see it as abuse, I'm sure. They have a huge problem and they are trying to solve it. Anyway, Ming Fang put an ad in the paper when Lee Hong's photos were ready. And, it seems to me that if the photos Lee Hong took and the visa application photos are of the same people, then probably Sam Gross ordered them."

"Why would he have done that?"

"I don't have any idea."

"You folks ready for dessert?" Jenny had arrived again, unnoticed.

Glad of the interruption, Sadie answered, "I don't think so. I'll make a birthday cake for tonight."

"Birthday? You get a free dessert on your birthday, sir," Jenny said assuming that it was Mike's birthday.

"No, no dessert. Thanks anyway. Just the check," Mike said.

Finally zeroing in on the tension at the table, Jenny put the black folder with the bill down and left without clearing the dirty plates.

As he dug through his wallet for a credit card, Mike said, "So, since you seem to know more about all this than I do, what do you suggest we do?"

Sadie was taken aback. Was Mike actually asking for her opinion? She didn't detect any sarcasm in his voice but—well, a problem shared, is a problem halved. She answered: "It would seem to me that we should start by comparing the photos, and then, if they are of the same people, we should try to find those people."

"Black Hawk again?"

"A starting place, certainly. Want to do it tonight?"

"No," Mike stood up. "I think this is a job for the feds who are overrunning our department. Besides which, we've got other plans for tonight. I'll be over about six."

Twenty-Eight

On the way back to campus, they agreed to graze for dinner. "I'll pick up something at Wild Oats," Mike said. "And, of course, a birthday cake."

"No, let me bake a cake."

"You can bake a cake?" He slammed on the brakes as a student ran into the pedestrian crosswalk on Broadway. "Someday, someday ... someone is going to get killed here," Mike muttered.

"Pedestrians do have the right of way in crosswalks, you know."

"I know, but it wouldn't hurt if these kids at least looked before they ran into traffic."

"You were questioning my cake-baking skills?"

"Not questioning your skills, just wondering why you hide them so well."

"I can bake a cake. I just don't often choose to bake a cake ... or anything else for that matter," Sadie laughed.

Mike turned off Broadway onto Euclid, heading toward the Language Arts Building.

"You can let me off here if you want," Sadie said. "My class starts in the Terkel Building in a few minutes." She checked her watch.

"You don't have to go back to your office first?"

"No, this is a writing class, and I don't have anything to return to the students but I'll have a lot when the class is over." She was not looking forward to the coming marathon of reading and grading a five-page proposal from each of the eighteen students in her ESL writing seminar. But until then, her classes could continue to be minor interruptions in her day-long birthday celebration. After all, soon she'd have to stop acknowledging her birthdays. By forty, certainly, she thought.

Mike pulled the car into a No Parking spot in front of the Faculty Club. Sadie hopped out and headed east along Euclid toward the Terkel Building. As she rounded the corner onto 18th, she saw Ling hurrying toward her. They met at the front door of Terkel.

"Hi. Was it a good surprise?" Ling asked with a deferential grin.

"It certainly was. Both good and a surprise."

They hurried past the line at the coffee bar and entered the classroom. It was already filled with students who had their laptops fired up and ready. Terkel was the Institute's latest excursion into high-tech teaching. The new building had something for everyone. In Sadie's case, the "something" was a totally wired classroom with long tables. Students could easily work together and did so enthusiastically on in-class collaborative writing assignments.

Sadie didn't know how she rated the use of a classroom in the much-sought-after building, but she certainly appreciated it.

"Today you have a final draft of a proposal ready. What's the first thing you should do?" Sadie asked the assembled students.

"Reread it?" someone said in a tremulous voice.

"And after that?"

"Ask someone else to read it?" the same voice offered.

Sadie was pleased. That was exactly the answer she was looking for. "Right! So let's do that first. Let's exchange proposals and look at each other's ideas. Can you all do that electronically?"

"You mean e-mail it to someone else?"

"Yes, let's do that."

Eighteen pairs of hands flew across the laptop keyboards. Eighteen heads lowered to consider the incoming e-mails. "I got too many. Which one should I look at?" someone asked.

"Pick one that interests you and e-mail back to the author that you'd like to critique that one. Maybe we'll get lucky and everyone will choose different proposals."

But, of course, they didn't get lucky, and both Ling and Sadie had to make a few explicit assignments. It took ten minutes before each student had a single proposal to critique.

"Now, you remember how to critique on-line in Microsoft Word?"

"*Tools*, right?"

"Yes, click on *Tools* and then select *Track Changes.*"

The room fell silent as the students bent their heads to read. They were quiet, intent on their task. Occasional bursts of muted keystrokes were the only sounds in the room.

Sadie gave them twenty minutes before interrupting their work. "Okay, now send your comments back to the author."

Again, heads dropped. A few keystrokes later, they were all reading what their colleagues had written. Some were pleased, judging from the smug expressions. Some wore puzzled frowns, others scowled.

"Okay," Sadie said. "Now you've gotten some feedback on your writing. What are you going to do with it?"

"They misunderstand," a Korean woman said. "I think they are wrong."

"Yes, but why did your reader misunderstand? Do you know?"

"They are stupid?"

Everyone laughed.

"Not necessarily. Your readers do not know what you know. They only know what you write. So if they misunderstand, maybe you need to change your writing."

"How?"

"In this case, you are lucky. You can talk to the person who misunderstood. Let's all do that now. If you have questions, ask the person who critiqued your proposal."

Fingers flew again as the students queried each other and read the answers. The clock clicked off another fifteen minutes.

"It's a bit early, but this is a good time for a break," Sadie said. "Take ten minutes, then come back and make any changes you'd like to on your proposal before you turn it in."

The class now charged with their final instructions, Sadie skimmed through her incoming e-mail. Among the inevitable spam and department announcements, there was a message from Mike. Sent just minutes before, it said, "Just FYI, the donkey didn't do it. Details at dinner."

The next hour flew by as the class worked on their laptops. One by one, the draft proposals began to appear in Sadie's in-box. Finally, at 5:30, she had all eighteen proposals in her box ready to be downloaded, reviewed, and graded. But not tonight. No, tonight was still her birthday, Sadie thought as she packed up her computer and prepared to leave.

"You have birthday still?" Ling asked.

"Yes, still. And I stupidly said I'd make my own birthday cake. So, I'd best get home and do that."

The two women parted ways. Ling headed east, and Sadie set out northward across campus toward home. As she walked, she considered her ill-advised promise to bake a cake.

She regretted her decision even more when she detoured into Wild Oats and stood in front of the glass bakery case. The scent of buttery cinnamon was almost more than she could stand. Why not just buy a cake? A cake is a cake is a cake.

No, she had said she'd do it herself. The natural foods grocery did carry cake mixes, but the selection was not large. And there didn't seem to be any frosting. After much deliberation, Sadie bought a box of angel food cake mix and a generous-sized can of cherry pie filling.

It was almost 7:00 when Sadie got home. Tiger had been waiting too long—at least that was the message he seemed to be trying to convey as he writhed on the carpet in greeting.

"Okay, Tiger, out you go." Sadie opened the sliding door to the tiny garden of her condo. Tiger tore out in pursuit of a squirrel that had been loitering on the ground just inside the fence.

The squirrel escaped over the fence and up a large tree by Arapahoe, Tiger went about his business, and Sadie hurried back into the kitchen.

"Let's see," she said to herself as she studied the cake mix box. "I think this will work, it's about the right proportion of wet stuff and dry stuff."

She set the oven for three hundred fifty degrees, poured the cake mix into a large bowl and plopped the bright red pie filling on top of the mound of white mix. She stirred but the cake mix resisted absorbing the gooey pie filling. Several hundred paddles of the spoon later, she succeeded in producing a cherry-red paste. Decanting it into a square glass pan required a lot of spatula work but it was ready for the oven just before Mike arrived, laden with two large Wild Oats sacks.

"Dinner, birthday dinner," he said cheerfully, putting the sacks on the kitchen counter. "I got bits of a lot of things. But," he grinned, "no birthday cake, right?"

"Right." Sadie wasn't as confident as she sounded. "It's in the oven."

Mike looked surprised. "Really? I figured we'd have to forget the birthday cake part. Well, great! Happy birthday, again." He hugged her. "Shall we eat?"

"Sure."

Mike started to unpack the bags. "First, wine," he said flourishing a bottle of Kendall-Jackson. "A Vintner's Reserve Chardonnay. What more could you ask?"

Sadie got out two wine glasses, set the table, and sat down. Mike uncorked the wine, poured two glasses, and handed one to Sadie. "And many, many more," he said, joining her at the small kitchen table.

"Thank you. This has been a really nice day. I wish all work days could be this relaxed." Sadie felt mellow and at peace.

"Hors d'oeuvres." Mike opened containers of guacamole, kalamata olives, and a box of crispy almond rice crackers.

They sipped wine, enjoyed the hors d'oeuvres, and sipped some more wine. A sweet, cherry smell wafted from the oven.

"There's dinner too," Mike said. "We have one more whole Wild Oats bag to go." He tipped his chair back and reached for the other bag just as the oven timer went off.

Sadie jumped up, yanked open the oven door, and looked at her cake concoction. It appeared to be done. Pink cake swelled above the glass dish. A faint brown crust rimmed the dish, and a bright pink gash had opened in the middle of the cake. She turned the oven off and took the cake out. It jiggled in the dish as she set it down on a hot pad.

"That's really pink," Mike said.

"Well, cherries are pink, you know."

"Right, but that's a rather intense pink. What kind of cake is it?"

Indeed, what kind of cake? The odd jiggle said it wasn't angel food cake. "It's cherry," Sadie said, "Cherry Wiggle Cake. A sort of special birthday cake."

"Cherry Wiggle Cake?"

"Ummm, yes. So what's for dinner?"

Mike resumed his emptying of the bag. There was lasagna, spinach salad, garlic bread, roasted veggies, and two pieces of flan. All were the perfect temperature thanks to Wild Oats' careful packaging.

They ate in companionable silence. It was delicious, as always. Wild Oats could certainly be depended on, Sadie thought.

"How come you got the flan?" she asked Mike.

"Well, you said no cake. But I thought … just in case, maybe dessert."

"We can save the flan." Sadie stood up and put the plastic container in the refrigerator. "It's time for Cherry Wiggle Cake." She gathered up their dirty plates, took them to the sink, and looked at her cake. It didn't look like the same cake. Where once it had been tall and plump, it was now concave. The Cherry Wiggle Cake had fallen, big time. "Maybe the flan after all," she said.

"No, I want to try this Wiggle Cake. Let's have it." Mike was almost smirking. "After all, you're such a good cake baker. It would only be right."

Sadie got a knife from the top kitchen drawer and two dessert plates from the cupboard. She cut two small squares of cake and tried to lift the first one onto a plate. The piece didn't want to come out of the dish. She ran the knife back and forth underneath it a few times until she got the semi-sodden-looking cake onto the plate. A repeat of the process produced a second, dumpy-looking plateful.

Mike looked at his plate. A small frown began to show between his eyes, but he picked up his fork and took a bite. His eyes lit up.

"This is great! Looks terrible but tastes wonderful."

Sadie put a bite of the sticky dessert into her mouth. She too was pleasantly surprised. It was good.

Mike was laughing. "You didn't think it was going to be edible, did you?" He whooped and banged the table with his hand. "I love it. You said you'd bake a cake, so you did. And then you thought it was dreadful. And it's not. You are just too much. Or maybe you're just lucky?"

"Not lucky. I just treat cooking like basic chemistry. Mix some wet stuff and some dry stuff, bake until done. It usually works."

Mike paused, a forkful of cake halfway to his mouth. "Basic chemistry?"

"Sure, that's all cooking is. There are just a few rules."

"Like what?"

"Well, as I said, it's all about wet and dry—and color, of course. Most recipes use ingredients that are white and sticky or white and pasty or red and runny. So you just need to follow a few basic rules."

Cherry Wiggle Cake

1 can cherry pie filling
1 white cake mix

Mix ingredients, put in greased
glass dish, and bake until done.
(About 35 minutes at 350°.)

Sadie's notes:

Cake will fall when it cools. If
this concerns you, top with Cool
Whip to make an even, smooth
appearance.

"Like what?" Mike repeated, pushing his empty cake plate toward the middle of the table and settling back in his chair.

"First, and I think probably most important, is the fact that any white, runny substance can be substituted for any other white, runny substance. Likewise, with red, runny stuff."

Waving a hand dismissively, Mike said, "I say again, like what? Examples would be helpful."

Sadie pursed her lips and thought before answering. "Say your recipe calls for milk but you don't have any milk. So what else is white and runny?"

Mike shrugged. "Buttermilk?" he guessed.

"No, that's too easy. How about yogurt? Just beat it up a bit, add water if you really want it runny, and it'll substitute fine. Egg whites may work also. Or run some cottage cheese through the blender. Lots of things will work.

"There are other categories of ingredients of course—like white, pasty stuff; white, fluffy stuff; green, crunchy stuff ..."

"Enough," Mike said. "I don't think I want to know any more about this."

"Color and texture, these are my basic parameters of cooking. I could go on," she invited.

"Not right now. I'd like to enjoy this cake without finding out what's in it."

Sadie got up, turned on the coffee maker, and washed out Tiger's dish. As she was assembling the dog's dinner, Mike picked up the Year of the Dog card from Ling and read it aloud.

"The Dog will never let you down. Born under this sign, you are honest and faithful to those you love. You are plagued by constant worry, a sharp tongue, and a tendency to be a fault-finder. You would make an excellent activist, businessperson, teacher, or secret agent.

"Hmmm," he said. "This profile is certainly interesting. And, you know what?" His tone was playful as he collected the dirty cake plates from the table. Figuring he was going to make some crack about fault-finding or constant worries, Sadie laughed when he said, "I've never slept with a secret agent before."

Twenty-Nine

"Details at dinner," Sadie teased the next morning. "We forgot about the donkey last night. So let's have details at breakfast, please."

Mike opened the cupboard and surveyed the available cereal options. "Not much in here," he said, shaking a box of raisin bran.

"There's other cereal."

He took down three more boxes and shook them. "Yeah, right. Other almost-empty cereal boxes."

"Good grief. Just sit down. I'll figure it out for you while you tell me about the donkey." Sadie took two bowls out of the next cupboard and poured half the raisin bran in each. The flakes barely covered the bottom of the bowls.

"There's nothing to tell except that Lee Hong wasn't kicked. He was bludgeoned. First with a small object, then several times with a log. The log was there in the pond, sunk into the muck near his body. There were wood fragments in the head wound and traces of his blood on the log."

"So the muddy hoof prints on Lee Hong's back didn't mean anything?" Sadie poured the contents of a Cheerios box into the bowls. They still didn't look very full. She rummaged in the back of the cupboard and found a box of shredded wheat. It too was almost empty.

Mike continued, "There were muddy hoof prints but no real trauma. A three-hundred pound animal can't walk on you without leaving a bruise or two. It looks as though the donkey just panicked and ran across the body."

"Why would she have done that, I wonder?" Sadie broke a pillow of shredded wheat into four pieces and added it to Mike's bowl. "I'd think she would have tried to avoid stepping on him, like she did when we found the body."

"As you have no doubt noticed, I don't know much about donkey behavior," Mike shrugged. "I suppose something scared her so much she just took off. Maybe it happened right after Lee Hong was killed."

That makes some sense, Sadie thought as she tore apart a second cereal pillow, put it in her bowl, and stirred the resulting mix. The contents of both bowls looked exactly like the leftovers they were.

Maybe I need an overall food rule, she thought. Something like: If it looks weird, cover it up. With what? She opened the refrigerator and saw the flan. Of course. Flan is made with eggs and milk. Eggs, milk, and cereal—a perfect breakfast. She laid a piece of flan on top of each bowl of cereal and delivered the bowls to the table.

"What is this?"

"Eggs, milk, cereal … a balanced breakfast."

"It looks like flan on top of leftover cereal."

"Yep, but it's very good," Sadie said, savoring a spoonful of crunchy flan. "So what will happen to the donkey now?"

"I don't suppose anything different."

"Didn't you have some sort of hold on her?"

"Not any more." Mike took his second spoonful. "Flan certainly makes most anything edible. But snap-and-crackle flan is a new taste treat for me."

"So now she will be up for adoption?"

"I don't know. The donkey has never been something I worried about much."

"I know. But I did, and I still do."

Mike tipped his bowl to get out the last bits of flan-laced cereal. "So, what do you want to do today? I don't have to be in until noon. What's your schedule?"

"I have a class at noon—Frank Shopnick's out of town so I'm covering for him—and I do have some prep to do and papers to grade."

"You have to prep for Shopnick's class?"

"Really not—it's just beginning ESL."

"So we both have time to go visit the donkey? Want to?"

Surprised and pleased that Mike was actually interested in the donkey, Sadie readily agreed. She fed Tiger and let him into the garden for a few minutes; then the three of them left for the Humane Society.

When they arrived, Tiger was more than happy to stay in the car. He curled up in the back and shut his eyes. Sadie and Mike found the donkey in the farmyard behind the main shelter. She wasn't alone. Quite a crowd surrounded her. As they got close enough, Sadie heard two conversations, both in French.

A small boy grasped the donkey around the neck while a taller girl stroked the animal's nose. Both were speaking in happy, excited tones. Eyes shut, withers relaxed, the donkey seemed content. Behind her, Georges LeBourne and Lila exchanged short remarks. Neither of them looked relaxed or content.

Doug, the groom, met Sadie and Mike at the gate. "Have you filled out a visitor's form? Actually, it doesn't matter. Too many people are in here now. You'll have to wait."

"I don't think so," Mike said, taking his badge wallet from his pocket and flipping it open.

Doug's eyes bulged. "Sure, okay … come in, I guess." He opened the gate.

"I've got a few questions," Mike said, stepping aside as Doug closed the gate.

"I do too," Sadie put in, "but they're for Lila." She left Mike talking with Doug and headed into the barnyard.

The donkey opened her eyes and watched Sadie walk toward Lila and Georges LeBourne, who were now glaring at each other.

"Hi, Lila. What are you doing here?" Sadie asked.

"Better ask what is he doing here." Lila gestured with her thumb at LeBourne.

"Okay." Sadie smiled at him. "What are *you* doing here? Are these your kids? Is this your donkey?"

"Yes, it is our donkey. And we must pay a lot of money to take her home."

"And?"

LeBourne was silent.

"Are you going to take her home?"

"Yes, sure, we will take her home. You can see the children love her."

"How did she get here?" Sadie asked.

"She was lost. Someone found her."

"Lost? Lost in a tiny pen on Institute property?"

"I do not know. She was stolen, I think." LeBourne tugged at the collar of his T-shirt.

"Someone stole the donkey and penned her up near the Institute gravel pits? Why would anyone do that?"

"So, … yes …"

"*Non*, not so," Lila interrupted. "The children say that is not so."

"*Allez, allez, maintenant*, time to go." LeBourne spoke gruffly to his children.

Tears welled in the little boy's eyes, and he clung even tighter to the donkey's neck. His sister handled the verbal dissent. Her defiance was apparent, even though her French baffled Sadie.

"We must pay for Eloise's food. Then we can take her home. Let's go do that," LeBourne coaxed.

"It's more than her food, sir." Doug had joined the group around Eloise. "You have to pay for the pickup, the trailer and all, and the impound fees, and her vet check … and …"

"Enough. I know I must pay." LeBourne interrupted Doug's explanation of fees. "Where do I do this?"

"I'll take you to the office." The groom started toward the gate. "It's nice to know her name. Who would have thought her name was Eloise?"

Sadie didn't hear LeBourne's response as he and Doug walked away toward the building.

"So, Lila," Sadie said. "What did the children say? How did the donkey get lost?"

"Catherine, that's the little girl, she said her papa took the donkey away last weekend. He said they were going to the vet, but he came back without the donkey. She said it was just like Cindrillon."

"Cindrillon? You mean Cinderella?"

"Yes, Cinderella. She left her glass slipper behind. Eloise left her halter behind."

Thirty

"So what do you think?" Sadie asked Mike as they drove away from the Humane Society.

"I think it's about time I got back to town."

"You know that the kids said Eloise forgot her halter? Catherine says it was in Eloise's stall after her dad and Eloise left last weekend. So how did LeBourne get Eloise into the horse carrier?"

"Obviously, with another halter."

"Yes, but why? In the last few days she's had at least three halters that I know of. There's the one Eloise had on when we found her at the pond. The stretchy one with the glass rosettes. Then there's the too-tight leather one she had on here the other day. And now she has another one. The Cinderella one that she left at home."

Mike's subject change was abrupt. "You have a class soon, don't you? Do you want to go right to campus?"

"Yes, I should."

Mike turned the Honda south on Broadway, made the left turn light at Euclid, and swung into the No Parking space at the loading dock of the Language Arts Building before responding to Sadie's comments about the donkey and her halter.

"You know, I just don't understand your obsession about the donkey's halter."

"Halters, that's my obsession. Why so many halters?"

193

"Why not?" Mike shrugged. "Time to go to work," he said. "I'm off at eight. Is that too late for dinner?"

"It's a good thing you're so cute. Because you can be a real jerk." Sadie unbuckled her seat belt and opened the car door. "Eight's good. That will give me time to get caught up on some of my grading. And we can finish the donkey conversation over dinner."

Mike blew her a kiss before he drove off, leaving her to rush into Shopnick's noon class, which went very well. Sometimes no prep pays off, Sadie thought much later as she strolled toward home down the sunny sidewalk.

Tiger got a short run before Sadie settled down with her laptop to download the first of the eighteen proposals she had to read before next week's writing seminar. The first proposal was seeking funding to fabricate ultra-small chips for quantum computers.

Interesting, Sadie thought. Aren't ultra-small chips what Georges LeBourne is working on? This guy must be one of LeBourne's grad students.

She closed the proposal file and opened her browser. A quick search of the Institute Web site turned up the fact that the proposal writer, Dak-Ho Kim, was indeed a student of LeBourne. Sadie went back to the proposal file and read the Executive Summary with renewed interest. The subject matter made it a slow read.

> *Present-day computers use thousands of transistors to store, manipulate, and process information. These transistors are actually tiny switches that are either "off" (if electrical current is not allowed to flow through them) or "on" (if it is). These two "states" can represent 0 and 1, respectively: a "bit" of information.*
>
> *The next revolution in computing will use quantum mechanical devices that can store not just a single ON or OFF, but a more complex code representing a packet of information, a "qubit" (quantum bit). As a way of visualizing the difference, think of a globe. A transistor can specify only two points on this globe: the North Pole "ON" and the South Pole "OFF." By*

contrast, a quantum device could specify any spot on the globe by its latitude and longitude.

Consequently, qubits can make computers billions of times more fast. To build a quantum computer must overcome the inherent fragileness of the quantum device. Any interaction with the environment causes "quantum decoherence," which means that the information gets too much scrambled. We propose to develop a reliable way to eliminate decoherence. Then quantum computing can be a practical reality. Our research is near to achieving this reality. Our device to test has stacks of crystal pods in arrays. Each pod check on its neighbors. Read/write is with laser pulses.

Whew! Sadie now knew more than she wanted to know about quantum computers. But, she also knew something about Dak-Ho Kim that she hadn't known before.

The man had no idea about intellectual property rights. He was not the only author of the short Executive Summary that mixed awkward Korean-to-English syntax and smooth, clear technical English. He had not written it, and he hadn't credited any sources. She had discussed proper credit, paraphrase, and plagiarism many times in class, so it wasn't possible that Kim didn't know better. Was it possible that he didn't understand? Or, more likely, that he didn't care?

What to do? Sadie decided to consult Georges LeBourne, Dak-Ho Kim's advisor about his student's glaring plagiarism. Using the standard Institute address system, she composed a short, to-the-point e-mail.

Georges:

I am concerned about a paper I have received from one of your students. Dak-Ho Kim submitted a proposal in my 6080 seminar that is at least 60% plagiarized. I plan to return his paper ungraded, pointing out some of the passages that he did not write himself. Can you please encourage him to rewrite a properly credited proposal? If you have any questions, please let me know.

Thank you,
Sadie

Five minutes later, her computer bonged to report an incoming e-mail. Sadie checked and saw that it was from LeBourne.

Sadie:

I called your office and got voice mail. Where can I call you? We need to talk about this.

Georges

She fired off a reply giving him her home phone number. The phone rang two minutes later.

"Sadie," the liquid voice of Georges LeBourne didn't disguise a hint of anxiety as he got right to his point. "I am worried that you do not understand what Dak-Ho Kim is doing. So how can you judge what he has written?"

"I'm not judging what he has written, only how he has written it. And, my point is that he didn't write most of it. Someone else did. He needs to credit the author."

"Yes, well, perhaps so. But are you sure?"

"Of course I'm sure." Sadie bristled at his condescending tone and bit back without thinking: "I'm as sure about the plagiarism as I am that you didn't lose your donkey. Why did you take her away and leave her at the gravel pond? She must have been terrified out there all alone."

"You sound like Lila. She, too, was angry about the donkey. But she understood I had to do it. No choice. But Eloise is home now and almost everything is okay again."

Sadie had no idea what he was talking about, but before she could think of another, less hostile question, LeBourne swung back to the issue of Dak-Ho Kim.

"Give him back his paper; I will speak to him about it. I will explain that Americans are super-sensitive about these things. We will fix it."

A dial tone replaced his voice. He had hung up.

"Well, what did I expect? Super-sensitive indeed! About the plagiarism? Or the donkey?" Sadie spoke out loud, Tiger cocked his head and looked at her. Was she talking to him? Always hopeful of attention, he came over and put his head in Sadie's lap.

She scratched Tiger's ears and thought about Georges' answer to her outburst about the donkey. The fact that he had "no choice." What could that comment mean?

The phone interrupted her thoughts. It was Lila.

"Allo, Sadie. Can you go to the airport with me tonight?"

"Why? Who's coming in?"

"No one. No one is coming, but I must pick something up for Georges."

"You're running errands for Professor LeBourne?" Sadie frowned at the thought.

"My, my. I think you don't like Georges very much. Why?"

"Mostly I guess because he was just pretty high-handed with me. And I also think he doesn't treat his donkey very well."

"You mean, because he lost her?"

"He didn't lose her, he left her. Why did he do that?"

"You think so? You think he left her?"

"You tell me. I don't know. But I don't like him." She changed the subject, "What are you picking up for him?"

"Left luggage."

"Left luggage? Why left luggage? And why you?"

"He asked me to. And I want to be nice. Daniel introduced us because he thought I would like to talk to someone from home. He was right. It's nice to find a Frenchman besides my brother to talk to and," she hesitated, "to cook for also."

"It looked to me like you were doing more arguing than talking the last time I saw you with him."

"Yes," Lila sounded sad. "We argued about Eloise. But, we French always argue, *non*?" Lila sounded almost wistful.

"Over-emote is more like it, I think. LeBourne is still married, isn't he?" Sadie had to ask.

"Yes, but his wife is still in France. He is all alone and so worried about his children and the donkey. He did not want to leave home tonight. So he asked me could I do this. I said yes."

"And you don't want to go alone?"

"No, I don't. I promised Daniel I would cook tonight. So, probably I cannot go before six. It will be dark. I don't like the airport parking garage at night. Please, Sadie. Can you not go with me?"

"I'm seeing Mike at eight. Can we be back by then?"

Lila clucked her tongue, making a peculiarly French sound of annoyance. "I think so. Daniel and I will eat early because he leaves for the films with Rick. I will pick you up at six. You can't drive because we must use Georges' car."

"I don't want to drive," Sadie said. "I'll be ready at six, but I do want to be back by eight."

"Okay!" Lila sounded her usual cheerful self, unlike Mike, who grumbled when Sadie called to tell him that she might be late getting home.

Thirty-One

Missing the overhead signs to Arriving Passengers, where short-term but expensive parking was available, Lila and Sadie wound up on the road to the airport garage instead. At the first garage entrance, a sign proclaimed all levels of the huge parking structure **FULL**, in red neon letters. Similar red signs glowed in the twilight at the other garage entrances ahead of them.

"Full? We will see about that," Lila said wheeling LeBourne's dark blue Honda Accord into the first entrance. She drove straight up from level one to level two and onward toward level four.

"Where are we going?" Sadie asked.

"Left luggage is on five. No one can park on level five, so we are going to four."

"But the garage is full."

"How does that sign know the garage is full? The garage is not full."

Sadie was pressed back into her seat as Lila accelerated up the ramp to level four.

"*Voila*! See, there, someone leaves." Lila slammed on the brakes as the backup lights of a large green SUV lit up. The driver of the SUV tried to back out but didn't have enough room to maneuver the big vehicle out of the narrow parking space. So he pulled back in, cranked the wheel and tried again. The second time he started to back out, a black car approached from the other direction and stopped.

"No way," Lila said. "He cannot have this space. We saw it first." She edged the Accord closer to the SUV and snapped the turn signal on. From the other direction, the black car moved closer also.

"This isn't going to work," Sadie said. "Maybe I should just get out and go get LeBourne's luggage while you look for a parking place."

"I have found a parking place," Lila said. The SUV backed out of the parking space momentarily blocking the black car. Speeding the Accord behind the SUV and into the parking space, Lila stomped on the brakes and jammed Sadie against her seat belt buckle. The driver of the black car responded with an indignant, prolonged honk that bounced back from the concrete walls of the garage.

"Never mind," Lila said. "He was cheating. He knew we were waiting." She busied herself gathering up purse and keys while the black car sped off. Sadie unbuckled her seat belt and climbed out.

They were very near the terminal. Crossing the pedestrian crosswalk, they went in a door marked 416. It was the first door of the terminal, and this far end of the airport was deserted.

Once inside the isolated airport, Sadie punched a button to summon the elevator and, when it arrived, it too was empty. They rode to Baggage Claim on level five and emerged near carousel ten, one of the many serving United Airlines. Right now, it wasn't serving anything. No one was there.

They walked along the marble corridor to the center of the airport, their footsteps echoing in the long hallway until they reached the carpeted atrium. Silence enveloped the usually bustling, cavernous space.

Looking across a sea of empty chutes for the closed security lanes, Sadie saw their goal.

How could she not have noticed this before? A sign—Airport Baggage Center—spanned two storefronts. Rows of gleaming new bags, backpacks, waist packs, fanny packs, and all manner of containers filled the windows from top to bottom. How much luggage could this place sell? Who would come to the airport to buy luggage? Maybe, if the airlines destroyed your bag, you would need to replace it immediately. But the size of this establishment suggested a brisk trade in luggage—luggage of all sorts. That certainly seemed unlikely. Maybe the store made their money on left luggage.

"There it is." Lila's voice broke into Sadie's thoughts. They hurried toward the brightly lit store. A bell announced their entrance.

Inside, display racks reached almost to the ceiling. At the far end, an Asian man perched on a high stool behind an imposing counter. Lila went toward him, opening her purse.

"I want to pick this up," she said extending an orange cardboard ticket to him.

He took the ticket and looked at it carefully. "You owe eight more dollars. This is over-long."

"Eight dollars? All right." Lila reopened her purse and pulled out a wallet. After she gave him the bills, he pushed off his stool and went through a door behind the counter. Soon he was back with a small black suitcase on wheels. "Your name is Georges?" he asked Lila.

"No, Georges asked me to pick this up."

"You know his last name?"

"LeBourne."

The man looked at the orange slip again, shook his head, and trundled the suitcase behind the counter with him. He yanked open a drawer below the counter and sorted through a pile of orange tickets before settling on one.

Pushing his glasses back on his nose, he looked at Lila. "Who left this suitcase here?"

"I do not know. Georges asked me to pick it up. I suppose he left it."

"No, not him."

"Does it matter? I have the receipt."

The man looked at the receipt. Then he peered at Lila again. "You sign release?"

"Certainly."

"Okay, you can have it." He brought out the bag again and left it in front of Lila.

"Where's the release?" Lila demanded.

"No release."

"You want a release, I will sign a release."

"No release. Just wondered if you would sign one."

Lila scowled at the man.

"Let's just take the suitcase," Sadie said.

"I do not understand. He wants a release, then he says no release."

"It doesn't matter. We've got LeBourne's suitcase. Let's go." Sadie didn't know whether to be amused or worried. But she did want to get going. At this rate, they would be late getting back to Boulder. She reached around Lila, grabbed the suitcase handle, and started to roll it toward the door. She'd reached the marble floor again before Lila caught up with her.

"Were you still hassling that man?" Sadie asked.

"Not hassle. Just curious."

They rounded the corner into the baggage claim area and encountered a near-explosion of noise. Disheveled passengers swarmed around the now-spinning United carousel.

"So much for the quiet end of the airport," Sadie said. They crowded into an elevator with several other baggage-laden people.

When they arrived at the car, Lila popped the trunk open. Sadie collapsed the handle and picked up the suitcase. It was unexpectedly heavy, and she fumbled it. The suitcase landed on its side on the garage floor with a heavy thud.

"What's in here? This tiny suitcase has to be packed with bricks to be so heavy."

"I do not know. Here, you take the other end." Lila grabbed one end of the suitcase, and between them, they managed to hoist it to the lip of the trunk. It started to slide in, but a tear in the suitcase fabric caught on the trunk latch.

"It's damaged." Sadie ran her fingers over the tear. It was more of a slash than a tear. Sadie tried to pull the suitcase off the impediment, but something inside the suitcase was now entangled in the latch.

"Help me hoist this back out." She and Lila wrestled the suitcase back out of the trunk. A ripping sound accompanied their effort.

Sadie froze, staring at the red and white halter that now hung from the trunk latch. Decorative rosettes reflected the overhead garage lights.

"Lila! Look at this. Could this be the missing halter?"

"I don't think Eloise has been to the airport," Lila replied.

"No? Look at this." Sadie picked up the halter and turned it over and over. Several of the rosettes had been damaged, and one was missing, seemingly ripped out of the fabric of the halter. "Why would anyone destroy a halter? And then leave it in left luggage?"

"Let's go, or you will be late for your date. Pick up your end of the suitcase again."

Sadie tossed the halter into the trunk before helping Lila lift the suitcase.

"I want to know what else is in this suitcase," she said. "It's already torn, so a bit more won't matter." She grabbed the torn cover and pulled.

"*Mon Dieu,*" Lila swore at Sadie. "*Mon Dieu,*" she repeated in astonishment when she saw the bundles of hundred dollar bills that filled the suitcase. "How much money is that?"

"A lot. This suitcase must weigh more than a bag of Tiger's dog food. And that's fifty pounds."

"Maybe it's not all money."

"What else would it be?" Sadie dug to the bottom of the suitcase. "Feels like money all the way."

"All big bills?"

"Do you want me to unpack it?"

"No. Do not do that. But what should we do?"

"You ladies leaving or not?" The driver of a blue minivan stopped behind them. He would be able to see into the trunk if he looked. Sadie slammed the open trunk shut.

"Right away. We're leaving right away."

"We are?" Lila had the wide-eyed stare of a deer trapped by headlights.

"Yes, come on, Lila." Sadie marched around to the passenger side. Lila went to the driver's side more slowly and climbed in.

"What will we do?" she asked Sadie again in the car.

"First, we get out of here." The blue minivan backed up to give them room to leave.

"After that?"

"Find Mike."

Thirty-Two

$\mathbf{F}$inding Mike was easy. He was sitting in his car in front of Flatirons Vista when Lila and Sadie arrived shortly after eight o'clock. He returned a laconic salute to Sadie's wave before opening his car door to stand and watch Lila's repeated attempts to parallel park the unfamiliar car in the small space in front of his Honda. Each attempt was a bit worse than the last. The hood of the Accord refused to tuck into the curb.

Mike walked up to the car. "You two look like you could use some help. Did you buy a new car, Lila?"

Lila threw her hands up in resigned defeat. "*Non*, it is Georges'. You park it. I cannot." She slid the seat back, got out of the car and held the door open for him. Mike got in and pulled the car back onto Arapahoe, coming to a stop very close to the car in front of the space.

As he expertly swung back toward the curb, Sadie spoke. "We have a problem."

Mike pulled the key out of the ignition, tossed it into the air, and caught it. Pointing to Lila, he said, "Yes, the problem is dancing around on the curb. Perhaps Lila wants us to get out of the car. Then she could go home."

"Not yet. She can't go home yet."

"Oh, yeah, that's right. She has to deliver something to Professor LeBourne."

"That's the problem. I want you to look at Professor LeBourne's luggage." Sadie opened the door and got out. Lila, already standing beside the trunk, wasn't exactly dancing, but she was shifting from one foot to the other nervously.

"Did you tell him?" she demanded as Sadie and Mike arrived at the trunk.

"Not really."

"Tell me what?" Mike's infectious grin was replaced by a frown.

"You have the keys. Please just open the trunk. Then you'll understand." Sadie shoved her chilly hands into the pockets of her jacket.

Mike found the trunk key, inserted it, and pulled the lid up. He stared at the torn suitcase before reaching in to riffle through the bills. "I don't believe it! This is what LeBourne asked you to pick up at the airport?"

"Yes." Sadie and Lila both answered.

"Was it torn like this when you picked it up?"

"Not exactly." Sadie looked in the trunk. "It sort of caught on the lock when we put it in the trunk. It was so heavy. We didn't expect it to be so heavy."

"Money is heavy. Did you know you were picking up a suitcase full of money?"

"No." Again both women replied in unison. "But," Sadie went on. "It isn't just money. Look." She pulled the halter from beneath the suitcase. "It's Eloise's missing halter. It was in the suitcase with all this money. And someone has torn it apart. Why would it be here? And how much money do you think this is, anyway?"

Mike hefted the suitcase. "Sixty maybe seventy pounds. Probably several hundred thousand dollars if it's all big bills. Certainly more than your average bear would check in left luggage. I think we need to talk with your Professor LeBourne." He unclipped his cell phone from his belt and keyed in a number.

After reporting the suspicious suitcase full of money, he slammed the car trunk shut. Sadie and Lila moved away from the car.

"What is he going to do?" Lila whispered. "What will I tell Georges?"

"I think Mike will have the suitcase impounded. And you won't have to tell LeBourne anything. I'm sure Mike will take care of that. Quite soon."

"Oh dear! Georges is going to be unhappy with me."

"It's you who should be unhappy with him." Sadie bristled. "He's the one who involved you. What was he thinking? Here we are strolling around with all this money. Anything could have happened to us."

"I guess so." Lila didn't sound so sure. "Maybe Georges did not know what was in the suitcase."

"Whose suitcase is this, anyway?" Sadie's voice rose as she continued, "Why was it in left luggage? Why did LeBourne ask you to pick it up?"

"All excellent questions. Any you care to answer?" Off the phone, Mike had come up behind them unnoticed.

"Both of you … this is not my fault." Lila was unusually defensive.

"Let's go inside and talk about this." Mike gestured toward the courtyard of Flatirons Vista. Sadie and Lila turned and headed for Sadie's condo.

Once past Tiger's enthusiastic welcome, they settled around Sadie's kitchen table. No one looked at anyone else. The general unease spread to Tiger, who crouched on the floor by Sadie's feet. No tail wagging, no calling attention to himself, the dog waited and watched.

"Okay," Mike started. "Tell me everything you know about this suitcase."

Sadie looked at Lila.

"Umm, Georges asked me at the Humane Society."

"Asked you what?"

"To pick up the suitcase?"

"Did he say why he couldn't pick it up himself?"

"He said he didn't want to leave the children alone. His wife is not here yet. The children are alone too much. And, he said they were overexcited."

"Overexcited?"

"Yes, because of Eloise."

Mention of Eloise reminded Sadie about the halter. "Mike, the halter in the suitcase with the money. I think it was the halter Eloise had on when we first saw her that night at the pond. The stretchy one with shiny rosettes. She never had it on again after that."

Mike grimaced. "Sadie, let's stay on the topic here."

"That halter may be the topic. Why was it in with the money? Did you look at it at all?"

"No, I didn't. I'm trying to find out why a respected engineer would send someone else to collect a suitcase full of money for him. I really don't think it has anything to do with his donkey's halter."

Sadie sat back in her chair, arms crossed. "I don't see how you can say that. That halter could have everything to do with the money."

"Sadie, please!" Exasperated, Mike thumped the table.

With Mike's attention off of her, Lila rose. "I think we all need a drink." She opened the refrigerator and peered inside. "There's orange juice or apple juice. And milk for coffee. What would you like?" She turned with a wide smile to address the two people glaring at each other across the table.

"Nothing for me."

"Me either," Sadie said.

"Well, I will have some apple juice." Lila removed a glass from the drying rack and was pouring the golden liquid into it when Sadie's doorbell pealed. Whoever it was hadn't needed to buzz from the lobby.

"I'll get it." Mike stood but Tiger beat him to the door. "Back, boy, back." Mike had his hand on the doorknob but Tiger was having none of it. He stood his ground, nose ready to thrust out the door when it opened.

"Tiger," Sadie called from the kitchen. "Sit."

The dog slowly complied. Sitting cost him his primary position at the door. Sadie's further command to stay stripped him of any hope of challenging the visitor. Tiger squirmed in place as Mike opened the door and acknowledged a colleague from the Boulder Police. "It's in a car on Arapahoe. I'll show you."

Tiger whined, appealing to Sadie for release from his enforced sit and stay. She complied, and the dog exploded toward the door. Too late. Mike shut the door firmly in Tiger's face.

Sadie turned to find Lila rummaging in the refrigerator again. "What did you plan for dinner? I find not much in here." Lila continued to move things about on the shelves of the refrigerator.

"I didn't have any plans, really. We usually just get takeout from Wild Oats."

"I see. Maybe I will do takeout myself and go home with Georges' car. Is that okay with your policeman?"

"You can ask him. He's probably still out at the car with that other person from the police department. If they're finished, you can probably even have the car back."

Lila put down her empty glass and headed for the door. Once again, Tiger got there first. But once again, he was left behind.

"Too bad, boy, it's just you and me," Sadie consoled him after Lila left. "Maybe we could just chill for a few minutes." She went into the living room, sat down and patted the couch beside her. Tiger didn't need any more than that. He hopped up, circled once, and settled down with his head on Sadie's lap.

Sadie stroked the dog's black-and-white fur. It was comforting, and both she and Tiger relaxed until the doorbell rang. It rang again before Sadie could untangle herself from Tiger and get off the sofa.

"All right! Give me a chance." She yanked the door open. Mike stood there alone.

"We're going to go talk to LeBourne. I thought I'd just let you know I won't be here for dinner."

"Later?"

"Maybe. I'll try. But this looks to be a real mess."

"Yes, I suppose so. Did you figure out how much money is in the suitcase?"

"The evidence tech thinks it's at least half a million dollars. I'll call you when we're done at LeBourne's." Mike turned and walked away.

As Sadie shut the door, "half a million dollars" echoed in her brain. The same amount that Wayne Chen offered to "find" for Lila if she would apply for an E-2 visa. I wonder, I wonder.... She headed into the kitchen as she mulled over the coincidence of half a million dollars in a suitcase left for Georges LeBourne. Left with Eloise's halter. A mangled halter at that. Sadie sat down, her thoughts racing.

Thirty-Three

Why would someone leave half a million dollars in a shoddy suitcase at the airport? It couldn't have anything to do with whatever scam Wayne Chen was running with E-2 visas. The suitcase was left for Georges LeBourne, who certainly didn't need any help with his immigration status. He was a well-known computer engineer. It had been quite a news splash when LeBourne moved from CEDEX in France to Boulder to run the Institute's burgeoning quantum computing research program. Even Sadie, ensconced as she was in Language Arts, had heard of LeBourne long before Rick Baines introduced them in the Faculty Lounge last Monday.

A new thought checked in: If LeBourne knew about the money, why would he ask Lila to pick up the suitcase?

"Risky! Very risky!" Sadie's voice startled Tiger. Assuming she was talking to him, the dog got up and headed toward his leash in the kitchen.

"No, Tiger. Don't get your leash. We're not going anywhere." Sadie laughed at the puzzled dog. "I'm sorry. I guess I'm confusing us both. Come here." She waggled her fingers, and Tiger returned to sit at her feet. He sighed as Sadie scratched his ears.

"So, do you have any ideas?" Sadie asked Tiger, who ignored her as she continued to muse aloud.

"Why did LeBourne ask Lila to pick up the suitcase? Would he do that if he knew there was so much money in it? After all, Lila is very nosy. She'd be likely to look in the suitcase."

Sadie laughed again. It wasn't Lila who had been nosy. Remembering those tense moments in the airport parking garage, she thought about the halter. Why was Eloise's halter in the suitcase? Why was a rosette torn off? Why tear a single rosette off a well-used halter?

This last question triggered a cascade of questions that ended with a heart-stopper: Could something have been in the rosette? It would have to be something very small. And something very valuable—half a million dollars valuable?

Yes! There may be, could be, something very small and very valuable. A quantum chip.

Sadie sat, stunned. Of course. How obvious. Georges LeBourne must be stealing proprietary technology. And—Sadie gritted her teeth—distressing his own kids in the process. She remembered the children's joyous reunion with Eloise at the Humane Society. What a jerk! Using his kids' pet that way. What if Eloise had gotten out of that fence at the pond? What if she'd really gotten lost?

And … Sadie stopped cold as she remembered Lee Hong. Her blood chilled. Lee Hong had gone to photograph Eloise and somehow gotten caught up in LeBourne's plot.

"Oh my God. Oh my God." She didn't understand everything but she understood enough. She had to talk to Mike. Grabbing the phone, she dialed his cell. It rang through to voice mail. Of course, she thought, he's probably talking to LeBourne right now. And, if I know Mike, he's not going to ask anything about Eloise or her halter. Nonetheless, Sadie left a message.

"Mike! I think I know what's going on. Well, at least part of what's going on. I think LeBourne is a thief. The missing rosette on Eloise's halter—I think it had a quantum computer chip in it. And someone paid him half a million dollars for that chip—after they killed Lee Hong."

She stood up and began to pace around her living room. Tiger joined her, wagging his tail expectantly. Sadie zeroed in on what she knew, and what she could surmise.

Lee Hong had been in the wrong place at the wrong time. He must have seen the person who took Eloise's first halter. But, why was it necessary to kill Lee Hong? Taking a halter off a stray donkey couldn't be that suspicious. Or could it?

What if Lee Hong knew the person who took the halter? Worse yet, what if the person knew Lee Hong? And knew about the workplace "portraits" he had been taking in Black Hawk.

It had to be Wayne Chen! But how could she prove it? Sadie's thoughts raced. Chen had asked Lila to apply for an E-2 visa. What would happen if she did? Sadie reached for the phone.

Thankful that Lila herself answered, Sadie blurted out her suspicions. "I think Wayne Chen is buying technology from Georges LeBourne. Probably using money that should be going into developing the ski resort. Money from E-2 visa holders."

"But," Lila said slowly, "what does that mean? That Georges is doing something wrong?" She sighed. "I hope not."

"Why else would his suitcase be stuffed with money?"

Lila had no answer. Sadie held her breath as the silence lengthened. When she finally spoke, Lila sounded defensive. "Maybe Georges did not know. If he did, why would he ask me to pick up the suitcase?"

"The obvious answer is that he didn't want to take any risk."

"So I take the risk? And do not even know it?"

"Well yes. You ... and Eloise, of course."

"Eloise?"

"Yes, I think Georges hid something—probably a quantum chip—in Eloise's halter before he left her at the pond."

"And Mr. Chen took the halter at the Humane Society? How did he know Eloise was there?"

"There's a lot I don't understand yet. But, one thing I am very sure of is that Mr. Chen is up to his Taiwanese neck in this. He may even have killed Lee Hong."

Lila's sharp intake of breath told Sadie that her friend was finally listening. Her next words confirmed this. "What does your policeman say?"

"I couldn't reach him, but I left a message. Mike's with LeBourne now, I think."

Silence again. Sadie seized the initiative.

"Lila, would you be willing to tell Chen you want an E-2 visa?"

"Why? You want me to be murdered also?"

"No, of course not. I don't think Chen murders his visa holders. He just turns them into floor sweepers and garbage collectors."

Lila sniffed audibly. "I do not think I care to do that."

"He wouldn't need to do that with you. After all, you have a place to live, and someone to take care of you. Besides which, we'll solve this long before your E-2 visa comes through. I just want you to exercise Chen's system, so we can see how it works."

Sadie heard Lila's quiet cluck, the sound her friend often made when thinking how to answer a difficult question.

"Can you at least call Chen? Tell him you're interested in knowing more?" Sadie urged.

"Right now?"

"Yes."

"No."

"Why not?"

"Daniel is home. He would not understand."

"Hmmm, you're probably right about that. And probably it's better that no one else know."

"So, I can do this tomorrow morning?" Lila sounded relieved.

"No, I think you should call him tonight. Just do it somewhere Dan can't hear you."

"Such as?"

"Here. Come over here. We'll talk about what you should say and then you can call from here."

Sadie waited through yet another long silence before adding, "Besides which maybe Mike will call. Then we can see what he thinks."

Sadie knew what Mike would think of the idea. He wouldn't like it at all. But, the thought of Mike's input reassured Lila. At least, she agreed to return to Sadie's. "Within the hour," she said.

"We've got time for a short walk," Sadie said to Tiger after she hung up.

"Walk" was Tiger's favorite word, even though he had the semantic content a bit muddied. "Walk" to Tiger was a command. It meant: Find your leash and bring it here, then we'll go to the movies or, at least whatever passes for movies in a dog's world.

Soon, Sadie and Tiger were tromping along the path beside Boulder Creek. As Tiger explored the creekside bushes, Sadie remembered Sam Gross. Did Chen kill him as well as Lee Hong? If so, why? She had no answer. But she did have a lot of qualms. Maybe this wasn't such a good idea, meeting with Chen, a possible murderer. No, it wasn't a good idea at all.

Sadie yanked Tiger's leash, "Let's go. We have to get home. Now!" She started running for home, the dog trailing behind her.

Thirty-Four

The timing was perfect. Sadie and Tiger came up the grassy hill from Boulder Creek just as Lila pulled into the residents' lot at Flatirons Vista. Sadie watched as she rummaged in the glove compartment to produce a parking permit. Waving at Sadie, Lila threw the permit on the dashboard and climbed out of the little car.

"Daniel still has a permit to park his car here. Did you know that?" she asked.

"Yes, I guess I did know. And I would like it back sometime but that's not important right now. What's important is that we need to really rethink what we're doing. I'm not sure it's such a good idea after all."

They walked together through the lobby and turned the corner toward Sadie's condo.

"Why?"

"Let's just get in the house." She led the way through the lobby into the courtyard and toward the door to her condo.

Once they were inside, Sadie busied herself taking off Tiger's leash and hanging it up. She rinsed his water dish, refilled it, and put it back on the kitchen floor.

Lila watched, eyebrows arched in question. "What are you doing? I had to come right away to call Mr. Chen. And all you are doing is ... well, what is it you are doing?"

Sadie threw her hands up. "I know, I know. I'm procrastinating, I guess. I'm not sure this is a good idea. But it's the only idea I have."

"Yes, it is not a good idea. But I think we must do it." Lila sat down in the pink recliner next to the phone. "Let us decide what to say."

"Lila, it's possible this man is a murderer."

"*Non*! Why do you say that? He is just a salesman."

"I'm not so sure. We need to be careful."

"I won't ask him if he murders anyone." Lila brushed off the idea. Too lightly. "I will just ask about the visa. Nothing more. How do you think I should do it?" She settled back in the recliner.

Maybe it would work. Just the visa. Just the visa. Sadie paced as she thought about it. "I agree. Just tell him you have thought about his offer, and you want to take him up on it."

"Up on it?"

"Idiom, sorry." Sadie waved her right hand in a dismissing gesture. "Tell him you want to apply. Then just play it by ear … Oh, that's another …"

"Idiom. But that one I know. Okay. I brought the brochure he gave me. It has his phone number, I think." Lila pulled a crumpled brochure out of the pocket of her cardigan. "Ready?"

"Ready," Sadie replied. "I'll pick up the extension in the kitchen after you dial." She hurried into the kitchen and stood by the yellow wall phone, waiting while Lila took the pink handset and punched in the eleven-digit long-distance number that would reach Chen's sales office in Nederland.

When she picked up the receiver from the wall phone in the kitchen, Sadie heard the soft *brrr* of a ringing phone. So apprehensive she found it hard to breathe, she collapsed into a chair by the table. The phone rang a few more times before a recording came on. Lila hung up and came into the kitchen.

"What should I do?" she asked Sadie. "If I leave a message, he will call me back at Daniel's. I don't want that."

"Tell him the truth. Tell him that you don't want Dan to know, so he has to call you back here. That's a good idea anyway because he probably has caller ID. He'll know you called from here."

"Okay." Lila went back into the living room and resettled in the recliner. They did it all over again: Lila punched in the numbers, Sadie picked up the phone, and they waited. When Chen's recorded message finished, Lila said, "Mr. Chen? Mr. Chen, this is Lila Simone. You talked to me the other day? I have been thinking. I would really like to stay in the United States, and maybe your E-2 visa would work for me. I would like to talk …"

"Madame Simone?" Chen's smooth tones interrupted Lila midsentence. "How nice to hear from you. Even though it is rather late, isn't it?"

"Yes, but now is when I can call. I have not yet told my brother about this."

"Of course, of course. I understand."

"So, please. Can you tell me what I should do? How do I apply for this visa … the E-2?"

"It's easy. I have the form. We just fill it out and submit it to the authorities."

"That is all? There is a fee, no?"

"It is not a fee, exactly. It is a guarantee. A guarantee to bring money when your visa is granted."

"Oh dear." Lila cooed. "It is complicated, *non?* Can we do this soon? Can we do it tonight?"

"Tonight? It's almost nine o'clock. I'm in Nederland and you're in Boulder. Let's meet tomorrow."

"Tonight, please. I want to get this started. My visitor's visa is almost expired."

Chen was silent. Sadie held her breath. Lila broke the silence with another plaintive coo. "Oh dear, I don't know what to do. Maybe I should not do this at all. I should not bother you."

It was the right thing to say. Chen responded immediately. "Maybe now is okay. I can come to Boulder. You are calling me from the home of S. Wagner, is that correct? Do you want me to come there?"

He is getting that from caller ID, Sadie thought. She leaned away from the table and nodded vigorously at Lila through the kitchen door. It was unnecessary. Lila had everything under control.

"Yes, can you come here? It is easy to find. It is right across the street from the library. The condos called Flatirons Vista. It's number four-twenty-four. You have to buzz from the lobby."

"I'll find you. It may take an hour." Chen hung up.

Lila kicked her shoes off and leaned back in the chair. "Oh, my goodness, that was exhausting."

Joining her from the kitchen, Sadie said, "You look more exhilarated than exhausted. We need to decide what you should tell Chen."

"Tell him? I already told him. I want to apply for the visa."

"Yes, but you'll have to explain me. He may not want a witness. Remember when he talked to us at the sales office? He talked only to you. In fact, he probably thought I didn't speak English very well."

Lila wrinkled her forehead. "Why would he think that?"

"Because I didn't say a word when you talked with him. Anyway, he may be surprised to find me here and to find out that I'm an American."

"You cannot leave me here alone."

"No, I'll be here. I just think we should be ready to explain why I'm here. Or, rather, why you are here at my house."

Hands in front of her, fingers curled as though she were clutching two of Tiger's tennis balls, Lila rocked back and forth on the edge of the chair. "This is too hard. I think maybe we should not do this."

"Calm down. It will be okay." Sadie wasn't so sure but she needed to reassure Lila. "Would you like a cup of herb tea?"

"Abomination! Herb tea! *Non!*"

"Regular tea, then?"

"Please."

Sadie busied herself brewing a pot of Yunan gold. Lila continued to rock back and forth on the edge of the chair. Because Tiger stayed out of the way in his bed, Sadie gave him a reward biscuit when she carried the tea tray from the kitchen to the table in front of the couch.

Thirty-Five

They sipped the warm, golden beverage in silence, each harboring her own apprehensions until Sadie voiced hers. "What's the worst that could happen?"

"I could end up being a garbage person in Black Hawk." Lila giggled. Her laughter relieved the dark mood.

"The worst that could happen is that he won't believe you want a new visa. I hope that's the worst that could happen." Sadie poured the last of the tea into Lila's cup and stood up to return the tray to the kitchen.

"And then he will just go away?" Lila didn't sound too sure but there was no more time for discussion. The doorbell from the lobby entrance chimed.

Sadie looked at her watch. If it was Chen, he'd certainly made good time. She walked over to the intercom keypad, touched it and responded, "Yes?"

Chen's voice replied from the tinny speaker. "I am to meet Madame Simone. She is there?"

"Yes, Mademoiselle Simone is here." Sadie emphasized the correct title as she buzzed Chen in. "We're in four-twenty-four, to your left."

Lila opened the door and waited for Chen to stride across the courtyard from the lobby.

"Mademoiselle!" Chen took Lila's outstretched hand, raised it to his lips, and kissed it in an overdone Continental flourish that caught Tiger's attention. The dog rose and stood in his bed, seeming to assess the situation.

"And," Chen added, "your friend. Miss Wagner is it? We did meet before. I recognize your dog." As he gestured at Tiger, the dog growled. It was a long, low, warning snarl.

"Tiger, it's okay." Sadie moved quickly to the dog's side.

Tiger clearly did not think it was okay. The anger ruff down his back stood on end as he continued to growl quietly. Sadie grabbed his collar.

"You are not French, Miss Wagner. Why did I think that you were, I wonder?"

"I … I don't know," Sadie spoke loudly to mask Tiger's continuing objections. She didn't know what to do. Tiger had good judgment and he must be picking up vibes from Chen that he didn't like. The dog was also undoubtedly keying into her own apprehension about the whole situation.

"Sometimes he's just crabby at night." Sadie smiled as she lied. Smiled and towed Tiger toward the garden door. "I'll put him outside until he remembers his manners." Even though she would much rather have Tiger present, she certainly couldn't afford the possibility that the dog would derail the conversation.

Tiger resisted Sadie's tugs on his collar. He looked at her as though he couldn't believe what was happening. She was actually going to put him outside. Outside! While this odd man was in the house. He sat down and refused to move.

"Tiger, come on!" She opened the garden door, waiting for the dog to comply. Instead, Tiger lay down and looked at Sadie with large, accusing eyes.

"Maybe he is hungry," Lila suggested.

"I don't want to bribe him to obey." While Sadie was losing patience with Tiger, Chen was losing patience with the entire situation.

"Ladies," he said in a firm tone, "it's getting late. I'd like to get started, but I cannot stay here if that dog doesn't go outside."

That did it. Sadie grabbed a box of Milk Bones off the kitchen counter and shook it in Tiger's face before throwing the entire box out the door. The dog got up, shot one last glare at Chen, and stalked into the garden to claim his dog biscuit bonanza. Sadie slid the door shut behind him and pulled the curtain closed.

In the living room, Chen sat down on the couch and opened his small briefcase. "I have an application right here, Mademoiselle. It has to be filled out in your own handwriting." He handed a thin sheaf of papers to Lila, who studied the top page carefully.

"This says I must submit a letter of credit. I do not have that. And also it wants my passport number. I do not have my passport here."

Chen scowled. "The credit is not a problem."

"No?"

"No." Chen stood and went to bend over Lila. He pointed to a footnote. "You check here to say you will use cash instead."

"Yes, but I do not have cash either."

"Of course not. But I do."

"And you will give it to me?"

"Of course."

"You will give it to me and then, I will give it back to you. After I get the visa. Is that it?"

"Exactly." Chen clapped his hands and grinned his toothy, gold-accented grin.

Still worried by Tiger's attitude, Sadie couldn't keep still. "It seems to me that Lila would have to do more than just give you the money back. If she's a limited partner, doesn't she have to work for your corporation? Isn't that what E-2 visas are for? Working partners?"

Chen turned and cast a narrow-eyed look at Sadie. "You know about visas? Most Americans don't. Why do you ask this?"

"I work with foreign students. They sometimes have trouble with their visas and … I don't want Lila to get into trouble."

"Ah, no trouble, no trouble." Chen waved his hands in front of him as though wiping away any troubles. "She cannot get into trouble. What trouble?"

"So, let me get this straight." Sadie held up her left hand and ticked off the points on the outstretched fingers with her right forefinger as she spoke. "First, Lila applies for an E-2 visa to become a limited partner in your ski resort development. Second, you give Lila half a million dollars. Third, when she gets the visa, she gives you the money back. Presumably, you put it back into your development and Lila becomes a limited partner. Then what?" Sadie wagged her fourth finger. "What's next?"

"Next?"

"Yes. I don't see what good this does you, Mr. Chen. Maybe it does Lila some good. Maybe she has a better visa than her current one. But maybe she doesn't. What if your development fails? Will Lila still have a good visa if she has no job? Not, of course, that she really has a job with you anyway."

Chen turned to Lila. "I don't know how to reassure your friend. Are you also worried?"

"No, I mean, yes. Yes, I am worried also." Lila's eyes flitted back and forth between Chen and Sadie.

Chen's attitude changed. No longer accommodating, he seemed to have made a decision. "Mademoiselle Simone, you said you don't have your passport. You must have your passport. We cannot do this without your passport. Go home now and get it."

"Now?"

Chen stood up, strode to Sadie's kitchen door—the one he had entered just minutes before—and yanked it open.

"Now. I will wait here."

Lila stood up hesitantly. "It will take me a half hour or so."

"That is fine. Miss Wagner and I will wait for you. Now go."

Uneasy at the prospect of being alone with Chen, Sadie couldn't think of any other reasonable way to respond. "It's okay, Lila," she said. "He's right. You do need your passport. Go ahead."

"If you are sure. I will hurry." Lila went out the open door, which Chen shut firmly behind her.

"Now, Miss Wagner," he said in a quiet voice. "You want to talk about visas, we have some time to talk." He leaned against the closed door and crossed his arms.

There was nothing to do but continue her role of concerned friend, so Sadie returned to the issue of how Lila would benefit from an E-2 visa.

"I know what you could do," she said, as though it had just occurred to her. "Is there someone else Lila could talk to? Some other limited partner in your ski resort? Another E-2 visa holder?"

"No."

"No? Lila would be the first limited partner you have? Really?"

"No, not the first but the others do not speak English—or French."

"They are all Chinese?"

Chen's steely glare seemed to bore into her eyes. "Yes," he said after too long a pause. "How do you know this?"

Nervous, Sadie's swallow caught in her throat. When she did manage to speak, it was little more than a croak. "I just guessed."

Chen continued to glare at her, pursing his lips into an ugly grimace. "I don't think so. I don't think you just guessed."

His gaze softened as he thought out loud. "I saw you yesterday in Black Hawk, first in the casino, and then later with your dog. And your friend. She does not bring her passport with her when she is going to apply for a new visa?"

Having reviewed the facts, Chen switched to a verbal assault. "No one is that stupid. What do you two think you are doing?"

His arms were no longer crossed over his chest. His fists now flexed at his side. "She doesn't really want a new visa, does she? Why do you want to meddle in my business?"

"It isn't about your business. It's about my business." Sadie thrust her right forefinger into her chest.

"What do you mean? Why is any of this your business?" His response was immediate and punctuated by hostile body language as he shifted his weight forward.

Sadie took a step backward, toward the garden door.

Chen read her mind. "Stop. You're not going out that door. I want an answer, Miss Wagner. Why do you meddle? You have a French friend. But you ask questions about Chinese people. Why?"

"My teaching assistant who works with me is Chinese. Her brother-in-law was a photographer. He was killed."

"Her brother-in-law? Did he work with you also?"

"No, he worked for Naval Intelligence," Sadie blurted out without thinking. The ugly look on Chen's face said she had made a major mistake.

"Naval Intelligence," he said in a sotto voice. "Just so. Naval Intelligence. What do you know about Naval Intelligence, Miss Wagner?"

Sadie thrust her chin up. "Nothing really, except that Commander Gross was asking questions about Lee Hong and then both he and Lee Hong were murdered."

"If the photographer worked for Naval Intelligence, why would Commander Gross ask you questions about him?"

"How do you know Commander Gross?" Sadie slipped her question into the opening Chen had left her. "He doesn't seem a likely prospect for a limited partner."

"No? He was very interested in our real estate plans."

"Interested, maybe. But perhaps for the wrong reasons?"

"Who are you really, Miss Wagner?"

"I'm just a teacher."

"I don't think you are just a teacher. You ask too many questions."

Ignoring Chen's threatening words, Sadie plunged ahead. "I'm curious about Commander Gross. He was killed, you know. Lee Hong was taking photographs for him. Both of them were killed. Whoever killed Commander Gross stole the memory card out of

Lee Hong's camera. But, you know what? Lee Hong had already printed the photos. And now the government has them."

"That is not possible." Chen's eyes narrowed and glinted like obsidian.

"Not only possible, but true." Sadie hoped to derail Chen's threatening attitude by showing him it was no use. She knew everything. He had no secrets, from her or, she decided to exaggerate just a bit, from the authorities.

"I've seen the photos and so have the police. Lee Hong's photos are very different from the ones on the gentlemen's E-2 Visa applications."

Chen had heard enough. In one quick movement, he produced a gun. It was a very long gun.

Sadie froze. A gun! And was that a silencer? What had she done? What was Chen going to do? A tsunami of fear washed over her.

He answered her unspoken question. "We are leaving here. You will walk out the door in front of me. If you do anything to attract attention, I will kill you. Right here. Right now. Do you understand me?"

Sadie understood. Too well. "How can you do this? Lila will come back. She will know what happened."

"She may not come back, but if she does, I will kill her, too." He stalked over to her, grabbed her arm, and shoved her toward the kitchen door.

"Open it," Chen ordered, tightening his grip. Sadie eased the door open. There was no one in the courtyard. Across the way, TV lights flickered behind her neighbor's closed curtains. Muted music came from next door, also from behind closed curtains. A scream for help would go unheard, she realized with a lurch in the pit of her stomach.

"Where are we going?" she asked.

"Not far. Just through the parking lot out there and down to the creek. Just a short walk." Chen's gold tooth glinted in an evil look. "Let's go, Miss Wagner."

Sadie moved slowly toward the lobby, trying hard to think of something to do.

"Go!" Chen repeated.

She turned toward the lobby. A shadow moved to the left in her peripheral vision. Her hopes soared and then fell as she saw that it was just a vine blowing in the gentle breeze moving through the courtyard.

Sadie, with Chen's gun jammed into her side, could see no safe haven as they approached the lobby. Her last hope of encountering anyone else was dashed. There was no one there. They passed through the lobby and moved into the parking lot. Streetlights from Arapahoe provided only dim illumination that faded well before the back of the lot where they were headed.

Despair overwhelmed the fear coursing through her body. Behind the parking lot, the grassy lawn stretched toward the trees edging the Boulder Creek Path. Their dense branches made the darkness ahead even darker. Chen urged her forward, toward the creek, the same creek where Commander Gross's body had been found.

With that thought, Sadie decided there was nothing to be gained in continuing to cooperate. She stopped and wrenched around to face Chen. "I won't do this. I think you killed Sam Gross down there and I won't make it so easy for you to kill me too. I won't go one step further."

"Then I'll kill you here." Chen's tooth glinted in the dim streetlight. As the gun rammed into the soft flesh below her ribs, a black and white whirlwind exploded out of the darkness. Tiger crashed full-force into Chen, shoving him into Sadie. She stumbled and fell to her knees, skidding in the slightly damp grass. The gun was no longer jammed into her side, but Chen, standing over her, still had an iron clasp on her arm.

Shadows cast by the trees around the creek moved across the damp grass. Sadie, struggling to stand up, felt Chen's grasp loosen as he attempted to deal with Tiger. The dog had latched onto Chen's other hand, the one holding the gun. He held on, gnawing and writhing to avoid the man's vicious attempts to kick him.

Sadie pulled away from Chen. Too breathless to scream, she stopped on all fours, engulfed in sound, frightening sound: her own panting, Chen's cursing, Tiger's growls melded together.

Chen's blood welled around Tiger's grip and dripped on the grass. Tiger, teeth sunk in Chen's hand, shook his head hard, loosening Chen's grip on the gun. It fell to the ground

It was a chance. She had a chance! Sadie grabbed the gun and scrambled away in a crablike crawl. She had no idea how to use the cumbersome weapon. It was awkwardly heavy and now warm and sticky with Chen's blood. Chen followed her, dragging Tiger with him.

With no time to figure out how to use the gun, she stood and heaved it toward the creek. The big gun ripped through the shrubbery along the Creek Path and splashed into the water beyond.

The sound of the gun hitting the water caught Tiger's attention. Ears piqued in curiosity, he let go of Chen and turned to Sadie, wagging his tail proudly.

Chen grasped his bleeding hand. "We are not finished," he hissed through clenched teeth. Holding his damaged hand to his chest, he turned and ran down the sloping grass toward the creek.

Sadie took off the other way, toward the parking lot, with Tiger on her heels. Where was the gun? Did it hit deep water and sink? Or was it in the mud at the edge of the creek? And would it fire all wet and full of mud? All she had was questions. No answers. Why was it so hard to think? For that matter, why was it so hard to breathe?

Frantic, Sadie couldn't focus. She was in the parking lot now, Tiger circling around her, ecstatic with his off-leash freedom. Where should she go? Chen might find his gun at any moment. And, for sure, he would come looking for her. Home seemed like a bad idea. The street would be better. Was Wild Oats still open?

Questions roiling through her panic, Sadie ran through the parking lot toward Arapahoe. She heard a noisy altercation behind her. Was Chen coming back? Throwing a quick glance over her shoulder, Sadie saw Tiger wheel around and tear back into the darkness.

"No, Tiger. Come back!" She stopped, reluctant to let Tiger dive back into danger. "Tiger! Tiger!" she called frantically expecting to hear the dog re-engage Chen at any moment.

Tiger started barking. Sadie couldn't see him but he sounded both hysterical and happy.

What was going on? Standing near the entrance to the parking lot, Sadie began to shake so hard she had to sit down. When she did, Tiger was back. He climbed into her lap, whimpering happily and trying to lick her face.

"Are you okay?" Sadie hugged the dog. Chen's blood, spilled across Tiger's chest, smeared onto her blouse.

"He's okay. Are you okay?" Mike's calm voice cut through her consciousness. Sudden relief swelling her heart, Sadie looked up. Cell phone in hand, Mike stood over her. Concern was etched in his face. Behind him, down on the lawn at the edge of the parking lot, Chen was face down, thrashing about, his hands cuffed behind his back.

What happened? Where did Mike come from? How did Mike know? She was unable to voice any of these questions. She seemed to be transported to another layer of reality: her thoughts perfectly calm, her body quaking. Many questions rushed through her mind and were gone. They could wait. There was no hurry about anything now. She held Tiger so tightly the dog complained.

Mike turned to talk to the uniformed officers who had just arrived. One officer hauled Chen to his feet while a second read him his rights.

"I threw his gun that way." Sadie pointed toward the creek. "I heard it splash."

The second officer looked surprised. Probably not used to seeing a woman sitting in a parking lot hugging a bloody dog and babbling about a gun, Sadie thought.

The officer disappeared down the sloping lawn. Sadie watched the pool of light from his powerful flashlight as he scanned the creek edge. Apparently the gun was easy to find. The officer bagged it and came back in what seemed like no time at all.

"A silencer!" He showed the bagged gun to Mike. "What went down here, anyway?"

"Long story," Mike answered. "Long story, short ending." He reached down, extricated Tiger from Sadie's grasp, and helped Sadie up before drawing her into an embrace. She was still shaking.

"How did you know?" Sadie asked, her voice caught in her throat.

"Easy," answered Mike. "When I got your message about LeBourne and his donkey, I hurried back here. When I saw Tiger in your yard ignoring a whole box of Milk Bones, I knew for sure that something was wrong. I opened your gate and he took off toward the parking lot like a rocket. I couldn't keep up."

Thirty-Six

Sadie and Mike, along with Tiger, had just returned to the condo when Lila buzzed. "I've got my passport," she shouted into the intercom.

"Passport? Is Lila leaving?" Mike sounded almost hopeful.

"No, it's part of the long story," Sadie replied, buzzing Lila into the courtyard. "I know part of the story, but I'm sure you know more. Maybe we can fill each other in?"

"Okay, maybe. But you start. You and Lila." Mike swung Sadie's door open on an astonished Lila.

Her questions tumbled over each other. "Where is Mr. Chen? Why are you here? Did you talk to Georges? Is he okay? He did not know about that money, did he?" Then her glance swung to Sadie's disheveled appearance—scraped and grass-stained knees, torn clothing, and wide-eyed shock. "What happened? Did your policeman attack you? And why did not Tiger protect you from him?"

"Tiger did protect me, Lila. But not from Mike. From Chen. He was going to kill me. And he was going to kill you, too, when you got back."

Lila collapsed on the couch. "Kill you? Kill me? Why?"

"This is all very interesting, but let's do this debriefing in a more regular way. That is, after we get you fixed up." Mike steered Sadie toward her bedroom and the adjoining bathroom.

"Those knee abrasions need to be washed out. Do you need help?"

"No, I can manage." She shut the bathroom door and looked at herself in the mirror. Sure, she could manage. Just as soon as her guts stopped quaking. She held onto the sink until the wave of nausea washing over her subsided.

Then she ran a basin of hot water, sat down on the toilet seat, and dabbed at her scuffed-up knees. It hurt, but she persisted. Finally, an antibiotic cream slathered on both knees, she stood up and reassessed her appearance.

Brushing her hair helped a bit. Washing her face made her feel cleaner. Maybe she needed to change out of her torn and bloody clothing? As she contemplated this last thought, it occurred to her that the condo was very quiet. Surely Mike was still there.

Panicked, she yanked open the bathroom door and hurried through her bedroom. Mike, Lila, and Tiger were all in the living room, tension evident in their stilted, silent poses. Mike leaned on the wall near the bedroom door, Lila huddled on the couch wringing her hands, and Tiger sat bolt upright in the middle of the living room, the best place to watch both of them and the bedroom door at the same time.

"We were all getting worried." Mike stepped away from the wall to embrace Sadie. The tip of Tiger's tail wagged and blossomed into a full body wiggle of excitement. Lila let out a "whoosh" of relief.

"You look better. I hope you feel better." Mike motioned for Sadie to sit in the recliner. "Before we get to why Lila showed up here with her passport at ten o'clock at night, tell me how you wound up in the parking lot with Chen."

"Parking lot?" Lila interjected.

"Quiet, or I'll separate you." Mike scowled Lila into immediate silence.

Sadie started her answer slowly. "Remember, I called you and left a message. I said I thought Georges LeBourne was stealing industrial secrets and selling them? Then I started thinking about who he would sell them to. Obviously, people who have neither the skills nor the time to develop similar technology on their own."

"And that would be Chen?" Mike sounded dubious. "What would he want with computer technology? He's developing a ski area."

"Is he?" Sadie shrugged. "I wonder about that. Anyway, I don't think Chen wanted the technology for himself. I think he wanted it for China."

She turned to Mike. "Remember, Chen wanted to sell Lila a limited partnership in his new ski resort. He didn't get interested in Lila until he found out she was here on a limited visa, and that she wanted to stay. Then he told her about the E-2 visa and even told her he'd help her get the money for it."

"So where would he get that much money?" Mike sounded as though he didn't believe it was possible.

"Exactly. There's only one place. It has to be coming from Chinese industry, maybe even the Chinese government itself."

"The Chinese government would give money to me? Surely that is not possible." Lila sounded amazed.

"Yes," Sadie argued. "It is possible. If we assume that the money comes from someone in China who wants American technology, it explains a lot of things."

She began to tick off her points on raised fingers again. "First, it explains why Commander Gross hired Lee Hong to take pictures of Chinese men working in menial jobs in Black Hawk. Second, it explains why we found pictures of these same men on E-2 visas in Gross's briefcase. These guys weren't limited partners. They were money mules, bringing money into the country, laundering money Chen could use for bribes."

Sadie sat forward in the pink recliner, emphasizing her next point to Mike. "If these guys came over here with half a million dollars each, why were they dumping garbage and washing dishes in Black Hawk? Because they didn't really have any money. They weren't really limited partners in anything. It was just all too fishy."

"So you decided to go fishing? And you needed Lila's pass-port as bait?" Mike shook his head in disbelief.

"Yes and no. I asked Lila to call Chen and say she wanted to apply for the E-2 visa and that she had to do it tonight. He agreed to come here to talk to her and to bring the proper forms to fill out. But Lila didn't bring her passport. After Chen sent her home for it, I started asking questions about why he would give her the money for the visa, and he explained that he would give it to her, but once she had the visa, she would give the money back to him to build his resort.

"Of course, that's what a limited partner would do, put the money into the partnership. But I think a good part of that money probably becomes bribe money for people like Georges LeBourne. I asked too many questions, and that's when he got suspicious." Sadie started to shake again as her memory replayed the last hour.

"Georges? He is not honest? Is that the truth?" Lila's voice quavered.

"I'm afraid that's the truth, Lila. I'm sorry." Mike replied. "He has been selling quantum computing information to Chen. Claimed he didn't know what Chen did with it, but that's hard to believe. For the last year or so, he'd been selling information, but Chen suddenly demanded a piece of actual hardware."

"Hardware?" Lila's eyebrows knitted together as if she were beyond understanding.

"Yes, a prototype quantum computer chip."

Sadie pounced on the memory of the donkey's mysterious eyes. "Was the chip shiny?"

Mike turned to her in surprise. "What are you talking about? I haven't seen it. And why on earth ..." His words slowed as com-prehension dawned. "The donkey's eyes? They weren't eyes. It was a quantum computer chip ... in a glass rosette on her halter."

It was too much for Lila. She jumped up, throwing her hands into the air. "The donkey's eyes. What are you two talking about?"

"Okay, your turn." Mike turned to her. "What role did you have in all this? Besides picking up a suitcase full of bribe money from China?"

Lila sank back onto the couch under the onslaught of Mike's angry questions. "Bribe money? Georges? I cannot believe it."

"Yes, not only was he taking bribe money, he sent an innocent friend to collect it. You *are* an innocent friend, aren't you? What do you think of your precious Georges LeBourne now?"

"And," Lila asked hesitantly, "did he steal his children's donkey?"

"Not exactly steal," Mike answered. "I'd say he didn't want to risk carrying the actual chip to Black Hawk because he'd seen Lee Hong taking photographs of some of his Chinese contacts there. So he told Chen that he'd put the chip in one of the rosettes on the donkey's halter and leave her where Chen could get it without their having to actually meet each other."

"So he put his children's donkey in that terrible place?" Lila's violet eyes darkened in anger. "What did you do to him? Did you arrest him?"

"Yes, but not because of the donkey. Because of the industrial espionage, although we're calling it theft until the Feds decide what to do."

"What about the children?"

"There's a matron with them. But if you want to go out to LeBourne's place, I'm sure the kids would prefer you. The donkey would too, probably."

"I just cannot believe he would do that to his children. Make them think their pet was lost."

"He thought it would just be for overnight." Mike relented a bit. "He expected Chen to collect the chip and then call him and he'd go back for the donkey. He didn't know what to do when Chen didn't call."

"Such a smart man does not know what to do when his children are missing their pet?" Lila stood. "I am going right now. Those children need me. Their mother is still in France, remember? You are finished with me, yes?"

Mike nodded, and Lila rushed out, clutching her passport to her chest.

Sadie picked up where Lila had left off. "I do agree that he was pretty cavalier with an animal his children adore. But I guess he was pretty cavalier about a lot of things."

Mike shrugged. "I think the pet was the last thing on his mind. Especially after Chen called him the next day and said he didn't get the chip because the donkey bolted after he killed Lee Hong."

This was just too much. Sadie couldn't believe it. "Chen actually told LeBourne that he killed Lee Hong?"

"That's LeBourne's story. He says Chen went to the pond the second time to get the chip and found Lee Hong there taking pictures. Since Lee Hong had already shown so much interest in the Chinese working in Black Hawk, Chen decided the game was up. He snuck up behind Lee Hong and socked him in the head with his gun. Then, to cover that up, he hit him a few times more with a wet log from the pond's edge."

Mike continued. "That's probably when the donkey spooked. She ran over Lee Hong's body into the water and wouldn't let Chen get near her. So he couldn't get to her halter to get the chip."

"Wait, you said that was the second time he went to the pond. When was the first?" Sadie was afraid she knew the answer.

"I think you guessed it. It was about when we came along. He was hiding back in the Russian olives while we were placating the donkey on the other side of the pond."

That was too much for Sadie. "He could have shot us both. Right then."

"Yes, but why? He'd only have a lot of explaining to do. LeBourne said that Chen got a good idea watching you."

"Me?" She sat upright, tension running through her entire body. "I gave Chen a good idea? I hope not."

"Yes, he remembered how silly Americans can be about animals. So he decided to just call the Humane Society the next day and report an abused donkey. Then he could stroll in and remove the chip from its halter. Which, as you recall, is exactly what he did the next day."

"Sort of. What he actually did was exchange the halters."

"Yep." Mike finally sat down. Spreading his hands across his knees, he said, "So easy, so hard. And," casting a slightly apologetic look at Sadie, he added, "I guess the halter was important after all."

"And Gross?" Sadie couldn't stop without knowing it all.

"In for a dime, in for a dollar, I guess. Chen just decided to eliminate all his problems at once. LeBourne was probably next on his list—until you caught his attention, that is." Mike's eyes softened as he looked at Sadie.

"This could have turned out really badly. You know that, don't you?"

"It *is* bad. For a lot of people: Lee Hong. His family. Commander Gross. LeBourne's family. Probably even Eloise."

Mike nodded. "Yes, but you're okay and that's who I care about." He stood and pulled Sadie out of the recliner into his arms.

Relaxing into Mike's warm embrace, Sadie started to shake again.

"Wow, am I that scary? Or do we need to worry about posttraumatic stress syndrome here?"

"You're not scary, and you know it."

"Want to get some fresh air? It might help."

"Just so it's not in the parking lot."

"Okay, let's try going through the garden to the gate. I have one more thing to take care of tonight. It's in the car."

Tiger cocked an ear when Mike slid the garden door open but he made no move to come along. "Tiger's had too much excitement for one night, I guess," Mike said.

"Actually, he just doesn't want to go into the garden again. Now if we offered him a real k-l-a-w it would be a different story." She had to spell "walk" backwards since Tiger had perfected recognition of w-a-l-k a few years earlier.

Arm in arm, they walked through the garden to the gate. Mike opened it and steered Sadie toward his car, parked on Arapahoe. As they walked up to the Honda, she noticed that the windows were slightly open. Unusual for lock-up-everything Mike. Then she saw why. Curled up on the front seat, sound asleep, was a smallish brown dog.

"I found her in the road right after I left LeBourne's. She doesn't have any tags, and I think she's just a puppy."

"What is she, I wonder?" Sadie lifted the little dog into her arms. "Maybe Dachshund. A little bit, anyway." The sleepy puppy nuzzled Sadie's cheek.

"I'll let the Humane Society know we have her, but if no one claims her, I think she'll make a great addition to our household. That's assuming you'll have us ... both of us." Mike again enfolded Sadie in a tight embrace.

She wasn't shaking any more. She was smiling.

* * *